great thoughts
of great people

great thoughts
of great people

Daily wisdom for modern times

EKNATH EASWARAN

The Teacher of Timeless Wisdom

JAICO PUBLISHING HOUSE

Ahmedabad Bangalore Bhopal Bhubaneswar Chennai
Delhi Hyderabad Kolkata Lucknow Mumbai

Published by Jaico Publishing House
A-2 Jash Chambers, 7-A Sir Phirozshah Mehta Road
Fort, Mumbai - 400 001
jaicopub@jaicobooks.com
www.jaicobooks.com

Published in arrangement with
Nilgiri Press
P.O. Box 256
Tomales, California 94971
www.easwaran.org

To be sold only in India, Bangladesh, Bhutan,
Pakistan, Nepal, Sri Lanka and the Maldives.

GREAT THOUGHTS OF GREAT PEOPLE
ISBN 978-93-86348-85-2

First Jaico Impression: 2017

First published as *Words to Live By* by Nilgiri Press

Printed by
Snehesh Printers
320-A, Shah & Nahar Ind. Est. A-1
Lower Parel, Mumbai - 400 013

Table of Contents

Introduction

TO LIVE at our best, each day we must renew our faith, find strength to meet challenges, and draw inspiration from a living source. This book of daily readings is meant to help us face the challenges and opportunities of every day with courage and wisdom.

Some days we are offered a gentle reminder to slow down the hectic pace of our lives, to discover the richness of being mindful and patient. Other days give inspiration to change habits, or advice about a troubled relationship. At times, we read the words of a sympathetic friend who can help us through a dark day with timeless wisdom about the nature of life. And on some special days we have a glimpse of what it might be like to live on those peaks of spirituality that the teachers of all religions point to in every age.

The insights into daily life given here are stated in simple words. Some of the suggestions concern the spiritual foundations of our lives; some are on a much more mundane level. But they all form a beautiful whole, a unified approach to life. Inspiration is drawn from all the world's great religions, though it is not necessary for us to be religious in the conventional sense for this book to speak to our needs. Many of the sources are, in fact, not "spiritual" at all, but all show a glimpse of true wisdom, sometimes with a little humor as a welcome bonus.

However we see life, to find encouragement here, all that is required is an open mind and a desire to know ourselves.

To use this book, read the entry for the day, reflect on it, and then recall it to mind now and then during the day. Try to bring its message into your life day by day.

It is not necessary to begin reading on January 1st. The book is designed so that we can pick it up and begin at any time of the year. Basic concepts are repeated at intervals throughout the year to support the continuity of our inner life. We can return to this collection year after year, each reading taking the inspiration deeper into our hearts.

Taken from the talks and writings of Eknath Easwaran, the readings at times refer to his Eight Point Program for meditation and spiritual practice. A brief description of the Eight Point Program has been included at the end of the book.

For those already acquainted with Easwaran's books, this collection will serve as a reminder of familiar themes. Those who have not read Easwaran before will find a warm introduction here. For those who want to read more, we recommend *Meditation* and *The Mantram Handbook*. A complete list of books suitable for spiritual reading can be found at the back of the book.

As we go through the year with Easwaran, we take a new step on the path every day. Some days will be blessed with happiness and some will be marked by hardship, but each day can further our journey.

One day at a time is enough.

–THE EDITORS

January

Of all that is wonderful in the human being, our most glorious asset is the capacity to change ourselves.

EKNATH EASWARAN

January 1

As an irrigator guides water to the fields, as an archer aims an arrow, as a carpenter carves wood, the wise shape their lives.

THE BUDDHA

THE GLORY of the human being is our ability to remake ourselves. The Buddha is very rightly called the Compassionate One because he holds out hope for everybody. He doesn't say our past has been dark, therefore our chances are dim. He says whatever our past, whatever our present, the sky is bright for us because we can remake ourselves.

The Buddha says, be a good woodworker. Consciousness is the wood, and you can make it take any shape you like. Just as a carpenter works the wood to build a house or a fine piece of furniture, similarly we can fashion the responses and attitudes we desire: love, wisdom, security, patience, loyalty, enthusiasm, cheerfulness.

 RELATED PAGES *April 7, October 12*

January 2

As human beings, our greatness lies not so much in being able to remake the world – that is the myth of the "atomic age" – as in being able to remake ourselves.

MAHATMA GANDHI

IF WE have a particular weakness, life has an uncanny way of trying us at just that vulnerable spot. The man who is anger-prone finds himself forced to work with aggravating people. The woman who can't resist sweets can find no job but one as a pastry cook.

This can seem like sheer perversity on a cosmic scale, until we catch sight of the tremendous opportunity it provides. Between our inner need for growth and our external circumstances, a kind of dovetailing can often be detected. There almost seems to be a master hand behind it all, thrusting us time and time again into the same frustrating situation until finally we relent: "All right, you win – I'll grow if you insist!" This is all that is really expected of us. Once we have made the firm resolve to get ourselves out of the old trap, we will be amazed how quickly our circumstances begin to change, how quickly new opportunities open up for us.

RELATED PAGES *October 22, November 8*

January 3

Familiar acts are beautiful through love.

PERCY BYSSHE SHELLEY

BY GIVING full attention to one thing at a time, we can learn to direct attention where we choose. Simple, yet essential to the practice of love! Being one-pointed means we can give the person we are with our complete attention, even if she is contradicting our opinion on tax reform or explaining the peculiarities of French grammar. Once we can do this, boredom disappears from our relationships. People are not boring; we get bored because our attention wanders. When we can give someone our full attention, our attitude says clearly, "You matter to me. You have my respect."

 RELATED PAGES *January 15, August 1*

January 4

Try to treat with equal love all the people with whom you have relations. Thus the abyss between "myself" and "yourself" will be filled in, which is the goal of all religious worship.

ANANDAMAYI MA

LOVE IS a skill, a precious skill that can be learned. There are many other skills that are useful, even necessary, but in the end, nothing less than learning to love will satisfy us.

The saints and mystics of all religions tell us that life has only one overriding purpose: to discover the source of infinite love and then to express this love in daily living. Without love, life is empty; without love, life is meaningless. The only purpose which can satisfy us completely, fulfill all our desires, and then make our life a gift to the whole world, is the gradual realization of the divine Self within, which throws open the gates of love. We cannot dream what depth and breadth of love we are capable of until we make the discovery that this divine spark lives in every creature.

RELATED PAGES *January 21, November 5*

January 5

The seed of God is in us. Given an intelligent and hard-working farmer, it will thrive and grow up to God, whose seed it is; and accordingly its fruits will be God-nature. Pear seeds grow into pear trees, nut seeds into nut trees, and a God seed into God.

MEISTER ECKHART

THE SEED of goodness and creativity is in everyone. This seed does not need to be planted on a particular date, for it is already within us. It is indestructible. In the depths of the Dakota winter, this seed, the God-seed, can thrive; in the heat of Death Valley it can still flourish. No matter what our past has been, no matter how many mistakes we have made, the God-seed is still intact.

When at last we begin to search for it, we discover it is covered with weeds – weeds of fear and anger, giant thistles of greed. We shouldn't feel discouraged. Once we cease to water them, the weeds begin to wither and droop, and finally they fall to enrich the soil where the God-seed is growing. This God-seed within us will grow into a God-tree of love and service if we nurture it carefully.

 RELATED PAGE *June 7*

January 6

The soul is made of love and must ever strive to return to love. Therefore, it can never find rest nor happiness in other things. It must lose itself in love. By its very nature it must seek God, who is love.

MECHTHILD OF MAGDEBURG

SPIRITUAL FULFILLMENT is an evolutionary imperative. There comes a time in the growth of civilizations, as with individuals, when the life-and-death questions of material existence have been answered, yet the soul still thirsts and physical challenges cease to satisfy. Then we stand at a crossroads, for without meaningful aspiration, the human being turns destructive. Like a snake that must shed its skin to grow, our industrial civilization must shed its material outlook or strangle in outgrown ideals whose constructive potential has been spent.

RELATED PAGES *February 8, March 12*

January 7

Genius . . . means little more than the faculty of perceiving in an inhabitual way.

WILLIAM JAMES

ATTENTION IS very much like a searchlight, and it should be mounted in such a way that it can be trained on any subject freely. When we are caught up in some compulsion, this searchlight has become stuck. After many years of being stuck like this, it is hard to believe that the light *can* turn. We think that the compulsion has become a permanent part of our personality. But gradually, we can learn to work our attention free.

As an experiment, try to work cheerfully at some job you dislike: you are training your attention to go where you want it to go. Whatever you do, give it your best concentration. Another good exercise is learning to drop what you are doing and shift your attention to something else when the situation demands. For example, when you leave your office, leave your work there. Don't let it follow you home and come into the dining room like an untrained dog, barking at your heels.

All this is the spiritual equivalent of kicking exercises in a dance lesson or knee bends in an aerobics class. By practicing these exercises, anybody can learn to direct attention freely.

RELATED PAGES *May 8, December 19*

January 8

When we try to pick out anything by itself, we find it hitched to everything else in the universe.

JOHN MUIR

WHEN WE see the world with new, spiritual eyes, we realize it is God's beach, God's ocean, God's world. We see ourselves as waves in the ocean of love that is God. We are not separate from one another, we realize, but we all exist as part of the sea, as a wave of the infinite ocean. This is seeing spiritually: seeing everything joined together – the waves of the sea, the light in the sky, the birds skimming along the whitecaps, the dogs running, the children playing, the warmth of the sand – everything together.

It is impossible to put this experience into words, but all those who try to do so describe it as a deep sense of fellowship with all creatures, from the little sandpipers to the mighty leviathans of the deep.

RELATED PAGES *August 12, December 2*

January 9

We are what our thoughts have made us; so take care about what you think. Words are secondary. Thoughts live; they travel far.

SWAMI VIVEKANANDA

THE ANCESTOR of every destructive action, every destructive decision, is a negative thought. We do not have to be afraid of negative thoughts as long as we do not welcome them. They are in the air, and they may knock at anyone's door; but if we do not embrace them, ask them in, and make them our own, they can have no power over us.

We can think of thoughts as hitchhikers. At the entrance to the freeway, we used to see a lot of hitchhikers carrying signs: "Vancouver," "Mexico," "L.A." One said in simple desperation, "Anywhere!" Thoughts are a lot like those hitchhikers. We can pick them up or pass them by. Negative thoughts carry signs, but usually we see only one side, the side with all the promises. The back of the sign tells us their true destination: sickness and sorrow.

Nobody is obliged to pick up these passengers. If we do not stop and let them in, they cannot go anywhere, because they are not real until we support them. There is sympathy in the world: pick it up. There is antipathy in the world: don't pick it up. Hatred destroys. Love heals.

 RELATED PAGES *January 24, May 11*

January 10

It is here, my daughters, that love is to be found, not hidden away in corners but in the midst of occasions of sin. And believe me, although we may more often fail and commit small lapses, our gain will be incomparably the greater.

SAINT TERESA OF AVILA

THE WIDEST possibilities for growth lie in the give-and-take of everyday relationships. The truth of this is brought out sweetly in a story about Saint Francis of Assisi. Three young men approached Francis and asked his blessing to become hermits and seek God, each in his own cave, deep in the mountains of Umbria. Francis smiled. He instructed them to be hermits indeed, but hermits all together in a single hut. One should take the role of father; a second should think of himself as the mother; and the third should be their child. Every few months they should exchange roles. Living in this way they were to establish among themselves perfect harmony, thinking always of the needs of one another.

We can almost see the three would-be recluses exchanging sidelong glances. Their teacher had issued them a greater challenge than any they had bargained for. Yet they carried out Francis's instructions, discovering that human relationships are the perfect tool for sanding away our rough edges and getting at the core of divinity within us. We need look no further than our own family, friends, acquaintances, or even adversaries, to begin our practice.

RELATED PAGES *September 6, September 21*

January 11

Love seeks no cause beyond itself and no fruit; it is its own fruit, its own enjoyment. I love because I love; I love in order that I may love.

SAINT BERNARD

IT TAKES a good deal of experience of life to see why some relationships last and others do not. But we do not have to wait for a crisis to get an idea of the future of a particular relationship. Our behavior in little everyday incidents tells us a great deal.

We only need to ask ourselves, "Am I ready to put the other person first?" If the answer is yes, that relationship is likely to grow deeper and more rewarding with the passage of time, whatever problems may come. If the answer is no, that relationship may not be able to withstand the testing that life is bound to bring.

Relationships break down, not because we are bad, but because we are illiterate in love.

 RELATED PAGES *March 9, May 12*

January 12

All that we are is the result of what we have thought.

THE BUDDHA

OUR DESTINY is in our own hands. Since we are formed by our thoughts, it follows that what we become tomorrow is shaped by what we think today.

Happily, we can choose the way we think. We can choose our feelings, aspirations, desires, and the way we view our world and ourselves. Mastery of the mind opens avenues of hope. We can begin to reshape our life and character, rebuild relationships, thrive in the stress of daily living – we can become the kind of person we want to be.

RELATED PAGE *May 17*

January 13

This is the true joy in life, the being used for a purpose recognized by yourself as a mighty one.

GEORGE BERNARD SHAW

ALL OF us have tasted the freedom and happiness that self-forgetfulness brings. In watching a good game of tennis or becoming engrossed in a novel, the satisfaction comes not so much from what we are watching or reading as from the act of absorption itself. For that brief span, our burden of personal thoughts is forgotten. Then we find relief, for what lies beneath that burden is a still, clear state of awareness.

The scientist or the artist absorbed in creative work is happy because she has forgotten herself in what she is doing. But nowhere will you find personalities so joyous, so unabashedly lighthearted, as those who have lost themselves in love for all. That is the joy we glimpse in Saint Francis or Mahatma Gandhi. To look at the lives of men and women like these is to see what joy means.

 RELATED PAGE *March 6*

January 14

Loss of discrimination is the greatest source of danger.

SANSKRIT PROVERB

THE GREATEST source of danger to a human being is loss of discrimination, and this is the main malady in our modern civilization, where we have lost our capacity to differentiate between what is necessary and useful, and what is unnecessary and harmful.

How often do we stop and ask, "What is really important? What matters most to me?"

If every one of us starts asking this simple question, it will transform our daily lives and even the world in which we live. After all, we need clean air and water more than we need microwave ovens. Doing work that is meaningful and of service to others is more important than owning luxury cars. We need loving human relationships more than we need home entertainment systems.

Many modern conveniences make life more pleasant and can save time. We needn't live without them, but when we begin to think such things are not merely useful but prized possessions, we may gradually lose our discrimination.

In order to understand what is important in life, what our real priorities are, discrimination is essential.

RELATED PAGES *October 19, November 24*

January 15

When one is rising, standing, walking, doing something, stopping, one should constantly concentrate one's mind on the act and the doing of it, not on one's relation to the act, or its character or value. . . . One should simply practice concentration of the mind on the act itself.

ASHVAGHOSHA

THERE IS a close connection between deep concentration and love, and with the practice of one-pointed attention we can greatly increase the precious capacity to remain loving and loyal no matter what the vicissitudes or circumstances we encounter.

We can practice this one-pointedness throughout the day by doing one thing at a time, and giving our full attention to whatever we are doing. While having breakfast, for example, we can give our complete attention to the food and not to the newspaper. If we are listening to a friend, even if a parrot flies down and perches on his head, we should not get excited, point to the parrot, and burst out, "Excuse me for interrupting, but there's a bird on your head." We should be able to concentrate so hard on what our friend is saying that we can tell this urge, "Don't distract me. Afterwards, I'll tell him about the parrot."

 RELATED PAGES *February 14, August 1*

January 16

Remember that you ought to behave in life as you would at a banquet. As something is being passed around, it comes to you. When it comes to you, stretch out your hand gently, take a portion of it politely, but pass it on. Or, it has not come to you yet. Do not project your desire to meet it. So act always in life.

EPICTETUS

THIS IS the nature of desire: it jumps out from the present to the future. When you have a very pleasant event planned, the desire has jumped out already to meet it. Even though this particular event will take place on Saturday, and today is Monday, half of you is already living in Saturday.

And next Monday morning, you will be at your desk, remembering the great day you had Saturday.

Epictetus says, don't ever let your desire jump out to the future, and don't let your mind wander to the past, because you will never be present in the here and now.

If, for example, you are going to the theater to see *Anthony and Cleopatra,* it is only when you get into the theater that you let your attention dwell on it completely. Until then, you don't think about it. And when you are watching the play, you are there completely, with no wisp of consciousness wandering to what your boss said to you yesterday about the project that is late, and no wandering to what you would like for breakfast tomorrow. You are there completely, sailing down the Nile with Cleopatra.

RELATED PAGE *February 21*

January 17

He that loveth not, knoweth not God, for God is love.

I JOHN

THESE WORDS sound so ethereal that most of us cannot connect them with daily life. What, we ask, do personal relationships have to do with the divine? I would reply that it is by discovering the unity between ourselves and others – *all* others – that we find our unity with God. We don't first get to know God and then, by some miracle of grace, come to love our fellow human beings. Loving others comes first. In this sense, learning to love is practicing religion. Those who can put the welfare of others before their own small personal interests are religious, even if they would deny it.

RELATED PAGES *January 21, June 7*

January 18

There is no greater trouble for thee than thine own self, for when thou art occupied with thyself, thou remainest away from God.

ABU SA'ID

DO YOU want to be free? Most of us are held hostage in life by our likes and dislikes. We are bound by countless little preferences in food, clothing, decor, entertainment – the list goes on and on.

The person with rigid tastes in one area, for example in food, is likely to have rigid tastes elsewhere as well. He will probably enjoy only one kind of music, she will appreciate only one style of art, and when it comes to people, he has very definite allergies. In any case, a rigid person is conditioned to be happy only so long as he gets everything the way he likes it. Otherwise – which may be most of the time – he is unhappy over something.

The way we respond to small matters reflects the way we will respond to the larger matters of life. If we can begin to release ourselves from our little likes and dislikes, we will find that we are gaining the capacity to weather emotional storms. Then we can begin to face whatever comes calmly and courageously.

RELATED PAGES *October 2, October 16*

January 19

Love bears it out even to the edge of doom.

WILLIAM SHAKESPEARE

MOST OF us can spend years in personal pursuits without ever taking time to know the needs of people in our own home, in our neighborhood, at work. It may be rarely that we give our energy to serving their needs. We sometimes forget that our nascent capacity for love is the greatest thing we shall ever have. To nurture it, we may have to forget our private adventures in profit and pleasure for the sake of others, but that is how love grows.

It takes a lifetime to learn to love. Love does not burst forth one morning with a display of fireworks. It grows little by little every day, by bearing with people, as Shakespeare's sonnet says, "even to the edge of doom." That is what love requires. But if we make it our first priority, no matter what difficulties come our way, our love cannot help but grow.

 RELATED PAGES *January 20, March 7*

January 20

You learn to speak by speaking, to study by studying, to run by running, to work by working; in just the same way, you learn to love by loving.

SAINT FRANCIS DE SALES

IN LEARNING to love, we start where we are – somewhat selfish, somewhat self-centered, but with a deep desire to relate lovingly to each other, to move closer and closer together. Love grows by practice; there is no other way. There will be setbacks as well as progress. But there is one immediate consolation: we don't have to wait until our love is perfect to reap the benefits of it. Even with a little progress, everyone benefits – not only those we live with, but ourselves as well.

RELATED PAGES *May 14, October 14*

January 21

We have to take the whole universe as the expression of the one Self. Then only our love flows to all beings and creatures in the world equally.

SWAMI RAMDAS

YOU AND I appear to be separate. We differ in color, size, and shape. Differences in ideas, tastes, and prejudices mark us as individuals to be reckoned with. Beneath this apparent division, however, hidden deep within each of us is the one Self – eternal, infinite, ever-perfect. This is the closely guarded secret of life: that we are all caught up in a divine masquerade, and all we are trying to do is take off our masks to reveal the pure, perfect Self within.

In our present condition, we have forgotten we are wearing masks. Fortunately, the Self will not allow us to forget him, but keeps on calling to us. In order to find the Self, we must look deep within ourselves. When we succeed, our purpose in life will be fulfilled, and all our anger against others will melt into unfathomable love, all our fear of others into unshakable security.

 RELATED PAGES *October 20, October 28*

January 22

Love is patient and kind; love is not jealous or boastful; it is not arrogant or rude.

I CORINTHIANS

TO EXCEL in anything you have to have patience; but if you want to love, patience is an absolute necessity. You may be dashing, glamorous, fascinating, and alluring; you may be tall, dark, and handsome, or whatever the current fancy may be. Without patience, you can never become a great lover; it would be a contradiction in terms.

"Well," most of us say, "I guess that leaves me out. Patience has never been my strong point." Very, very few of us are born patient. Our age has been called the age of anxiety, the age of anger; but we could just as easily say the age of impatience. You see it in supermarket lines, on the highway, on the tennis court, in the schoolyard, in the political arena, on the bus. With all this we have begun to believe that impatience is our natural state. Fortunately, love is our natural state, and patience is something that everybody can learn.

RELATED PAGES *April 4, October 1*

January 23

Just as a fire is covered by smoke and a mirror is obscured by dust, just as the embryo rests deep within the womb, wisdom is hidden by selfish desire.

BHAGAVAD GITA

THIS VERSE is taken from the Bhagavad Gita, a short Sanskrit work of seven hundred verses that has fascinated and inspired mystics, physicists, psychologists, and philosophers of many countries for three thousand years. Set on a battlefield on the morning before a fierce battle, the Gita uses warfare as a metaphor for our personal struggle with the challenges of life.

The Gita's message is simple but profound: our native state is freedom. What we want most from life is to be free of all the mental compulsions that keep us from living in peace with ourselves, with others, and with the environment. This desire for freedom is at the core of our personality, says the Gita, and our failings only hide our real nature like dust obscuring the face of a mirror.

 RELATED PAGE *September 27*

January 24

They live in wisdom who see themselves in all and all in them, who have renounced every selfish desire and sense craving tormenting the heart.

BHAGAVAD GITA

THE GITA'S hypothesis is that it is possible, by mastering the thinking process, to leave behind unwanted habits and negative thoughts. To accomplish this, the Gita outlines a daily course of training in which we acquire conscious control of our attention, strengthening our will at such a deep level of the unconscious that no compulsive desire or addiction can sweep us away. What is the predicted result? When your will is linked to your intellect at the very depths of your personality, you discover yourself as you really are – secure, wise, compassionate, and intimately connected with all of life.

RELATED PAGES *April 15, May 11*

January 25

Be strong and of a good courage, fear not, nor be afraid . . . for the Lord thy God, he it is that doth go with thee; he will not fail thee, nor forsake thee.

DEUTERONOMY

WHENEVER WE worry about something in the past or the future, we are setting up our own little haunted house and peopling it with our own special ghosts.

Most of us live very little in the present. If we could watch our thoughts, we would be surprised to see how much time we spend in the past or future – or simply daydreaming, out of time altogether.

Very seldom can we say we are fully present in the present moment. Yet now is the only time there is. The present is all we have. If we feel we don't have enough time, the first thing to do is not throw it away. Instead of ceding it to the past and future, we can take steps to give our undivided interest to here and now.

Attention flowing to the past is not energy used; it is energy wasted. The same is true of the future: looking forward to things, worrying about what might happen, fantasizing about dreams coming true is energy drained away. When the mind stays in the present, all this vitality comes back to us.

 RELATED PAGES *February 3, December 13*

January 26

Love the whole world as a mother loves her only child.

THE BUDDHA

MY GRANDMOTHER could not read or write, and she was a woman of few words, but by her example, by the very power of her presence, she taught me that we are all children of God, no matter what our country, religion, race, or sex. To use the language of traditional Hinduism, she was aware of the unity of life that binds us all together, and she was able, gradually, to transmit her awareness to me.

A favorite expression of my granny's was, "Life cannot make a selfish person happy." It has taken me half a lifetime to understand the profundity of her simple words, warning that happiness cannot come from possessing another person, or from any selfish attachment. But she would also always add, "Life cannot help but make a selfless person happy." Like spiritual teachers of all the world's religions, she taught that happiness is to be found in learning how to love others more than I love myself.

RELATED PAGES *June 12, September 4*

January 27

Households, cities, countries, and nations have enjoyed great happiness when a single individual has taken heed of the Good and Beautiful. ... Such people not only liberate themselves; they fill those they meet with a free mind.

PHILO

JUST AS we live in a physical atmosphere, we are surrounded also by a mental atmosphere. And just as the air we breathe may become polluted, our mental atmosphere can be polluted by negative thinking. If trees were not always releasing oxygen into the atmosphere, scientists tell us, all life on earth would suffer. On a smoggy day the trees along the freeway look grey and drab in the haze; they do not seem to add anything valuable to the landscape.

Yet they are performing a vital function: they are taking in our carbon dioxide and giving us oxygen in return.

A person whose mind is free from negative thinking spreads a life-giving influence in much the same way that a tree gives oxygen. Although a selfless man or woman may seem to go through the day doing nothing extraordinary, without them nothing would revitalize the atmosphere in which we think. By being vigilant, and not encouraging negative thoughts, all of us can offer this vital service – which benefits everybody, including ourselves.

 RELATED PAGES *February 11, March 23*

January 28

Dreams are real as long as they last.
Can we say more of life?

HENRY HAVELOCK ELLIS

WHEN WE wake up from a dream into waking consciousness, we do not pass from unreality to reality; we pass from a lower level of reality to a higher level. And, the mystics of all religions say, there is a higher level still, compared with which this waking life of ours is as insubstantial as a dream.

Yet until we do wake up, nothing sounds more absurd than the assertion that we are dreaming, and nothing seems more solid than this world of the senses. Why should this be so? If original goodness is our real nature, why are we unable to see it? The answer is simple: because we see life not as it is but as we are. We see "through a glass darkly," through the distorting lenses of the mind – all the layers of feeling, habit, instinct, and memory that cover the pure core of goodness deep within.

RELATED PAGES *November 9, December 22*

January 29

On this path, effort never goes to waste, and there is no failure. Even a little effort toward spiritual awareness will protect you from the greatest fear.

BHAGAVAD GITA

TO BE truly secure, we must begin to find a source of security within ourselves. Even the bravest among us have many fears. Behind the attachment to money or possessions, for example, you will always find the fear of loss. Attachment to prestige brings the nagging fear of what others think of us. The thirst for power feeds the fear that others may be stronger. Every self-centered desire brings the fear that we may not get what we desire.

One could make a Sears catalog of these fears, but all stem from one fatal superstition: thinking of ourselves as merely physical creatures, separate from the rest of life. As our sense of oneness with the rest of life deepens, we step out of the world of fear to live in the world of love.

 RELATED PAGE *September 12*

January 30

And then there crept a little noiseless
noise among the leaves,
Born of the very sigh that silence heaves.

JOHN KEATS

TODAY I was walking with some friends in Armstrong Redwoods Park and I was astonished at those trees. The more I looked at them, the more I came to appreciate them. It was completely still, unlike our tropical forests in India, where elephants trumpet, tigers roar, and there is a constant symphony of sound.

Here everything was still, and I enjoyed the silence so much that I remembered these lines of John Keats. It is a perfect simile for the silence of the mind, when all personal conflicts are resolved, when all selfish desires come to rest. All of us are looking for this absolute peace, this inward, healing silence in the redwood forest of the mind. When we find it, we will become small forces for peace wherever we go.

RELATED PAGES *March 21, June 26*

January 31

A devotee who can call on God while living a householder's life is a hero indeed. God thinks: "They are blessed indeed who pray to Me in the midst of their worldly duties. They are trying to find Me, overcoming a great obstacle, pushing away, as it were, a huge block of stone weighing a ton. Such a one is a real hero."

SRI RAMAKRISHNA

TO FIND a spiritual path, it is not necessary to give up our job, leave our family, change our religion, or travel to distant lands. We start wherever we are, not running away from society, but right in the midst of life.

Whatever context we find ourselves in is a suitable one in which to overcome our problems and grow to our full height. We tend to look upon the *other* home as peaceful, the other couple as perfect, the other parent-child relationship as ideal, but this is not very likely. Everyone has certain liabilities as well as assets. Everyone has done some good, and made some mistakes as well. This is part of the human condition.

Saints and sages are loving realists. "Don't wait for ideal conditions. You'll never find them," they admonish. "Begin! And the conditions you need will come to you."

 RELATED PAGE *June 18*

February

At the very core of our being is a spark of purity, of perfection, of divinity.

EKNATH EASWARAN

February 1

We are formed and molded by our thoughts. Those whose minds are shaped by selfless thoughts give joy when they speak or act. Joy follows them like a shadow that never leaves them.

THE BUDDHA

THE METHOD of meditation I teach involves sitting quietly with eyes closed and going slowly, in the mind, through the words of an inspirational passage that appeals to you deeply. It may be a prayer, or a poem from one of the great mystics, or a piece of scripture from any of the world's religions. It must be a very positive selection. When you sit quietly like this every morning, concentrating completely on words that embody your highest ideals, you are giving your mind thoughts of the purest quality to work with during the day. These selfless thoughts begin to mold your life. Joy begins to follow you throughout the day.

It is meditation every morning that gives you the wonderful capacity to stay patient and forgiving no matter what the day brings. When you know from your own experience what the tremendous benefits can be, you look forward to meditation. When the alarm goes off in the morning, even in the dead of winter when the bed is warm and the blankets hold you down, you get up for your meditation with eagerness and enthusiasm every day, well or not so well, because you know that meditation is the key to the art of living.

 RELATED PAGES *February 26, July 27*

February 2

For the outer sense alone perceives visible things, and the eye of the heart alone sees the invisible.

RICHARD OF SAINT-VICTOR

THE SENSES – the eyes, ears, touch, and taste – are wonderful instruments for observing the outer world. But these instruments function at their best when they are trained. If they clamor for what is damaging to our health, it is not their fault. It is ours, because we haven't sent them to school.

"Why do you want to eat that?" we ask the palate in exasperation. "You know it's going to add to the pounds."

"I can't help it," the palate replies. "You never trained me."

It may take a long period of education, but the senses can be trained. Then, the palate might clamor briefly for the chocolate mousse, but a friendly "Careful!" brings it back to the fresh strawberries.

RELATED PAGES *February 23, May 24*

February 3

Time is what keeps the light from reaching us. There is no greater obstacle to God than time: and not only time but temporalities, not only temporal things but temporal affections, not only temporal affections but the very taint and smell of time.

MEISTER ECKHART

WE THINK that past and future are real because the mind keeps brooding over what we have done and what others have done to us, what we will do and what others will do to us. But it is not past and future that are real; it is our brooding on the past and the future that is real. If we could withdraw our attention from these ghosts, many of our problems would simply dissolve.

As our meditation deepens, we develop the ability to withdraw our attention more and more from the past and the future to focus it on the present. And as we begin to live more and more in the present, we make the exhilarating discovery that past and future exist only in our minds. It is a tremendous realization, for it means that we are released from any burden of guilt about the past and any anxiety about the future.

Every moment is unique and discrete. When our concentration is complete, we rest completely in the present. Then we do not live in time, we live in eternity.

 RELATED PAGES *February 21, December 13*

February 4

No man is an island, entire of itself; every man is a piece of the continent, a part of the main.

JOHN DONNE

THE UNITY underlying life is so complete and pervasive that when we inflict suffering on the smallest creature, we injure the whole. When we refrain from habits that harm others, when we take up jobs that relieve suffering, when we work to put an end to anger and separateness, we strengthen the whole.

There is nothing more important in life than learning to express this unity in all our relationships. Violence, war, and insensitivity to our fellow creatures are external manifestations of the disunity in our consciousness. When we begin to practice spiritual disciplines, right from the first day, however slowly, we begin to transform our character, conduct, and consciousness. When the divisiveness which has been agitating us and making life difficult begins to mend, we get immediate evidence in our daily life. Our health improves, long-standing personal conflicts subside, our mind becomes clearer, and a sense of security and well-being follows us wherever we go.

RELATED PAGE *January 8*

February 5

All spiritual disciplines are done with a view to still the mind. The perfectly still mind is universal spirit.

SWAMI RAMDAS

MEDITATION IS the regular, systematic training of attention to turn inward and dwell continuously on a single focus within consciousness. With practice, we can become so absorbed in the object of our contemplation that while we are meditating, we forget ourselves completely. In that moment, when we may be said to be empty of ourselves, we are utterly full of what we are dwelling on. This is the central principle of meditation: we become what we meditate on.

Eventually, meditation will make our mind calm, clear, and as concentrated as a laser which we can focus at will. This capacity of one-pointed attention is the essence of genius. When we have this mastery over attention in everything we do, we have a genius for life itself: unshakable security, clear judgment, and deep personal relationships.

RELATED PAGES *March 1, July 16*

February 6

Everybody today seems to be in such a terrible rush, anxious for greater developments and greater riches and so on, so that children have very little time for their parents. Parents have very little time for each other, and in the home begins the disruption of the peace of the world.

MOTHER TERESA OF CALCUTTA

IN GOING faster and faster and trying our hand at new adventures all the time, we hope we can forget our emptiness. We try to squeeze as many jobs as possible into a limited span of time. We're in some frantic race, not knowing just why or against whom we're racing.

There is no joy in work which is hurried, which is done when we are at the mercy of pressures from outside, because such work is compulsive. All too often hurry clouds judgment. More and more, to save time, a person tends to think in terms of pat solutions and to take shortcuts and give uninspired performances.

It is often said that life in our modern world is so complicated, so busy, and so crowded that just to survive we have to hurry. But I think we still have a choice. We can insist on working conditions that do not force us to hurry. It is possible to do our work and attend to our duties without being oppressed by time, and when we work free from the bondage of time we do not make mistakes, we do not get tense, and the quality of our living improves.

RELATED PAGES *April 19, May 18*

February 7

And God shall wipe away all tears from their eyes; and there shall be no more death, neither sorrow, nor crying, neither shall there be any more pain.

REVELATION

WE HAVE all seen those signs on the highway, "Go Back. Wrong Way!" Where roads are concerned, we all understand this warning. We turn around. If only we could understand life's signs so easily!

Sorrow is often a warning with the same message: "Go back. Change your direction. You are going the wrong way." Every creature is conditioned to avoid pain; this is a built-in safety mechanism to protect our bodies from harm. When you eat more than necessary, for example, you should feel reassured if your stomach hurts. Your body is telling you, "Please don't do this again; it's not good for me." Mental and emotional suffering often serve the same function.

Once we have connected our sorrow with particular patterns of behavior, we will remember to act wisely more often. Eventually, as we learn its lesson, personal sorrow will fade from our life.

 RELATED PAGES *June 17, November 8*

February 8

All mystics speak the same language, for they come from the same country.

LOUIS-CLAUDE DE SAINT-MARTIN

WHAT WE are all looking for, even though we are searching in the most improbable places, is infinite wisdom, infinite joy, infinite love. In other words, we are trying to discover our real nature. At the very core of our being is a spark of purity, of perfection, of divinity. When we learn to identify less and less with that which is subject to change and more and more with this core of perfection, we are gradually moving closer to this supreme goal.

Though different religions call it by different names, the goal is always the same. It is *nirvana* to the Buddhist, *moksha* to the Hindu; Jesus calls it "entering the kingdom of heaven within." To the Sufis it is union with the Beloved; to Jewish mystics it is the return to the Promised Land. No matter what they call it, all the great religions point to the same supreme goal.

RELATED PAGES *July 10, August 29*

February 9

Sages speak of the immutable Tree, with its root above and its branches below. . . . The limbs of this tree spread above and below. Sense objects grow on the limbs as buds; the roots hanging down bind us to action in this world. The true form of this tree – its essence, beginning, and end – is not perceived on this earth.

BHAGAVAD GITA

WE ARE all familiar with the unflattering expression, "He can't see the forest for the trees." Similarly, it can be said that most of us don't see the tree for the leaves, that we fail to see the Tree of Life because we are fascinated by the leaves. We are so obsessed by the leaves – the millions of little fragments that grow on the tree – that we are not aware of the tree at all. We do not see that without the tree the leaves do not have any life, that it is the sap, coming from the very life of the tree, that flows into the leaves and supports them.

In our modern world, most of the emphasis is on separateness, on the leaf rather than the tree. Daily we receive the message, "Find your joy in your own way; live your life in your own way; find your fulfillment in your own way." This drive for personal satisfaction is based on a cruel fiction: that the leaf can prosper without the living tree. In reality, none of us are separate; we are all part of the same creation, drawing our strength, happiness, and fulfillment from the cosmic tree.

 RELATED PAGES *March 21, August 19*

February 10

Among the attributes of God, although they are all equal, mercy shines with even more brilliancy than justice.

MIGUEL DE CERVANTES

IN KERALA, the state in South India from which I come, along the roadside there are stone parapets the height of a person's head. When people need to rest from carrying heavy loads of rice or fruit on their heads, they stand next to the parapet and shift their load onto it.

The Lord of Love who dwells in the hearts of all is the perennial parapet, standing at exactly the right height for each one of us. For those who are very selfish, he stands very tall to support an awesome load; for those who are average in selfishness, he stands about six feet high; and for the selfless, the parapet can hardly be seen because the burden is so light that almost no support is needed. Through the practice of meditation, we can gradually learn to shift our load into the Lord's mighty arms.

We like to think that we make big decisions and carry terrible responsibilities on our shoulders. Our shoulders are bent, our back gives us problems, and we are too tired to stand on our feet because of the mighty weight we try to bear. Few of us realize there is somebody standing with arms outstretched, just waiting to carry our burdens.

RELATED PAGE *February 24*

February 11

Faults and virtues arise from our companions.

SANSKRIT PROVERB

ACCORDING TO this ancient saying, what is good in us and what is bad, our strong points and our weak points alike, develop because of constant association. When we associate with calm people, we become calm; when we associate with agitated people, we become agitated. When we frequent the company of people who are wise, we become wiser; when our company is otherwise, we become otherwise too.

We've all experienced this. When we have spent an evening with someone who is overwrought, we come home so agitated ourselves that we can't get to sleep. But there is a positive side of the power of association: we absorb good qualities too, by spending time with people who embody them. Whenever we associate with people, we participate in their mental states.

 RELATED PAGE *November 7*

February 12

The enemy is more easily overcome if it be not suffered to enter the door of our hearts, but be resisted without the gate at its first knock.

THOMAS A KEMPIS

THE BODY is rather like a city with five gates, the five senses. We are fairly fussy about what enters the gate of the mouth. But just as food enters the mouth and goes on to nourish or damage the body, sense impressions enter consciousness through our eyes, ears, nose, and skin, and in most of us the traffic is somewhat unregulated. We all want to be open to experience, but we also need to be watchful. When impressions come knocking, we need to check IDs.

Take popular films, many of which glamorize violence. We can pretend this is only entertainment, bearing no relationship to real life, yet every year violent crimes enact with terrible precision episodes from television or movies. In our violent society, how can anyone argue convincingly that witnessing casual cruelty on television does not affect us? We all have a personal stake in not supporting any of the mass media when they give us poisonous food for our eyes, our ears, and our minds.

RELATED PAGES *April 16, August 22*

February 13

You are what your deep, driving desire is.

BRIHADARANYAKA UPANISHAD

DESIRE IS the key to life, because desire is power. The deeper the desire, the more power it contains.

Most people start life with many small desires. Their power and vitality trickle away in many different directions. None of their desires is deep enough to contain much power. But there are people whose lives are molded by only a few, consuming desires. Such people usually achieve their goals. Because their desires are unified, their will becomes nearly invincible. To desire something deeply *is* to will it, and to will is to achieve. If they want to become a great artist, build a bigger pyramid, explain the movements of the planets, they devote their life to that, and usually succeed. Wherever you find great success in life, it is fueled by the intense unification of desires.

But the most successful people of all are the rare men and women like Mahatma Gandhi and Saint Teresa of Avila who have but *one* desire. All lesser desires have been consumed in the great fire of love for God.

 RELATED PAGES *March 26, September 2*

February 14

Let me not to the marriage of true minds
Admit impediments. Love is not love
Which alters when it alteration finds,
Or bends with the remover to remove.

WILLIAM SHAKESPEARE

MANY OF the disruptions that take place in personal relationships can be prevented by learning to control our attention, for attention is closely linked with loyalty.

I can illustrate with that most fascinating of relationships, the romantic. Suppose *Romeo and Juliet* had turned out differently, and the two lovers had married and settled down to a normal domestic life. After a few years, as sometimes happens, Romeo's attention gets restless. Once the sight of Juliet made him think of flowers and bubbling brooks and the "light, sweet airs of spring"; now she reminds him of the laundry and his morning espresso. After a while, his attention falls on Rosaline, his old flame. Now *she* reminds him of flowers and brooks; his attention seizes her and will not let go.

Today, Romeo would most likely receive the advice, "Follow your desires. That is where happiness will be." But that is just where *un*happiness will be. If Romeo's attention cannot stay with Juliet, how is it going to stay with Rosaline? If he cannot get control over his attention, happiness can only recede farther and farther.

RELATED PAGES *June 28, November 2*

February 15

If God gave the soul his whole creation she would not be filled thereby but only with himself.

MEISTER ECKHART

TODAY, EVEN modern industrial societies are not always able to provide food and shelter for all of their people. These are very real and important needs. But there are other needs that sometimes are not so easily identified. Even when the most pressing requirements for food or clothing or shelter have been satisfied, that is not enough for the human being. There remains a hunger for something more. We want to be somebody. We want to feel secure. We want to love. Without any better way to satisfy these inner needs, we end up depending on possessions and profit – not just for our physical well-being but as a substitute for the dignity, fulfillment, and security we want so much.

Only by living for something that lasts, something real – rather than for passing pleasure and profit – can we achieve the lasting fulfillment, the limitless capacity to love, that is our birthright.

 RELATED PAGES *April 12, April 30*

February 16

As Plato sometimes speaks of the divine love, it arises not out of indigency, as created love does, but out of fullness and redundancy.

JOHN SMITH THE PLATONIST

IN INDIA, where families often make severe sacrifices to send a son or daughter to college, everyone is patient with a student who is out of cash. If you are waiting in line for tickets with two or three friends, for example, and your turn comes at the box-office window, everyone understands if you suddenly discover that your shoelace has come loose. You bend down to tie it, giving your friends a chance to buy your ticket, and everybody knows there is no question of generosity or stinginess; you simply do not have the capacity to pay.

Similarly, when someone suddenly gets angry, you can think to yourself, "Well, his shoelace has just come untied." He has just run out of inner resources. Whatever he was doing before, he has to bend down and look at his feet; he hasn't got attention to give to anything else. To grow rich in love – to make yourself into a real tycoon of tenderness – have patience with others.

RELATED PAGES *September 19, October 1*

February 17

I claim to be an average man of less than average ability. . . . I have not the shadow of a doubt that any man or woman can achieve what I have, if he or she would make the same effort and cultivate the same hope and faith.

MAHATMA GANDHI

WHILE MOST people think of ordinariness as a fault or limitation, Gandhi had discovered in it the very meaning of life – and of history. For him, it was not the famous or the rich or the powerful who would change the course of history. If the future is to differ from the past, he taught, if we are to leave a peaceful and healthy earth for our children, it will be the ordinary man and woman who do it: not by becoming extraordinary, but by discovering that our greatest strength lies not in how much we differ from each other but in how much – how very much – we are the same.

This faith in the power of the individual formed the foundation for Gandhi's extremely compassionate view of the industrial era's large-scale problems, as well as of the smaller but no less urgent troubles we find in our own lives. One person *can* make a difference.

 RELATED PAGE *March 23*

February 18

Do not let your peace depend on the hearts of others; whatever they say about you, good or bad, you are not because of it another, for as you are, you are.

THOMAS A KEMPIS

EVEN IF you have ninety-nine people cheering you, there will always be a hundredth to boo. That is the nature of life, and to deal with it, we need simply to learn not to be always on the lookout for appreciation and applause. If people say, "Oh, there is nobody like you," don't get elated. Don't pick up your telephone and call your friends to tell them what is being broadcast about you. That's what most of us do, you know; that's why telephones are so busy. It is also why so many people get dejected when fortune seems to frown.

My spiritual teacher – a simple, straightforward woman who didn't mince words – used to tell me, "You can't shut other people's mouths." It took me years to understand that. This unlettered lady knew that we don't have any control over other people's minds. You can control only your own mind. When you understand this, you know you needn't be concerned about what people say about you: it doesn't affect you, because your mind cannot be upset. You may feel hurt, but you will have an inner security that cannot be shaken.

RELATED PAGES *March 4, September 16*

February 19

We are all dependent on one another, every soul of us on earth.

GEORGE BERNARD SHAW

ONE OF the surest proofs of spiritual awareness is that you will have respect and concern for all people, whatever country they come from, whatever the color of their skin, whatever religion they profess.

When you become aware that you are a part of the whole, something amazing happens in your life: you will be able to act spontaneously, almost effortlessly, for the good of all. You won't have to do research about famine to understand the needs of children in Africa and Asia who are unable to find enough food. You will understand, and you will find it impossible to waste food. Now you know that when a community in South America suffers, the whole suffers. You will find ways and means to help: perhaps change to a vegetarian diet so that the grain that is used to feed animals may be sent to the countries that sorely need it. You will be impelled into action, which is what awareness of unity means.

 RELATED PAGE *May 4*

February 20

I tell you one thing – if you want peace of mind, do not find fault with others. Rather learn to see your own faults. Learn to make the whole world your own. No one is a stranger, my child; this whole world is your own.

SRI SARADA DEVI

WHEN WE get even the slightest glimpse of the unity of life, we realize that in tearing others down we are tearing ourselves down too. When you sit in judgment on other people and countries and races, you're training your mind to sit in judgment on yourself. As we forgive others, we are teaching the mind to respond with forgiveness everywhere, even to the misdeeds and mistakes of our own past.

RELATED PAGES *August 4, October 13*

February 21

The secret of health for both mind and body is not to mourn for the past, not to worry about the future, or not to anticipate troubles, but to live the present moment wisely and earnestly.

THE BUDDHA

WHEN THE mind is at rest, we are lifted out of time into the eternal present. The body, of course, is still subject to the passage of time. But in a sense, the flickering of the mind is our internal clock. When the mind does not flicker, what is there to measure change? It's as if time simply comes to a stop for us, as we live completely in the present moment. Past and future, after all, exist only in the mind. When the mind is at rest, there is no past or future. We cannot be resentful, we cannot be guilt-ridden, we cannot build future hopes and desires; no energy flows to past or future at all.

Past and future are both contained in every present moment. Whatever we are today is the result of what we have thought, spoken, and done in all the present moments before now – just as what we shall be tomorrow is the result of what we think, say, and do today. The responsibility for both present and future is in our own hands. If we live right today, then tomorrow has to be right.

 RELATED PAGES *January 16, January 25*

February 22

This life of separateness may be compared to a dream, a phantasm, a bubble, a shadow, a drop of dew, a flash of lightning.

THE BUDDHA

TIME RUNS out so soon! In our teens and twenties, even our thirties, we have ample margin to play with the toys life has to offer. But we should find out soon how fleeting they are, for the tides of time can ebb away before we know it.

As we grow older and our family and friends begin to pass away, we see how relentlessly time is pursuing all of us. There is no time to quarrel, no time to feel resentful or estranged. There is no time to waste on the pursuit of selfish pleasures that are over almost before they begin.

All-devouring time follows us always, closer than our shadow. As long as I live only for myself, as a little fragment apart from the whole, I cannot escape being a victim of time. It is good to bear in mind how evanescent life is so that we do not postpone the practice of meditation.

RELATED PAGES *November 22, December 27*

February 23

The control of the palate is a valuable aid for the control of the mind.

MAHATMA GANDHI

I FIRST BECAME interested in improving my diet under the influence of Mahatma Gandhi, who used to include articles on diet and health in his weekly newspaper along with all the latest political news. I had been brought up on traditional South Indian cuisine. I had enjoyed it all thoroughly, but I had never asked what the purpose of food is. At Gandhi's prompting, I started asking this kind of question and concluded to my great surprise that food is meant to nourish the body.

I started changing. I began to eat foods that wouldn't have appealed to me in earlier days. Now asparagus tastes better than chocolate torte.

The palate is the ideal starting point for getting some mastery over your senses. You have three, four, maybe more opportunities a day: breakfast, lunch, dinner, and any number of between-meal snacks. No need to talk of fasting or strange diets. Just resolve to move away from foods that don't benefit your health and begin choosing foods that do.

 RELATED PAGES *May 22, May 24*

February 24

The grace of God is a wind which is always blowing.

SRI RAMAKRISHNA

ALL THAT you and I have to do is to put up our sails and let the wind of grace carry us across the sea of life to the other shore. But most of us are firmly stuck on this shore. Our sail is torn and our boat is overloaded with excess baggage: our likes and dislikes, our habits and opinions, all the resentments and hostilities which we have acquired.

But just as it is we, ourselves, who have acquired this baggage, it is we who can gradually learn to toss it overboard. The wind is blowing, but we have to make our boat seaworthy. We can patch up our sail, and unfurl it to catch the wind that will carry us to the other shore.

RELATED PAGES *February 29, December 24*

February 25

Got no checkbooks, got no banks,
Still I'd like to express my thanks;
I've got the sun in the morning and the moon at night.

IRVING BERLIN

EVEN PEOPLE with money, power, prestige, and everything they have been seeking in their careers can have emotional problems. No amount of money and prestige can prevent profound dissatisfaction and boredom, as well as psychosomatic disorders and drug addiction for millions of people. To me, this is proof that money and power are not our need, that the human being cannot be satisfied by them.

It is natural to feel that a little status or recognition would not be unwelcome in addition to earning a good livelihood, yet all the world's great religions teach us that getting something out of life, whether it is money or recognition or power or prestige, is not our real need. Giving to life is our real need.

 RELATED PAGES *July 1, July 11*

February 26

Put your heart, mind, intellect, and soul even into your smallest acts. This is the secret of success.

SWAMI SIVANANDA

ONE OF the practical reasons for meditating is to tap its power to solve problems that come up throughout the day. It is very much like getting momentum in a track event. While watching the Olympics on television for the first time, I was surprised to see how far back some of the athletes went to get a running start. In the pole vault one chap walked up to the bar, then turned around and strode so far back that I thought he had decided to go home. If you didn't know about the pole vault you might think, "What's the matter with this fellow? Instead of competing, he's running away."

He's not running away; he's going back to get the momentum he needs for a really big jump. That is the purpose of meditation, too. Instead of getting out of bed and plunging directly into life's maelstrom unprepared, you sit down for a half hour in meditation to get a good start. Then when you go out into the world, you have a good reserve of energy and security on which to draw.

RELATED PAGE *February 1*

February 27

The body is mortal, but the person dwelling in the body is immortal and immeasurable.

BHAGAVAD GITA

WHEN I say that this body is not me, I am not making an intellectual statement. It is an experiential statement. If you were to ask me, "Who is this body?" I would make an awful pun: "This is my buddy. I give him good food and good exercise, and I look after him very well, but he is not me."

My body has always been my faithful buddy, through many trials, and during many difficult times; and I let him know how much I appreciate his faithful service. We have an understanding: I take very good care of him, and he looks up to me as the boss. As Saint Francis used to say, "This body is Brother Donkey. I feed him, I wash him, but *I* am going to ride on *him*." Whenever we use drugs, or smoke, or drink, or even overeat, the donkey is riding on us. Francis challenges us: "Don't you want to get that donkey off your back and ride on *it*?"

 RELATED PAGES *April 6, July 2*

February 28

To display His eternal attributes
In their inexhaustible variety,
The Lord made the green fields of time and space.

JAMI

THE LORD has strewn little signs of his presence throughout the universe. The person who is observant will see these signs and know where God is to be found.

There is a marvelous story about a man looking for the Buddha the way one follows the tracks of an animal in the jungle. He went around talking to people everywhere, and whenever he found a person whose life had been transformed he would exclaim, "Those are the tracks of a really big elephant!"

The men and women who have realized God leave big, unmistakable tracks. In a smaller way, when we see someone being extremely patient, someone who can listen quietly to criticism without retaliating or losing her temper, we might think, "Aha! That's not my friend Jane; that is the Lord in Jane." Jane is leaving a trail – broken twigs of patience, torn leaves of kindness – all subtle signs by which we can track the Lord's presence.

Though the Lord is everywhere, the expression of his creativity varies throughout the infinite variety of the universe. Wherever perfection is approached, this glory is revealed a little more – among people, among trees, among mountains, among stars.

RELATED PAGE *December 2*

February 29

Make yourself familiar with the angels, and behold them frequently in spirit; for without being seen, they are present with you.

SAINT FRANCIS DE SALES

WHEN THE word "angel" is used, we can understand it as a personification of the forces for good in the world. Who will deny that forgiveness is one of the greatest forces on the face of the earth? Show me a man or a woman who can forgive completely and I will show you an angel.

If you want to see an angel, you have only to see a person who can return love for hatred. He is not just a person, he is a force. Similarly, a woman who has boundless patience is a powerful force that can transform antipathy into sympathy, ill will into good will, hatred into love.

There is another meaning as well: there are beneficial forces in life, ready to support those who are sincere but who find their capacities not adequate to the challenges that life presents.

When you are needed by others, when you have something valuable to contribute, these beneficial forces will support you, and give you greater health, greater energy, longer life, and deeper creativity. Life may strike at you, and challenges can hurtle themselves against you, but you will feel equal to them. Deeper forces from within will support you, hold you up, and act as a shield.

We are not alone in the universe. We are surrounded by mighty creative forces.

 RELATED PAGE *March 23*

March

Desire is the key to life, because desire is power.

EKNATH EASWARAN

March 1

In deep meditation the flow of concentration is continuous like the flow of oil.

YOGA SUTRA

THERE ARE two basic tools for mastering the thinking process. The first is meditation, which is described in the yoga texts with a beautifully precise image: there should be a smooth, unbroken flow of attention on a single subject, like the flow of oil poured from one vessel to another. My method of meditation is to make the mind go slowly through the words of a particular passage from the scriptures or great mystics, as slowly as possible. Whenever the mind wants to slip off on another line of thought, bring the attention back to the words of the passage. It may take practice, but eventually thought flows smoothly without interruption.

The other tool is the mantram, or mantra, which is a name or phrase with spiritual meaning and power. Meditation on an inspirational passage for half an hour every morning slows down the thinking process. Then during the day, the mantram keeps the mind from speeding up again. The mantram keeps the stream of concentrated thought flowing throughout the day.

 RELATED PAGES *March 2, March 10*

March 2

The mantram becomes one's staff of life, and carries one through every ordeal. It is no empty repetition. For each repetition has a new meaning, carrying you nearer and nearer to God.

MAHATMA GANDHI

THE MANTRAM, in some traditions called a prayer word, is the living symbol of the profoundest ideal that the human being can conceive of, the highest that we can respond to and love. When we repeat the mantram in our mind, we are reminding ourselves of the Supreme Reality enshrined in our hearts. The more we repeat the mantram, the deeper it sinks into our consciousness. As it begins to connect with this Reality, it strengthens our will, heals old sources of conflict and turmoil, and gives us access to deeper sources of strength, patience, and love.

In every religious tradition we find hallowed prayer words and mantrams. In the Christian tradition, the name of *Jesus* is precious; in India we have the name of *Rama*; in Buddhism *Om mani padme hum* is an ancient mantram. Jews may use *Barukh attah Adonai,* and Muslims repeat the name of *Allah.* These are only a few selections from the many that have been established by long tradition. Select one that appeals to you, but don't make up your own. A mantram given to the world by Francis of Assisi or the Buddha has great power. The mantram or prayer word can be repeated in the mind at any time, anywhere. But to meditate we must sit in a quiet place and concentrate on a memorized inspirational passage.

RELATED PAGE *March 27*

March 3

People say, "What is the sense of our small effort?" They cannot see that we must lay one brick at a time, take one step at a time.

DOROTHY DAY

IT IS repeated acts of unkindness that make us unloving and repeated acts of kindness that can make us loving. How do I become patient? By trying to be patient every day, little by little, *poco a poco.*

We shouldn't expect to go to bed one night the most impatient man or woman in the county and get up in the morning flooded with patience. Every day, every night, it takes continuous practice, continuous striving. If you are doing everything to be patient, you are going to become inexhaustibly patient. If you are struggling everywhere to become loving, you are going to be unfailingly loving.

In the gradual development on the spiritual path, it is better to concede that most of us start with a good deal of inertia. This shows itself as an attitude of avoiding challenges, shutting our eyes to the problems that confront the world. This inertia is slowly transformed into energy, just as ice when heated becomes water that flows – which can be used for irrigation and harnessed for any useful purpose that we approve of. In the same way, all of that locked-up energy can be released. But it requires steady effort, one step at a time.

 RELATED PAGES *March 28, May 5*

March 4

It is no little wisdom for you to keep yourself in silence and in good peace when evil words are spoken to you, and to turn your heart to God and not to be troubled with the judgment of others.

THOMAS A KEMPIS

MOST OF us appreciate praise, but it is disastrous to become dependent on it. If we are going to allow our security to be bolstered up by the praise, appreciation, and applause of others, we are done for. I have heard about a well-known movie star who goes to sleep at night with a tape of recorded applause playing. This is going to make him more and more insecure.

Why should we get agitated if someone ignores us? There are, after all, advantages to being ignored. We can go anywhere in freedom. Nobody recognizes us – how good it is! In life, there are occasions when we are ignored and sometimes forgotten. That is the time for us to remind ourselves, "Why do I need anybody's attention?" This attitude can be cultivated skillfully.

Even those of us who are the most sensitive to praise and appreciation can learn to be so secure within ourselves that the word *rejected* can be expelled from our dictionary. The one person who will never reject us is the divine Self within, and that is enough to make up for all the rejections we may have to undergo at the hands of everyone else.

RELATED PAGES *February 18, March 17*

March 5

God loves a cheerful giver.

II CORINTHIANS

IN INDIA we have a story about a man who was the perfect model of respectability, who always did what the letter of the law demanded. When he died, he was taken before the cosmic auditor. The auditor looked at the man's record. There was not a single entry on the debit page. The auditor was impressed. Then he turned to the credit page and stared in astonishment. This page, too, was completely blank. He didn't know what to do. The man had never helped anybody; never hurt anybody; never offended anybody; never loved anybody. He couldn't be sent to heaven, but he couldn't be sent to hell, either.

So the cosmic keeper of the books took him to the god of creation, and said, "You made this guy. What shall I do with him?"

The Creator looked at the statute books and couldn't find a precedent to cover the case. And since this is a Hindu story, he said, "Take him to Krishna."

Krishna said, "The buck stops here." He examined the record very carefully and there, almost illegible, was an ancient credit entry: "Gave two cents to a beggar at the age of six." "There," Sri Krishna said, "return his two cents and send him back to earth to try again." Until we have learned to give freely of ourselves, we have not learned how to live.

 RELATED PAGES *March 29, September 4*

March 6

God expects but one thing of you, and that is that you should come out of yourself insofar as you are a created being and let God be God in you.

MEISTER ECKHART

IN THOSE moments when we forget ourselves – not thinking, "Am I happy?" but completely oblivious to our little ego – we spend a brief but beautiful holiday in heaven. The joy we experience in these moments of self-forgetting is our true nature, our native state. To regain it, we have simply to empty ourselves of what hides this joy: that is, to stop dwelling on ourselves. To the extent that we are not full of ourselves, God can fill us. "If you go out of yourself," says Johannes Tauler, "without doubt he shall go in, and there will be much or little of his entering in according to how much or little you go out."

RELATED PAGES *January 13, April 9*

March 7

Love, and do what you like.

SAINT AUGUSTINE

LEARNING TO love in the way Saint Augustine is talking about is the most demanding, the most delightful, and the most daring of disciplines. It does not mean loving only two or three members of your family. It does not mean loving only those who share your views, read the same newspapers, or play the same sports. Love, as Jesus puts it, means blessing those that curse you, doing good to those that harm you.

Most of us do not begin by blessing those that curse us. That is graduate school. We start with first grade – being kind to people in our family when they get resentful. Eventually comes high school, where we learn to move closer to those who are trying to shut themselves off from us. College means returning good will for ill will. Finally we enter graduate school. There we learn to give our love to all – to people of different races, countries, and religions, different outlooks and strata of society, without any sense of distinction or difference.

 RELATED PAGES *May 14, October 14*

March 8

The tree which moves some to tears of joy is in the eyes of others only a green thing that stands in the way.

WILLIAM BLAKE

ONE DAY, when I was a growing boy, my grandmother asked me a question, "Have you ever looked in Hasti's eyes?" Hasti was one of the elephants that frequently served in our religious ceremonies and that I had been learning to ride. Hasti's eyes, like the eyes of all elephants, were tiny – ridiculously small, really, for an animal so huge. "She has no idea how big she is," Granny said, "because she looks out at the world through such tiny eyes."

If the world seems hostile and lifeless, and if we seem insignificant in it, it is because, like the elephant, we look at it through such tiny eyes. Through those small eyes, shrunken by the desire for profit and personal gratification, we appear just as insignificant as all the green things – and all the other human beings, animals, fish, birds, and insects – that stand in the way.

When we are absorbed in the pursuit of profit, we live in the narrow world of the bottom line. In that world, our only neighbors are buyers and sellers, our only concerns property, profit, and possessions. Yet all around us is a world teeming with people, animals, organisms, and elements – a deeply interconnected environment that responds to all we do.

RELATED PAGES *January 8, November 9*

March 9

Who has not found the heaven below
Will fail of it above.
God's residence is next to mine,
His furniture is love.

EMILY DICKINSON

LOVE IS not physical; it is a state of consciousness. That is why I consider loving a skill, a great skill that can be learned. It calls for great effort and enthusiasm, but it can be mastered. And when it is mastered, every loving relationship grows richer and more romantic with the passage of time. You can be more romantic, more tenderly in love during the second part of your life than you were in your twenties.

Very, very few of us are born with this skill. We have to learn it, mostly by making mistakes. In my early days I too made many silly mistakes. Every one of us has made mistakes in our relationships and gone through difficulties which led us to move away from people who were dear to us.

A spiritual perspective on life is meant not to torment us with the past, but to comfort and console us. An untrained mind cannot be in love very long, while a trained mind can never fall out of love.

 RELATED PAGES *January 4, January 10*

March 10

Seek ye first the kingdom of heaven, and all else shall be added unto you.

THE GOSPEL ACCORDING TO SAINT MATTHEW

THE MANTRAM is one of the best of prayers – one that we say not just when we get up or when we go to bed, but countless times throughout the day, and throughout the night as well. This prayer is not addressed to someone outside us, but to our deepest Self, the Lord of Love, who dwells in the hearts of us all. When we repeat it, we are not asking for anything in particular, like good health or solutions to our problems or richer personal relationships. We are simply asking to get closer to the source of all strength and all joy and all love. To use Jesus' words, we are asking for "the kingdom of heaven," and we find at the same time that our health improves, our problems begin to be resolved, and our relationships blossom.

RELATED PAGES *March 27, April 14*

March 11

Life consists in what a man is thinking of all day.

RALPH WALDO EMERSON

A COMPULSIVE DESIRE is like any other thought over which we have no control. It flows continuously: "I want that; I want that; I want that." There seems to be no space between the thoughts. But when your meditation begins to deepen, two things happen. First, the thought process slows down. Second, you develop a new attitude toward desires – you begin to realize that you needn't give in to the desire. You have a choice.

Now, when a very strong desire starts to overtake you, and your mind is just one long string of "I want that," you catch sight of a tiny opening between the demands. It may be only a split second in duration at first, but in time it grows long enough for another thought, another *kind* of thought, to make itself known. "Hmmm," we think, "maybe part of me does want that – but do *I*? Is it really in my long-term best interest to gratify this desire?"

 RELATED PAGE *May 10*

March 12

Blessed are the merciful: for they shall obtain mercy.

THE GOSPEL ACCORDING TO SAINT MATTHEW

EVEN IF we agree intellectually with the Sermon on the Mount, how many of us act as if its words apply to us? We let mercy wait while we pursue goals we understand. A luxurious home overlooking the sea through a forest of pines, prestige in our job, success for our children: don't all of us dream that such things can make us happy?

"That is not enough," Jesus would say quietly. Our need is for love, and we can get it only in the measure that we give. Instead of pursuing external satisfactions, we need to let love and mercy rule our decisions from day to day, and our long-range goals as well.

Then the forces of life will rise up from within to protect us. They will protect our health by keeping us clear of physical addictions. They will protect our mind by keeping it calm. People will surround us with affection and support when they see we care about them more than we do about ourselves.

RELATED PAGE *January 6*

March 13

We need men who can dream of things that never were, and ask why not.

GEORGE BERNARD SHAW

IN AN Indian movie I saw recently, a villager leaves home for the first time to travel to the city of Bombay. When he returns, his family and friends crowd around him, asking what it was like in the big city. His laconic reply sums up our era: "Such tall buildings . . . and such small people."

If we were asked to give an accounting of our society's achievements, we could claim many great technological developments and scientific discoveries, plenty of skyscrapers, and the amassment of huge sums of money, but few truly secure, truly wise, truly great men and women. It is not for lack of ability or energy, though; it is because we lack a noble goal.

To grow to our full height, we need to be challenged with tasks that draw out our deeper resources, the talents and capacities we did not know we had. We need to be faced with obstacles that cannot be surmounted unless we summon up our daring and creativity. This kind of challenge is familiar to any great athlete or scientist or artist. No worthwhile accomplishment comes easily.

 RELATED PAGE *April 30*

March 14

You must learn an inner solitude, wherever or with whomsoever you may be. You must learn to penetrate things and find God there, to get a strong impression of God firmly fixed in your mind.

MEISTER ECKHART

TO GIVE full attention to whatever we are doing isn't easy when we have a job we dislike, or must work with people who are difficult. Then our attention wanders like a child's – looking at this glass for a moment, then at this table, then out the window. If we could only attend a little more to the work, even when we dislike it, it would become quite interesting. When we can give it our full attention, anything becomes interesting. And anything, when we do not give it our full attention, becomes uninteresting.

RELATED PAGES *January 3, April 29*

March 15

The world is too much with us; late and soon,
Getting and spending, we lay waste our powers:
Little we see in Nature that is ours.

WILLIAM WORDSWORTH

OUR MODERN way of life seems to be making us busier and busier about less and less. It is only after we begin to taste the joy of simple living that we realize how much all this frantic activity can stand between us and our fulfillment. The more we divide our interests, our allegiances, our activities, the less time we have for living.

Loving, loyal personal relationships take time. We cannot get to know someone intimately in a day or establish a lasting relationship during a weekend conference. If we spend eight hours a day at our job and the evening watching television, where is the time for cultivating close friendships? If we simplify our lives, we shall find the time and energy to be together with our family and friends, or to give our time to a worthy cause that needs our contribution. The simple life doesn't mean bearing with a drab routine; it means giving our time and attention to what is most important.

 RELATED PAGE *November 14*

March 16

***What we take in by contemplation,
that we pour out in love.***

MEISTER ECKHART

THE OLD dispute about the relative virtues of the active way to spiritual awareness versus the contemplative way is a spurious one. We require both. They are phases of a single rhythm like the pulsing of the heart, the in-drawing and letting go of breath, the ebb and flow of the tides. So we go deep, turn inwards in meditation to consolidate our vital energy, and then with greater love and wisdom we come out into the family, the community, the world. Without action, we lack opportunities for changing our old ways and we increase our self-will rather than lessen it; without contemplation, we lack the strength to change and are blown about by our conditioning.

RELATED PAGES *April 24, September 6*

March 17

To have courage for whatever comes in life – everything lies in that.

SAINT TERESA OF AVILA

FOR THE majority of us, uncertainty is worse than disaster, because disaster comes to us only rarely; worry depletes us often. We never know whether we are going to get a brick or a bouquet. If we knew for certain a brick was on its way, there would be no anxiety. We would just say, "Throw it and be done with it."

We can learn how to handle both bricks and bouquets, praise and censure, success and defeat. When we can say, "Whatever comes, we will not be afraid because the divine Self is within us," then this resoluteness and faith will enable us to work free from tension, agitation, and fear of defeat. The person who works in this way is at peace, because he or she is not anxious about results.

 RELATED PAGES *March 4, September 16*

March 18

My life is an indivisible whole, and all my attitudes run into one another; and they all have their rise in my insatiable love for mankind.

MAHATMA GANDHI

WE SHOULD be able to make all sorts of graceful concessions on things that do not matter in life and yet stand unshakable on essentials.

To do this, we have to be detached from our opinions. I'm not recommending that we be wishy-washy, or lack strength in our convictions, but that we cultivate the forbearance not to force our opinions on others. When we have strength of conviction we will not get rattled when people question or contradict us. Mahatma Gandhi, for example, was not in favor of tea or coffee, but he would make a cup of tea for his wife each morning just the way she liked it. This is bending gracefully on nonessentials.

When it came to essentials, however, Gandhi was unshakable. His dedication to nonviolence was so absolute that he would abruptly call off a successful nationwide program of noncooperation with the British if he heard any reports of violence committed by his countrymen, even those who did not acknowledge him as their leader.

RELATED PAGES *August 6, October 16*

March 19

Hatred does not cease through hatred at any time. Hatred ceases through love. This is an unalterable law.

THE BUDDHA

IN ORDER to work for peace, we should have an adequate sense of detachment from the results of our work. If we are going to get agitated when there is a reversal, we ourselves will become violent. As we know, sometimes even demonstrators against violence become violent.

To paraphrase the wise words of the Buddha, "Violence will not cease by violence. Violence ceases by nonviolence. This is an unalterable law." In order to win over opposition, we have to be serene and compassionate. Most of us look upon defeat and reversals as weakening us; but when we are defeated it is possible to go deeper into our consciousness to bring out greater resources. Mahatma Gandhi was at his best when seemingly defeated. He used to say that he struck his hardest bargains from prison.

Defeat is found very often in the lives of selfless people as an opening into opportunity. When you follow the spiritual path, living for others, there come to you increased challenges, to make you go deeper and deeper into your consciousness. If there were no difficulties, you would only be skimming on the surface of life. Gandhi, in a rare statement in which he gave himself away, said, "I love storms."

 RELATED PAGES *April 11, July 9*

March 20

He that can have patience, can have what he will.

BENJAMIN FRANKLIN

HERE IS a tip for keeping the palate on the middle path. When it is craving candy or a hot fudge sundae, go for a walk repeating the mantram you have chosen, and bargain for time. Tell your mind, "In two hours, on our way home we can go to an ice cream parlor for a deluxe sundae." Interestingly enough, two hours later the mind has forgotten ice cream sundaes and is thinking about the movie it will enjoy tomorrow evening. All you need do is put just a little break of time between the palate and its desire, for you can count on the mind to change its desires.

Treat the mind gently, patiently, and compassionately. Since it has been allowed free license for so many years, it is not fair to expect it to come round in a day or two.

RELATED PAGES *June 10, October 2*

March 21

A human being has so many skins inside, covering the depths of the heart. We know so many things, but we don't know ourselves! Why, thirty or forty skins or hides, as thick and hard as an ox's or a bear's, cover the soul. Go into your own ground and learn to know yourself there.

MEISTER ECKHART

BELOW THE relatively superficial levels of the mind – beneath the emotions we are ordinarily aware of – lie layer on layer of the unconscious mind. This is the "cloud of unknowing," where primordial instincts, fears, and urges cover our understanding. The deepest flaw in the mind is what Einstein called the "kind of optical delusion of consciousness" that makes us see ourselves as separate from the rest of life. Like a crack in glasses that we must wear every moment of our lives, this division is built into the mind. "I" versus "not-I" runs through everything we see.

To see life as it is, the mind must be made pure: everything that distorts must be quieted or removed. When the mind is completely still, unstirred even in its depths, we see straight through to the ground of our being, which is divine.

 RELATED PAGES *January 30, June 26*

March 22

Strength does not come from physical capacity. It comes from an indomitable will.

MAHATMA GANDHI

WHAT COUNTS most in life is not IQ but WQ, "Will Quotient." No one can plead that he or she lacks will. There is will in every desire. Every desire carries with it the will to bring that desire to fruition. When it comes to something we like, we have all the will we need. Someone says, "Hey, come on, we're going skiing!" and that is enough. We will get out of bed at three in the morning, drive for hours, stand cheerfully in the snow waiting for the ski lift, and in general suffer all kinds of discomfort with a will of iron. Yet as small a challenge as a letter to Aunt Gertrude will find the will against us.

To control our destiny, we need to harness our will, to do not what we *like*, but what is in our long-term best interest. If the will is strong enough, great things can be accomplished; if the will is weak, very little. In every endeavor, it is the man or woman with a firm will who excels.

RELATED PAGES *May 22, August 30*

March 23

I want to go on living even after my death! And therefore I am grateful to God for giving me this gift, this possibility of developing myself and of writing, of expressing all that is in me. I can shake off everything if I write; my sorrows disappear, my courage is reborn.

ANNE FRANK

WHEN YOU discover that everyone is contained in you and you are contained in everyone, you have realized the unity of life, which is the divine ground of existence. Then you are not just a person; you have become a beneficial force. Wherever you go, wherever you live, those around you will benefit from your life.

The life of such a person, such as Mahatma Gandhi in our own times, becomes a permanent, selfless force on this earth, because even after death his influence continues to bring people together, to make them aware of their trusteeship for the resources of the earth and for all creatures. Gandhi is still alive because he is still at work as a real force, advancing peace, good will, and unity.

Even one unassuming man or woman leading a selfless life, though he or she may live only a few years on earth, enriches all life for all time to come. Even if one person in a community is leading a selfless life, he will make his contribution, and she will slowly inspire others to make the same contribution, because human nature responds to such an example.

 RELATED PAGE *January 27*

March 24

Those whose consciousness is unified abandon all attachment to the results of action and attain supreme peace. But those whose desires are fragmented, who are selfishly attached to the results of their work, are bound in everything they do.

BHAGAVAD GITA

IT IS not so much work that tires us, but ego-driven work. When we are selfishly involved, we cannot help worrying, we cannot help getting overly concerned about our success or failure. The preoccupation with results makes us tense, and our anxiety exhausts us.

The Gita is essentially a call to action. But it is a call to selfless action, that is, action without any selfish attachments to the results. It asks us to do our best, yet never allow ourselves to become involved in whether things work out the way we want.

It takes practice to learn this skill, but once you have it, as Gandhi says, you will never lose your nerve. The sense of inadequacy goes, and the question "Am I equal to this job?" will not arise. It is enough that the job needs to be done and that you are doing your best to get it done.

RELATED PAGE *September 17*

March 25

The little unremembered acts of kindness and love are the best of a good man's life.

WILLIAM WORDSWORTH

OUR LIVES affect others, whether directly, through the environment, or by the force of our example.

For instance, we could say that smoking shows a lack of love. First, our capacity for love is actually caught in the compulsion to smoke. But more than that, the example tells even casual passersby, "Don't worry about what your doctor says. Don't worry about the consequences. If it feels good, do it!"

Pelé, the Brazilian soccer star, was in a position to command a king's ransom for endorsing commercial products. He never gave his endorsement to any cigarette, putting the reason in simple words: "I love kids." That is a perfect choice of words. He *does* love kids. He knows that in most of the world they will buy anything with his name on it. Therefore, though he came from a poor family, no amount of money can tempt him to do something that will mislead young people or injure their health.

To love is to be responsible like this in everything: the work we do, the things we buy, the food we eat, the people we look up to, the movies we see, the words we use, every choice we make from morning till night. That is the real measure of love; it is a wonderfully demanding responsibility.

 RELATED PAGE *April 2*

March 26

Thy desire is thy prayer; and if thy desire is without ceasing, thy prayer will also be without ceasing. . . . The continuance of your longing is the continuance of your prayer.

SAINT AUGUSTINE

I ONCE HAD a physicist friend who would gladly discuss electric power; but harnessing the power of a passion or a craving – well, that was not dynamics; that was poetry. "Power," he told me sternly, "is the capacity to do work. Work is the energy required to move a definite mass a definite distance. No movement, no work. No work, no power."

Day or night I had never seen my friend far from his desk. Then late one evening I came out of a movie theater and saw him striding along like an athlete, several miles from his office. "What got you up from your desk?" I asked. "You're breaking the habits of a lifetime."

"Coffee," he muttered. "I ran out of coffee."

"Here," I said, "a very definite mass has been propelled at least three miles, simply by one little desire for a cup of coffee." He got my point.

Every deep desire is a prayer. Every desire also contains a certain quantum of energy – energy to grasp the desired goal.

RELATED PAGES *February 13, May 2*

March 27

I go far away or near but God never goes far off; he is always standing close at hand, and even if he cannot stay within he goes no further than the door.

MEISTER ECKHART

IT IS so easy to repeat the mantram – *Jesus, Jesus,* or *Rama, Rama,* or whichever one we have chosen – that at first most of us cannot believe that it is charged with great power. Only after we use it for a while do we begin to see that repeating the mantram is not just a mechanical exercise; it is a direct line to the Lord, the Self within, somewhat like picking up the phone and calling him collect. We don't have to make any promises or commitments; we only have to repeat the mantram when we are agitated – angry, afraid, speeded up, or caught in worries or regrets – and the Self opens a little door to the reserves of our deeper consciousness.

 RELATED PAGES *March 2, April 13*

March 28

Have patience with all things, but chiefly have patience with yourself. Do not lose courage in considering your own imperfections, but instantly set about remedying them – every day begin the task anew.

SAINT FRANCIS DE SALES

WHILE WE were living on the Blue Mountain in India, we noticed that our local bank had a very neighborly arrangement for collecting funds from the villagers. Poor villagers have very little to save, only a few copper pennies at most. To encourage them to deposit even these few pennies every day, the bank employed a boy with a bicycle to go into the village to their homes, collect their few coppers, and enter the total in their account.

In meditation it is the same: when the Self comes, we can say, "We are no great saint, but a few times today we have tried to be patient. A few times today we have tried to put our family first. A few times today we have resisted some little craving for personal satisfaction." This is how most of us are going to make progress for a long time: a few pennies here, a few pennies there, collected every day. But in these innumerable little acts of selflessness lies spiritual growth, which over a long period can transform every one of us into a loving person. To quote the bank advertisement, "It all adds up."

RELATED PAGES *March 3, April 15*

March 29

Whatever you do, make it an offering to me – the food you eat, the sacrifices you make, the help you give, even your suffering.

BHAGAVAD GITA

WE CAN'T give anyone joy or security by increasing her bank account or adding to his collection of vintage wines. Of course, a well-chosen gift given at the right time is always welcome, but whatever the gift, we should guard against the nagging expectation of getting something in return. The moment we expect reward or recognition, we are making a contract.

Even parents and children suffer from this contractual relationship. Parents can help their children tremendously by avoiding the "I did this for you, therefore you do that for me" approach, encouraging them instead to follow their own star.

In the spiritual lore of India, it is said that God whispered only one word in our ears when he sent us into the world: "Give." Give freely of your time, your talent, your resources; give without asking for anything in return. This is the secret of living in joy and security.

 RELATED PAGES *March 5, September 8*

March 30

Cheerfulness strengthens the heart and makes us persevere in a good life; therefore the servant of God ought always to be in good spirits.

SAINT PHILIP OF NERI

WHEN THINGS go wrong, that's the time to be more cheerful. When things go right, of course we are cheerful. When nerves are getting frayed, that's the time to smile.

The practice of spiritual disciplines has a very useful purpose: they can make us so secure, so firmly rooted in our deepest Self that not only can we go and live in the midst of people who are difficult with cheerfulness and equanimity, we can even learn to change them for the better.

Even if you have a bad day in the office, or a very busy day on the campus, that's no cause for your courtesy to fail, for your consideration to fail.

I knew a little girl of three or four who was usually very nice to me. Then suddenly one afternoon she was looking at me like a storm cloud. I asked, "What's the matter?" and she replied, "You better watch out: I haven't had my nap."

Now imagine grown-up people coming home in the evening and telling everyone, "Don't bother me. I haven't had my nap."

It is one of the hallmarks of the spiritually aware man or woman that they will always be cheerful, not because they don't feel deeply, but because they do feel deeply.

RELATED PAGES *July 9, October 7*

March 31

Purity of heart is to will one thing.

SOREN KIERKEGAARD

THERE IS a Hindu story comparing the mind to the trunk of an elephant – restless, inquisitive, always straying. In our villages in India, elephants are sometimes taken in religious processions through the streets to the temple. The streets are crooked and narrow, lined on either side with fruit and vegetable stalls. Along comes the elephant with his restless trunk, and in one sinuous motion, he grabs a whole bunch of bananas. He opens his cavernous mouth, and tosses the bananas in – stalk and all. From the next stall he picks up a coconut and tosses it in after the bananas. No threats or promises can make this restless trunk settle down. But the wise elephant trainer will give that trunk a short bamboo stick to hold. Then the elephant will walk along proudly, holding the bamboo stick in front like a drum major with a baton. He doesn't steal bananas and coconuts now, because his trunk has something to hold onto.

The mind works in the same way. We can keep it from straying into all kinds of situations if we just give it the mantram.

 RELATED PAGE *May 8*

April

Only by living for something that lasts, something real, can we achieve the fulfillment that is our birthright.

EKNATH EASWARAN

April 1

A mind that is fast is sick. A mind that is slow is sound. A mind that is still is divine.

MEHER BABA

SOMEHOW, IN our modern civilization, we have acquired the idea that the mind is working best when it runs at top speed. Yet a racing mind lacks time even to finish a thought, let alone to check on its quality. When we slow down the mind, we work better at everything we do. Not only is the quality of our work better, we are actually able to get more done. A calm, smooth-running flow of thought saves a lot of wear and tear on the nervous system, which means we have more vitality and resilience in the face of stress.

 RELATED PAGES *April 19, May 18*

April 2

Just as there is no loss of basic energy in the universe, so no thought or action is without its effects, present or ultimate, seen or unseen, felt or unfelt.

NORMAN COUSINS

JUST AS the example of Jesus inspired Francis of Assisi a millennium later, Francis inspired thousands of people during his own lifetime, and continues to do so today. Francis was recognized as a powerful teacher, but it was his simple and selfless life that moved hearts. It was his life, and his experience of God, that gave power to his words.

Near the end of his life, while he was making a mountain journey, Francis's health failed. His companions went into a farmyard to borrow a donkey for him to ride. On hearing for whom it was intended, the peasant came out and asked, "Are you the Brother Francis there is so much said about?" Receiving a nod from one of Francis's companions, he added, "Then take care that you are as good in reality as they say, for there are many who have confidence in you." Deeply stirred, Francis kissed the peasant in gratitude for this reminder.

We are not poor friars living in medieval Italy, but the lesson is the same: let us remember that our lives set an example for others. No one can say his life doesn't matter, her words don't matter.

RELATED PAGES *March 25, June 9*

April 3

The Buddhas do but tell the way, it is for you to labor at the task.

THE BUDDHA

SPIRITUAL TEACHERS are like signposts pointing the way to immortality, but it is we who must make the journey. This is quite reasonable. After all, when we pass a signpost on the freeway, we don't expect it to get into the driver's seat and do the driving while we lie down in the back to take a nap. On the first half of the spiritual journey, we cannot expect other people to pick us up and carry us along. It is up to us to meditate regularly, and practice the allied disciplines.

Sri Ramakrishna says that the first part of the trip is the "way of the monkey." The little baby monkey has to hold on for dear life while his mother swings from tree to tree. If the little one loses his grip, he'll fall and hurt himself. But the second half is the "way of the cat." The little kitten just sits there on the road looking cute and helpless, saying, "mew, mew, mew," and the mother cat picks it up by the scruff of its neck and takes it to safety. It is only on the second half of the journey that we are carried by a power higher than ourselves.

 RELATED PAGE *May 7*

April 4

One who holds back rising anger like a rolling chariot, that one I call a real driver; other people are but holding the reins.

THE BUDDHA

IT TAKES two to quarrel: the other person can throw down the gauntlet, but we don't have to pick it up. When someone criticizes us or contradicts us or speaks in an unpleasant tone of voice, there is no quarrel as long as we remember that we have the choice not to reply in the same manner. Trouble starts only when we react on the stimulus and response level – which may be all right for two-year-olds but not for mature men and women. At such times, it will help us to be more patient, and our example will help the other person to be more patient too.

RELATED PAGES *January 22, June 5*

April 5

He insulted me, he cheated me, he beat me, he robbed me – those who are free of resentful thoughts surely find peace.

THE BUDDHA

RESENTMENT IS nothing more than compulsive attachment to a set of memories. If you could peek through the window of the mind when you feel resentful, you would see a production line turning out the same emotion-charged memory over and over: "He did that to me in 1993, he did that to me in 1993 . . ." You are dwelling on something that took place in the past – or, more likely, on how you misunderstood that event and reacted to your misunderstanding. When you keep pumping attention into an event in this way, a limp little memory gets blown up into a big balloon of hostility. When you withdraw your attention by repeating the mantram, the balloon is deflated. It's as simple as that.

 RELATED PAGE *May 8*

April 6

The first wealth is health.

RALPH WALDO EMERSON

WHEN YOU regard your life as a trust, you realize that the first resource you have to take care of is your own body. This can be startling. Even your body is not really your own. It belongs to life, and it is your responsibility to take care of it. You cannot afford to do anything that injures your body, because the body is the instrument you need for selfless action. That is the fine print of the trust agreement: when we smoke, when we overeat, when we don't get enough exercise, we are violating the terms of the trust.

If you want to live life at its fullest, you will want to do everything possible to keep your body in vibrant health in order to give back to life a little of what it has given you.

RELATED PAGES *February 27, July 6*

April 7

If one who enjoys a lesser happiness beholds a greater one, let him leave aside the lesser to gain the greater.

THE BUDDHA

THE BUDDHA, the most practical of teachers, says that wisdom is essentially discrimination – the precious capacity to see what is important in the long run and then choose our course of action accordingly.

Most of us are vigilant when making big decisions, but less so when dealing with little ones. We forget the cumulative effect of all those missed "little" opportunities. It is precisely on those thousand little occasions, and over a period of time, that the mind is taught to be calm and kind – not instantaneously or by great leaps. In the ordinary choices of every day we begin to change the direction of our lives.

 RELATED PAGE *January 14*

April 8

Happiness is not a goal; it is a by-product.

ELEANOR ROOSEVELT

IT IS only immature people who believe, "I am separate; therefore, I can manipulate you, even exploit you, to ensure my own happiness."

To think that we can pursue joy as a collector pursues butterflies, seeking it here and there, is folly. We can never go after joy because joy has got to come after us.

It's like the horizon. When you look from the Berkeley hills, the horizon looks as if it is just beyond the Golden Gate. You honestly believe that if you go there, you will reach the horizon. But as you pursue it, it recedes farther and farther, and that is the nature of pleasure. It peeps out from the store, the restaurant, the bank, but when you enter there you will find it recedes farther and farther.

When we begin to seek a higher goal – for the welfare of our family and community – joy slowly tiptoes after us. We don't have to say to joy, "Excuse me, will you please come to my house?"

Joy will come and put her suitcase down and say, "I am going to be here, whether you like it or not."

That is how happiness comes.

RELATED PAGES *July 4, August 8*

April 9

Nirvana is not the blowing out of a candle. It is the extinguishing of the flame because day is come.

RABINDRANATH TAGORE

THERE ARE many distinguished scholars who try to interpret as far as the intellect can what nirvana means. They will say that nirvana is the annihilation of the ego-concept.

But this definition is far from adequate. Nirvana is really an awakening, which is the meaning of the Buddha's name: "He who is awake," from the root *budh*, "to wake up." What happens is you wake up from separateness into the whole – from being a fragment to being the indivisible whole. A Buddha is one who becomes aware of the wholeness of life and lives for the welfare of all.

Yes, from the negative side, nirvana means you are completely empty of yourself. You have to empty yourself completely of all your likes and dislikes, of your selfish attachments, your self-will, your petty personal desires. So nirvana is emptiness. But it is also complete fullness. In order to be full you have to empty yourself completely of yourself. The intellect can never understand this. The only way to understand nirvana is to experience it.

 RELATED PAGES *March 6, June 12*

April 10

True love grows by sacrifice and the more thoroughly the soul rejects natural satisfaction the stronger and more detached its tenderness becomes.

SAINT THÉRÈSE OF LISIEUX

IF SOMEBODY is kind to us ninety-nine times and then does one hurtful thing, we are likely to forget the ninety-nine good things and remember the one bad thing. We can watch it happen in ourselves – no matter how absurd we know it is – when our parents or partner or children fail us and we blow a fuse. When we get angry, we suffer a curious, temporary attack of amnesia. For the time being, we just cannot remember that week when she nursed us when we came down with the flu. We forget the time he entertained us cheerfully when we were depressed and irritable. We don't see the hundreds and hundreds of white flags charting the course of good relations down the years. We see only this last crimson flag waving menacingly in our face.

This is not to say that we should close our eyes when someone is unkind to us. But if we can turn our attention away from that one act of unkindness and turn it to all the kindnesses we have received down the years, the incident will fall into its proper place. We will probably say to ourselves, "This hostility is so petty! I shouldn't even have let it come up."

RELATED PAGES *March 3, September 21*

April 11

Nonviolence is the supreme law of life.

HINDU PROVERB

THE SANSKRIT word for nonviolence is *ahimsa*: *a* means "not" or "without"; *himsa* is violence. This may sound negative, but in Sanskrit a word constructed in this way stands for a state both perfect and positive. Ahimsa implies that when every trace of violence is removed from the mind, what is left is our natural state of consciousness: pure love. Unfortunately, that love has been buried under layer upon layer of ill will and selfish conditioning. To have love bubble up to the surface of our life, all we have to do is systematically remove all those layers.

There are three kinds of violence: one, through our deeds; two, through our words; and three, through our thoughts. Most of what we call violence is in the form of action, and it is with our actions that nonviolence naturally begins. But as long as our minds harbor violent thoughts, that incipient violence will find its way somehow into our speech and behavior. The root of all violence is in the world of thoughts, and that is why training the mind is so important.

 RELATED PAGES *March 19, June 15*

April 12

There is hunger for ordinary bread, and there is hunger for love, for kindness, for thoughtfulness; and this is the great poverty that makes people suffer so much.

MOTHER TERESA OF CALCUTTA

OUR MODERN civilization is so physically oriented that when we hear the word *hunger*, we immediately think of vitamins and minerals and amino acids. It seldom occurs to us that just as the body develops problems when it does not get adequate food, the person who is deprived of love – or worse, who finds it difficult to love – becomes subject to problems every bit as serious.

This doesn't mean just emotional problems, which of course are included. More and more evidence indicates that lack of love not only leads to loneliness, despair, and resentment, but also contributes to the deterioration of physical health. When spiritual figures like Mother Teresa talk about our need to love and to be loved, the need is not metaphorical. She is not talking about some vague spirituality; she is talking about good nutrition. Resentment, hostility, alienation, and selfishness are deficiency diseases. You can have all the essential amino acids, vitamins, and minerals known and unknown but if you cannot love, you are not likely to remain in good health.

RELATED PAGES *February 15, May 14*

April 13

Let sleep itself be an exercise in piety, for such as our life and conduct have been, so also of necessity will be our dreams.

SAINT BASIL

ONE OF the best times to repeat the mantram is while falling asleep at night. Tuck yourself in, close your eyes, and start repeating your mantram until you fall asleep in it: *Rama, Rama, Rama,* or *Jesus, Jesus, Jesus,* or *Hail Mary, Hail Mary.* – whichever mantram you have chosen.

Other thoughts may try to push the mantram away. But through sheer persistence you can achieve a minor miracle. Between the last waking moment and the first sleeping moment, there is an arrow's entry into deepest consciousness. If you can send your mantram in through that narrow gate, it will go on repeating itself in your sleep, healing old wounds and restoring your peace of mind for the next day.

The Lord is quite happy to work all night. Those who have learned to fall asleep in the mantram go forward even in their sleep.

 RELATED PAGE *March 27*

April 14

The time of business does not with me differ from the time of prayer, and in the noise and clatter of my kitchen, while several persons are at the same time calling for different things, I possess God in as great tranquility as if I were upon my knees at the blessed sacrament.

BROTHER LAWRENCE

THE MIND has a tremendous natural capacity to dwell on things, and in repeating the mantram we are channeling this capacity to train the mind. It is the same capacity, only we are giving it a different focus. There is a story in the Hasidic tradition of Judaism in which a man asks his *zaddik* or spiritual teacher, "Do you mean we should remember the Lord even in the give-and-take of business?" "Yes, of course," the rabbi replies. "If we can remember business matters in the hour of prayer, shouldn't we be able to remember God in the transactions of our business?"

RELATED PAGES *March 10, May 31*

April 15

Luck is not chance –
It's toil –
Fortune's expensive smile
Is earned.

EMILY DICKINSON

TRAINING THE mind is just that – a matter of training. It's a little like tennis. Championship tennis players have amazing skills and can direct the ball wherever they like: along the sideline two feet from the baseline, precisely. But the untrained player is going to find that most of his or her strokes will be out-of-bounds. This is because he or she hasn't learned tennis.

In tennis, we understand perfectly that the person who hasn't practiced is not going to enter championship play at Wimbledon and win the prize. I have never heard of anybody talking about instant mastery of tennis. So why do we think that love will be instant, or spiritual growth will be instant?

All of this calls for a lot of hard work. If we start today with all the zeal and the enthusiasm we are capable of, we can undertake this greatest of adventures – training the mind. Then, like the tennis pro, we can direct our thoughts just as we like: over the net and just inside the court.

 RELATED PAGES *January 24, March 28*

April 16

Be vigilant; guard your mind against negative thoughts.

THE BUDDHA

TODAY, MANY people are very well informed about nutrition. We worry about "junk food," which is a legitimate concern, but shouldn't we be just as worried about the food we feed our minds? There is junk food, yes. But there are also "junk thoughts."

Take a close look at the entertainment pages of your newspaper, for example. We have become so used to this kind of fare that we seldom even question it. I can imagine what people who lived in the Dark Ages would say if they saw today's paper: "They think we lived in the Dark Ages! What about them?"

It is not just a few nude scenes or explicit language, which are often more juvenile than alarming, but the terribly unkind attitudes people display toward each other on the screen, on stage, and on the printed page, which they vent in harsh words and harmful acts. All this goes into our minds and gets absorbed; it cannot help but resurface in our behavior. It is not that we want to live in a germ-free world, which is impossible, but we need to remember that mental states are affected by what we see, hear, and read every day.

RELATED PAGE *February 12*

April 17

If the heart wanders or is distracted, bring it back to the point quite gently and replace it tenderly in its Master's presence. And even if you did nothing during the whole of your hour but bring your heart back and place it again in Our Lord's presence, though it went away every time you brought it back, your hour would be very well employed.

SAINT FRANCIS DE SALES

THE MIND does not like to meditate; it wants to wander. When someone is not doing very well in meditation, one explanation is simple: his or her mind is elsewhere. The early stages of meditation are like a primary school for the mind. At first we are simply trying to get the mind to stay on the school grounds until the last bell rings. This is all we can do at first. The mind has been playing truant for years; when we try to concentrate, it simply is not present. All we can do is stand at the doorstep and whistle, trying to call it back in.

Even if all we do in thirty minutes of meditation is to call the mind back thirty times, we have made great progress. We don't have to wait for the day when the mind is completely still to receive immense benefits from meditation. As the Bhagavad Gita says, even a little of this discipline protects us from great dangers.

 RELATED PAGES *February 1, March 31*

April 18

The best way to cheer yourself up is to try to cheer somebody else up.

MARK TWAIN

OFTEN, WHEN a low mood is coming on, sometimes it is because the mind has started to brood upon itself. The things that formerly seemed exciting now elicit no response. In a sense, we have closed down. A friend can talk to us and we will not hear; we can go to a movie and may not even follow the plot. We are utterly absorbed in a hall of mirrors inside, in which we and everyone around us are pushed, pulled, and twisted into fantastic shapes.

There are a number of effective ways of treating these dark moods where they start, within the mind. What helps is to do what your mind is crying out not to do: be with other people, work with them, make yourself take an active interest in what they are doing and saying. This turns attention away from yourself by directing it outward. Once you are more concerned with others, your melancholy is gone; you are alive again.

RELATED PAGES *July 3, September 24*

April 19

The disunited mind is far from wise; how can it meditate? How be at peace? When you know no peace, how can you know joy?

BHAGAVAD GITA

TODAY'S MANIA for speed strikes right at the root of our capacity for an even mind. How often we find ourselves locked into behavior and situations that force us to hurry, hurry, hurry! By now, most of us are aware that compulsive speed – "hurry sickness" – can be a direct threat to our physical health. But hurry has another alarming repercussion: it cripples patience.

When we lack patience, even a few moments' delay, a trivial disappointment, an unexpected obstacle, makes us explode in anger. We are not hostile people; we are just in such a hurry that keeping the mind calm is impossible. Without peace of mind, how can we enjoy anything, from a movie to good health?

When we go slower, we are more patient, and when we are more patient, we are capable of enjoying life more. All these benefits can come from just learning to slow down.

 RELATED PAGES *February 6, April 1*

April 20

Thou shalt understand that it is a science most profitable, and passing all other sciences, for to learn to die.

HEINRICH SUSO

AS LONG as there is something we want to get out of life before we go – a little more money, a little more pleasure, a chance to get in a parting dig at someone we think has hurt us – there will be a terrible struggle with death when it comes. As long as we think we are the body, we will fight to hold onto the body when death comes to wrench it away. The tragedy, of course, is that death is going to take it anyway. So the great teachers in all religions tell us, "Give up your selfish attachments now and be free." Then, when death does come, we can give him what is his without a shadow of regret, and keep for ourselves what is ours, which is love of the Lord.

There is great artistry in this. Death comes and growls something about how our time has come, and we just say, "Don't growl; I'm ready to come on my own." Then we stand up gracefully, take off the jacket that is the body, hand it over carefully, and go home.

RELATED PAGES *May 19, June 4*

April 21

Progress in meditation comes swiftly for those who try their hardest.

YOGA SUTRAS

GIVEN THE sheer impossibility of it, I always find it astonishing how swiftly the transformation of personality can proceed when we are meditating with sustained enthusiasm. It may have taken you thirty years to make yourself insecure, but in much less than thirty years you can become secure, loving, resilient. The key is simple: how much do we desire to change? Patanjali, the author of the Yoga Sutras, makes a deceptively simple understatement: they go fastest who try hardest. Whether it is tennis or transformation, the secret is the same: to achieve success, we need to master our desires.

 RELATED PAGES *June 23, July 23*

April 22

If thou canst walk on water
Thou art no better than a straw.
If thou canst fly in the air
Thou art no better than a fly.
Conquer thy heart
That thou mayest become somebody.

ANSARI

SOMETIMES WE are advised to let our frustrations express themselves when they build up. One of the biggest problems with this advice is that by venting negative feelings, we relive them – confirming our suspicions that an angry man or petulant woman is who we really are. This is a most devitalizing self-image. We may not even like such a person, but if we are not vigilant, we can reach a stage where we throw up our hands and say: "This is the real me; what can I do?"

To establish a more positive identity, we need a good deal of patience and a certain sagacious realism. On the one hand, it does no good to pretend that simply because we are made in the image of the Lord, our problems are not really there. We should be prepared to see our difficulties as clearly as possible, so that we do everything we can to work on them. But on the other hand, we should not allow ourselves to be overwhelmed by them.

RELATED PAGES *August 9, September 18*

April 23

Peace is not an absence of war. It is a virtue, a state of mind, a disposition for benevolence, trust, and justice.

SPINOZA

WHEN WE first set out to learn this "disposition for benevolence," the going may be rough. The conditioning of stimulus and response, "an eye for an eye," is strong. But as meditation deepens, you find there is a fierce satisfaction in letting go of your own way so that things can go someone else's way instead. Gradually, you develop a habit of goodness, a positive passion for the welfare of others. In terms of emotional engineering, you are using the mind's enormous capacity for passion to develop the power to put other people first: and not just verbally, but in your thoughts and actions as well. Eventually kindness becomes spontaneous, second nature; it no longer requires effort. There is nothing sentimental about this quality, either; kindness can be as tough as nails.

 RELATED PAGE *December 17*

April 24

The true saint goes in and out amongst the people and eats and sleeps with them and buys and sells in the market and marries and takes part in social intercourse, and never forgets God for a single moment.

ABU SA'ID

THERE ARE some who like to imagine themselves as pilgrims moving among the deer on high forest paths, simply clad, sipping only pure headwaters, breathing only ethereal mountain air. To meditate, we needn't drop everything and undertake an ascent of the Himalayas or Mount Athos or Cold Mountain. It may not sound glamorous, but you can actually do better right where you are.

Your situation may lack the grandeur of those austere and solitary peaks, but it could be a very fertile valley yielding marvelous fruit. We need people if we are to grow, and all our problems with them, properly seen, are opportunities for growth. Can you practice patience with a deer? Can you learn to forgive a redwood? Trying to live in harmony with those around you right now will bring out enormous inner toughness.

RELATED PAGES *March 16, September 6*

April 25

I have joined my heart to thee: all that exists art thou. O Lord, beloved of my heart, thou art the home of all; where indeed is the heart in which thou dost not dwell?

JAFAR

LOVING SOMEONE does not mean automatically acquiescing to their every whim. Sometimes love shows itself in saying no to an attitude or desire that is harmful. But your opposing must be done tenderly, without anger or condescension. This is a difficult art.

Go slowly. Remember that it is better not to react in the heat of the moment. Whenever time allows, don't respond immediately. Speak and act when you can do so with patience and kindness. Remember, too, that the very best way to change someone is to embody that change with your own example.

Great lovers of God, like Teresa of Avila or Mahatma Gandhi, see the Lord in the heart of every person around them. This is the vision that enables them to treat others with love and respect even in the heat of opposition. It may take time, but no one is immune to this kind of love.

 RELATED PAGES *June 1, July 9*

April 26

Place yourself as an instrument in the hands of God, who does his own work in his own way.

SWAMI RAMDAS

TO SPEND a certain amount of time working with people at a job that benefits others, in which our personal pleasure and profit are not at all involved, nourishes both us and the people we help. It helps them directly, but it helps us indirectly, by enabling us to realize that we are a part of life and have a contribution to make.

Today, there are so many places where help is needed. Open the daily paper – the news speaks for itself. All of us need to work together to put out the fires of hatred and violence that are burning throughout the world, threatening us and our children. I cannot imagine any human being who has love in his heart not trying to think of ways to make some contribution to the world. We needn't work on a large scale. The important thing is that each of us give some time to working for a selfless cause. It's good for the world, and it's good for us.

RELATED PAGES *July 19, August 19*

April 27

The philosopher is Nature's pilot. And there you have our difference: to be in hell is to drift: to be in heaven is to steer.

GEORGE BERNARD SHAW

THE REAL issue in life is choice. If you had a car that could only turn one way, would you say that it is free? If it ran around crashing into things, denting its fenders and wasting all its fuel, would you shrug and say, "That's the automotive nature. That's my car's mode of self-expression"? It would take you a long time to get anywhere, and where you arrived would not be up to you.

The other day I set out for a drive through the California wine country. With a car that did not obey me, I might have ended up about a hundred miles away at the River's End restaurant, where the Russian River empties into the sea. It is tragic, but many lives are like that. At the end of the line there is nothing to do but go inside, get something hot to drink, and recall a line or two from Swinburne: "Even the weariest river winds somewhere safe to sea."

Meditation and other spiritual disciplines are largely meant to give us the toughness required to take hold of our lives. Without this toughness, despite the better goals we may cherish in our hearts, we will not be able to take the road that leads where we want to go.

 RELATED PAGE *July 21*

April 28

Know the Self as Lord of the chariot, the body as the chariot itself, the discriminating intellect as the charioteer, and the mind as the reins. The senses, say the wise, are the horses, selfish desires are the roads they travel.

KATHA UPANISHAD

THE UPANISHADS say that your body is like a chariot drawn by five powerful horses, the five senses. These horses travel not so much through space as through time. They gallop from birth towards death, pursuing the objects of their desire. The discriminating intellect is the charioteer, whose job it is not to drive you over a cliff. The reins he holds are the mind – your thoughts, emotions, and desires.

This image is packed with implications. For one, the job of the intellect is to see clearly. The job of the mind is to act as reins. When everything is working in harmony, our highest Self makes all the decisions. The intellect conveys these decisions to the mind, and the senses obey the mind. But when the senses are uncontrolled, they immediately take the road they like best: personal satisfactions, mostly pleasure. Then we are not making the decisions; the horses are.

RELATED PAGES *February 27, June 29*

April 29

Learn self-conquest, persevere thus for a time, and you will perceive very clearly the advantage which you gain from it. As soon as you apply yourself to contemplation, you will at once feel your senses gather themselves together: they seem like bees which return to the hive and there shut themselves up to work at the making of honey.

SAINT TERESA OF AVILA

COMPLETE CONCENTRATION is complete relaxation. The ability to work on a job with total concentration, and then put it out of your mind when necessary, is a skill which can be cultivated. Through practice, we can learn to drop whatever we are doing and turn our attention to a more urgent need. When you are absorbed in a favorite book and your partner interrupts you, set the book aside and give your complete attention to what he or she is saying. If part of your mind is on the conversation and part on what you have been reading, there will be division and tension in the mind.

When we practice this one-pointedness during the day, it will greatly help our meditation. The mind will much more quickly become recollected.

 RELATED PAGES *January 3, March 14*

April 30

God is a Good without drawback, and a well of living water without bottom, and the soul is made in the image of God, and therefore it is created to know and love God.

JOHANNES TAULER

WHEN HUMAN beings reach a state in which their physical wants are more than satisfied, when the optimum level of material abundance and physical comfort is reached, something in us feels an unpleasant sense of satiation. Absorbed up to then in the pursuit of prosperity and material security, we begin to feel restless, dissatisfied with the limits of life as it is being lived, constrained by the lack of challenges – and of love.

Then it becomes possible to hear a still, small voice speaking from deep below the conscious level of our mind, from beneath the level of conditioned desires. The voice was always there, but we were so busy with other things that we did not hear it. "I want an earth that is healthy, a world at peace, and a heart filled with love," it is saying. "I want my life to count."

RELATED PAGES *February 15, March 13*

May

We all need warm personal relationships to thrive, and the promise for growth lies in the give-and-take of every day.

EKNATH EASWARAN

May 1

Who can map out the various forces at play in one soul? I am a great depth, O Lord. The hairs of my head are easier by far to count than my feelings, the movements of my heart.

SAINT AUGUSTINE

MOST OF us never really see the people we live with. Our boyfriend may be right before our eyes, but we do not see him. We see our idea of him, a little model we have made in our mind, and on that we pronounce our judgments.

That is why, when we quarrel with someone, the worst thing we can do is to avoid him or her. We are trying to avoid an image in our own mind, which cannot be done. The mind takes some exaggerated impressions, memories, hopes, and insecurities, draws a quick caricature like one of those sidewalk cartoonists, and then turns up its nose. The person in question should retort, "That's not me; that's your caricature of me. If you don't like it, you don't like your own mind."

To heal our relationships, we have to move closer to people we do not like, learn to work with them without friction. When we do this, we are remaking the images in our mind – which means we are literally remaking the world in which we live.

 RELATED PAGE *December 19*

May 2

Offer unto me that which is very dear to thee – which you hold most covetable. Infinite are the results of such an offering.

BHAGAVATAM

DESIRE IS will. Every strong desire has a great deal of will locked up in it; the problem is that usually we do not have any control over it. In a compulsive desire, all that will goes into satisfying *only* that desire. Every time you can turn against a strong desire, therefore, it immediately strengthens your will.

You will also find your physical and emotional health improving, your relationships deepening, and your energy increasing. These are signs that you are going forward. The desire to go against selfish desires is the surest sign of grace.

RELATED PAGES *March 26, October 2*

May 3

The self-existent Lord pierced the senses to turn outward. Thus we look to the world outside and see not the Self within us.

KATHA UPANISHAD

CONSCIOUSNESS FLOWS out through the senses, following desire; it goes where our attention goes. When you are listening, for example, to your favorite music, consciousness runs out of the mind and into the ear.

In reaching out through the senses, we travel away from the indivisible unity of life at the center of our being. To live a balanced life, we must be able to flow outwards when necessary, and to center inwards when necessary.

 RELATED PAGES *February 2, September 9*

May 4

The capacity to give one's attention to a sufferer is a very rare and difficult thing. It is almost a miracle. It is a miracle.

SIMONE WEIL

SUFFERING IS inherent in life, however we may try to conceal it, however often we may try to turn our eyes away from it. To any sensitive person who reads the paper, every morning can be a hard blow: murders, suicides, air crashes, war, violence, disease, poverty – in every country on the face of the earth.

If you are sensitive, your heart will melt in grief. Yet the greatest joy lies in devoting your life to the amelioration of this sorrow. The greatest fulfillment comes to you when you dedicate your life to bring some of these tragedies to an end, to wipe the tears away from the eyes of a few people.

We needn't rescue the whole world, or even a city, or neighborhood. We begin with those around us.

RELATED PAGE *October 7*

May 5

Nothing great is created suddenly, anymore than a bunch of grapes or a fig. If you tell me that you desire a fig, I answer you that there must be time. Let it first blossom, then bear fruit, then ripen.

EPICTETUS

ALL TRUE spiritual development takes place little by little. From day to day you seem to make no progress, but when you glance back to the year before, though you have vastly farther to go, you realize that your nervous system is more resilient, your will stronger, your senses more responsive, your mind and relationships more secure; your goal is that much clearer before your eyes.

It is not very helpful to ask, "Why am I not making much progress? Why are there still so many difficulties in my way? Why can't I surmount them?" It takes time and labor, but the tree will bear fruit.

 RELATED PAGES *March 3, September 11*

May 6

A seeker once asked Bayazid: "Who is the true Prince?" "The man who cannot choose," said Bayazid: "the man for whom God's choice is the only possible choice."

BAYAZID AL-BISTAMI

THE LORD is extending the gift of immortality to each of us, but we do not reach out to take it because we are holding a few pennies in our hands. I don't know if you have seen infants in this dilemma; it happens at a particular stage of development, when they have learned to grasp but not quite mastered letting go. They have a rattle in one hand; you offer them a toothbrush, and for a while they just look back and forth at the toothbrush, then the rattle, then the toothbrush again. You can almost see the grey matter working: "I want that toothbrush, but how can I take it? My hand is already full."

Similarly, all of us look at the Lord's gift for a long while, asking "What is this? How do I know it's real? Give it to me first; then I'll let the pennies go." The Lord smiles and waits. He can offer the gift, but for us to take it, we have to open our hands. And there comes a time when we want something more than pennies so passionately that we no longer care what it costs. Then we open our hands, and discover that for the pennies we have dropped, we have received an incomparable treasure.

RELATED PAGE *April 30*

May 7

Let us not believe that we have received the divine kiss, if we know the truth without loving it or love it without understanding it. But blessed is that kiss whereby not only is God recognized but also the Father is loved; for there is never full knowledge without perfect love.

SAINT BERNARD

IF I haven't come to have faith in the Lord within, who is my real Self, how can I be secure? How can I be at peace? How can I live for others? By "faith" I do not mean blind faith, but a deep belief based on personal experience.

It is not enough to have faith in spiritual ideals, based on the testimony of the scriptures or spiritual teachers. We must realize these truths for ourselves, in our own life and consciousness. As the Buddha was fond of saying, the spiritual teacher only points the way; we must do our own traveling. The personal example of others may plant the seed in our hearts, but faith can develop fully only when we begin to experience these truths in our own lives.

 RELATED PAGES *April 3, May 21*

May 8

Knowing that their past actions may try to overwhelm them, the devotees must be prepared to combat them. God will give them the strength: His Name will be an impenetrable armor.

SWAMI BRAHMANANDA

IN PRINCIPLE, the training of attention is simple: when the mind wanders, bring it back to what it should be doing. The problem arises when the distraction is not a stray thought, but a compulsive resentment, irritation, apprehension, or craving. Such thoughts dominate our attention. When a self-centered thought comes up, everything in our conditioning screams, "Hey, look at that! Pay attention to that!"

When tormented by painful thoughts, many of us have cried out, "If only I could stop thinking!" But we don't know how. The mind has gotten stuck, and we feel helpless to stop it. All the mind can do is repeat the same thought over and over.

Here again, our greatest ally is the mantram. Whenever a destructive thought comes up, repeat the mantram. When the mantram takes hold, the connection between the thought and your attention is broken. A compulsive thought, whether it is anger or depression or a powerful sense-craving, does not really have any power of its own. All the power is in the attention we give – and when we can withdraw our attention, the thought or desire will be helpless to compel us into action.

RELATED PAGES *January 7, March 31*

May 9

Entered into Divine Mind, herself made over to That, the soul at first contemplates that realm; but once she sees that which is higher still, she leaves all else aside. Thus when I enter a house rich in beauty I might gaze about and admire the varied splendor before the master appears; but once seeing him I would ignore all else and look to him alone.

PLOTINUS

THIS BODY is not me. It is the house in which I live. If you say that I am so many inches tall, or that I weigh such and such number of pounds, I will reply, "You are not describing me. You are talking about my address."

Since I don't identify myself with my body, I don't associate other people very much with their physical appearance either. If someone asks me, "How tall is John?" I have to take time to try to picture him, then use a mental tape measure to try to remember his height. When someone asks me how old a person is, it takes a certain amount of effort for me to recall even what decade he or she is in. The more we dwell upon the physical appearance and age of others, the more we are conscious of our own appearance and age.

We should be concerned less about these details of packaging and concerned more with the contents. When I look at people, I like to look at their eyes. These are the windows into the Resident: the Lord, the Self. Gradually, as we become more and more spiritually aware, we will be looking straight into people's eyes and deep into their souls.

 RELATED PAGE *November 19*

May 10

Have thy heart in heaven and thy hands upon the earth. Ascend in piety and descend in charity. For this is the Nature of Light and the way of the children of it.

THOMAS VAUGHAN

WHEN OUR hands are busy with a worthwhile task, and our mind is busy with the mantram, we won't have much chance to brood on our problems. Cravings will not have a chance to grow.

Self-centered desires need a lot of attention to thrive. They are like delicate houseplants, not very hardy. Unless their needs are met precisely, they cannot last long. If we do not water and fertilize them regularly – think about them, dream about them, plan and wish – they will wither and die. To get plants to thrive, it is considered helpful to talk to them in soothing, friendly tones. Destructive desires thrive on talk too; the more we talk about them, the stronger they get.

So whenever you feel driven by a compulsive, destructive urge, don't analyze it; don't talk about it; don't dwell on it. Turn your attention away from it by throwing yourself into work for others. It can starve the desire away.

RELATED PAGE *March 11*

May 11

All human evil comes from this: a man's being unable to sit still in a room.

BLAISE PASCAL

UNLESS WE train it, the very nature of the mind is to keep on hopping from one thing to another, almost at random. The mind can be very usefully employed, but it has to be trained for its job. Too much of the time the mind is engaged in negative thinking, either about others or about ourselves – a destructive occupation. Training the mind means establishing and maintaining sound shop standards: good, creative, consistently kind thinking, and no around-the-clock activity, either. When the mind has nothing productive to do, we need to learn how to close up shop and let it rest.

 RELATED PAGES *January 9, April 5*

May 12

The community of the living is the carriage of the Lord.

HASIDIC PROVERB

WHERE THERE is so little love that "the carriage of the Lord," our essential unity, is torn asunder, we must love more. The less love there is around us, the more we need to love to make up the lack.

A man once came to Rabbi Israel, the Ba'al Shem Tov, and said, "My son is estranged from God; what shall I do?" The rabbi replied simply, "Love him more."

Love him more. Make his happiness more important than your own. This was my grandmother's approach to every problem, and I know of no more effective or artistic or satisfying way to realize the unity of life in the world today. It is an approach to life in which everything blossoms, everything comes to fruition. Where there is love, everything follows. To love *is* to know, *is* to act; all other paths to Self-realization are united in the way of love.

RELATED PAGE *January 11*

May 13

Return from existence to nonexistence! You are seeking the Lord and you belong to him. Nonexistence is a place of income; flee it not! This existence of more and less is a place of expenditure.

JALALUDDIN RUMI

EVERY ONE of us has an enormous internal savings account of vitality. In our youth we have a margin for experimenting with this vital energy account, for learning through trial and error how it works. But after the age of, say, twenty-five, we need to begin to learn how to live on the interest of this account and not consume the principal. We need to be very careful about which desires we pursue, and not waste our energy in resentment or in fear.

Yet grace adds a whole new dimension to this account. The divine core in all of us is the very source of vital energy, and it is infinite. The more we draw on this divine deposit of wealth – so long as we are drawing from it not for ourselves, but in the service of all life – the more it is replenished.

 RELATED PAGES *February 24, October 19*

May 14

Lord, grant that I may not so much seek to be loved as to love.

SAINT FRANCIS OF ASSISI

MILLIONS OF people today suffer from loneliness. Here Saint Francis is saying, "I know the cause of the malady and I know the secret of its complete cure." No matter what the relationship may be, when you look on another person as someone who can give you love, you are really *faking* love. That is the simplest word for it. If you are interested in *making* love, in making it grow without end, try looking on that person as someone you can give your love to – someone to whom you can go on giving always.

Learning to love is like swimming against the current of a powerful river; most of our past conditioning is pushing us in the other direction. So it is a question of developing your muscles: the more you use them, the stronger they get. When you put the other person's welfare foremost every day, no matter how strong the opposing tide inside, you discover after a while that you can love a little more today than you did yesterday. Tomorrow you will be able to love a little more.

RELATED PAGES *January 20, March 7*

May 15

Thou must be emptied of that wherewith thou art full, that thou mayest be filled with that whereof thou art empty.

SAINT AUGUSTINE

IN INDIA we have a flaming-hot chili pepper called "little thing" in my mother tongue. It is smaller than your little finger, so small that you don't take it seriously; but even a tiny bite will burn your mouth. Self-will is like that; a little dose of it can cause harm for a long time.

The remedy, in the Buddha's language, is *nirvana*, from *nir*, "out," plus *vana*, "to blow." You don't snuff self-will out in one day; you have to keep blowing away, in meditation and then during the day, especially in your relationships. This world is a place where we learn to return good will for ill will and love for hatred, to work harmoniously with others, and to put other people's welfare before our own. You keep blowing for years and years and one day the fire goes out.

 RELATED PAGES *July 28, November 11*

May 16

What we hope ever to do with ease, we must first learn to do with diligence.

SAMUEL JOHNSON

PLAIN OLD inertia is the underlying cause of many of our day-to-day difficulties. You will be feeling listless, oppressed, weighted down by lassitude; you won't want to do anything at all. You may feel persecuted: "Why shouldn't I sit around if I feel like it?" You may feel you are not in the best condition physically, with aches and pains that nobody understands.

To release yourself from this inertia, the first step is physical. The worst thing you can do is rest. Rest is what you have been doing; what is required is to get moving on something. Superficial physical symptoms may come by way of protest: a dull, throbbing headache, nerves on edge, a head as heavy as your heart. Get up and go for a walk – and walk fast, even if you don't feel equal to it. Try to walk a little faster than you feel you can.

After ten minutes or so you will find yourself breaking through that physical lethargy. Keep walking, and you will see that the rhythm of your breathing has improved, your spirits are lighter, you are ready to face the next challenge of the day.

RELATED PAGES *March 3, December 10*

May 17

Perseverance is more prevailing than violence; and many things which cannot be overcome when they are together, yield themselves up when taken little by little.

PLUTARCH

WITH EVERY thought, we are working on our destiny. When a sculptor creates an elephant, each touch of the chisel shapes the stone. While carving an eye he barely strokes the stone, but those light strokes are as vital as the rough shaping blows. There is no such thing as an unimportant blow.

Similarly, every thought shapes our lives. There is no such thing as a little thought, no such thing as an unimportant thought. It may be heavy, it may be light, but it always should be well-directed, with discrimination and precision.

 RELATED PAGES *January 12, October 6*

May 18

Mental tensions, frustrations, insecurity, aimlessness are among the most damaging stressors, and psychosomatic studies have shown how often they cause migraine headache, peptic ulcers, heart attacks, hypertension, mental disease, suicide, or just hopeless unhappiness.

HANS SELYE

A GREAT DEAL of psychological stress comes from the rush and hurry of a turbulent mind, which jumps recklessly to unwarranted conclusions, rushes to judgments, and often is going too fast to see events and people as they truly are. Such a mind keeps the body under continual tension. It is constantly on the move – desiring, worrying, hoping, fearing, planning, defending, rehearsing, criticizing. It cannot stop or rest except in deep sleep, when the whole body, particularly the nervous system, heaves a sigh of relief and tries to repair the damage of the day.

Simply by slowing down the mind – the first purpose of meditation – much of this tension can be removed. Then we are free to respond to life's difficulties not as sources of stress but as challenges, which will draw out of us deeper resources than we ever suspected we had. A one-pointed mind is slow and sound, which gives it immense resilience under stress. With a mind like this, we always have a choice in how we respond to life around us.

RELATED PAGES *February 6, April 1*

May 19

I went to the woods because I wished to live deliberately, to front only the essential facts of life, and see if I could not learn what it had to teach, and not, when I came to die, discover that I had not lived.

HENRY DAVID THOREAU

EVERYONE WILL agree that someday the body must grow old, weaken, and drop away, but not many will face the fact that it will happen to them. If we really believe we will die, we will do something about it.

If we live each day as if it were our last, we will be preparing for death. The man or woman who repeats the mantram regularly is actually preparing for death. The person who has become established in the mantram, who has made it an integral part of his or her consciousness, is prepared for death at all times.

When we realize fully that we are not this changing body but the changeless Self who dwells in the body, we conquer death here and now.

 RELATED PAGES *April 20, November 22*

May 20

Who is wise? One who learns from all.

THE TALMUD

IN MANY disagreements – not only in the home but even at the international level – it is really not ideological differences that divide people. It is lack of respect. Most disagreements do not even require dialogue; all that is necessary is a set of flash cards. If Romeo wants to make a point with Juliet, he may have elaborate intellectual arguments for buttressing his case, but while his mouth is talking away, his hand just brings out a big card and shows it to Juliet: "I'm right." Then Juliet flashes one of hers: "You're wrong!" You can use the same cards for all occasions, because that is all most quarrels amount to.

What provokes people is not so much facts or opinions, but the arrogance of these flash cards. Kindness here means the generous admission – not only with the tongue but with the heart – that there is something in what you say, just as there is something in what I say. If I can listen to you with respect, it is usually only a short time before you listen with respect to me. Once this attitude is established, most differences can be made up. The problem is no longer insoluble.

RELATED PAGES *August 1, August 23*

May 21

If you go on working with the light available, you will meet your Master, as he himself will be seeking you.

RAMANA MAHARSHI

THE WORD *guru* has passed into the English language, but it is often misunderstood. Guru simply means "heavy," one who is so heavy that he or she can never be shaken. A guru is a person who is so deeply established within himself or herself that no force on earth can affect the complete love they feel for everyone.

It is good for us to remember that the guru, the spiritual teacher, is in every one of us. The outer teacher makes us aware of the teacher within.

We should select a teacher very carefully. We should not get carried away by personal appearance – because we like his hairstyle or her robes. There is a good test of authenticity: does their life accord with what they teach? We have to listen carefully, judge carefully, then make our own decision. Once we make a decision and select a teacher who is suited to our spiritual needs, we should be prepared to be loyal. To the extent we can be loyal to the outer teacher, we are being loyal to ourselves.

 RELATED PAGES *May 7, December 26*

May 22

The measure of your holiness is proportionate to the goodness of your will.

JAN VAN RUYSBROECK

THE WILL does not grow weak through neglect. Rather, we undermine it, usually through little indulgences, often concerning food. We say, "What does it matter?" What matters is the effectiveness of our will.

When we sneak down to the refrigerator at midnight, it's a guerilla raid on the will. As we find the slice of pizza, we ask, "After all, who's to know?" No one may know, but, to use Ruysbroek's language, the goodness of our will is a little more fragile.

Our will can withstand a lot of this kind of attack, but eventually it may go into hibernation. Then, the answer is to rouse it out of its sleep by resisting everyday temptations where food is concerned.

RELATED PAGES *February 23, March 22*

May 23

To be right, we must do one of two things: either we must learn to have God in our work and hold fast to him there, or we must give up our work altogether. Since, however, we cannot live without activities that are both human and various, we must learn to keep God in everything we do, and whatever the job or place, keep on with him, letting nothing stand in our way.

MEISTER ECKHART

WE CAN train our attention wherever we are, whatever we are doing. The benefits are well worth the discipline.

Everybody knows what it is like to share the highway with a bad driver. He is driving along in the lane next to you and suddenly, without warning, he wanders into your lane. Then, with equal abruptness, he realizes what he has done and overreacts – first with the brake, then with the accelerator – and darts back into his own lane. He's an accident waiting to happen.

If we could only see it, everything in life suffers like this when attention wanders. A mind that darts from subject to subject is out of control, and the person who follows its whims weaves through life, running into difficult situations and colliding with other people. But the mind that is steady stays in its own lane. It cannot be swept away by an impulsive desire or fear; it cannot be haunted by an unpleasant memory or by anxiety about the future. There is no skill more worth learning than the art of directing attention as we choose.

 RELATED PAGES *January 3, February 5*

May 24

Living creatures are nourished by food, and food is nourished by rain; rain itself is the water of life, which comes from selfless worship and service.

BHAGAVAD GITA

WE HAVE been conditioned to look to food for some kind of deeper fulfillment. Food can entertain us, we are told. It is exciting, romantic, adventurous, exotic. Vast sums of money are spent trying to get us to buy a certain brand of potato chip or to prefer one brand of frozen pizza over another. In the midst of this carnival atmosphere, it is easy to forget that the real purpose of food is to nourish our bodies.

Eating together with those we love, eating nutritious food that has been prepared with love – this *can* nourish our inner needs, as well as our bodies. Taking time at meals to talk to each other and enjoy the meal as a shared sacrament is rare today. People are so busy that even meals have become something to be got through as quickly as possible. We need to slow down, take the time to prepare nutritious meals and rearrange our schedules so that we can be together.

RELATED PAGES *February 23, June 10*

May 25

Love has no errors, for all errors are the want of love.

WILLIAM LAW

WITHOUT A sincere effort to get ourselves out of the way, we can't understand the needs of the people closest to us; we simply can't see them clearly. Often, for example, good parents have goals for their children that their children do not share, goals that may not be in anyone's best interests.

The summer I finished high school, living as I did as part of a large clan, I was barraged by many opinions – from uncles, aunts, brothers-in-law, everybody – about what I ought to do with the rest of my life. The only person who didn't try to put pressure on me was my grandmother; she kept her counsel to herself.

My grandmother never heard of educational psychology – or, for that matter, of any other kind of psychology. But at the very end of summer vacation as I was taking leave of my family to go off to college, she called me over to her and whispered in my ear, "Follow your own star."

 RELATED PAGES *March 29, September 8*

May 26

You are what you believe.

ANTON CHEKHOV

YOU ARE what the deep faith of your heart is. If you believe that money is going to make you happy, then you will go after money. If you believe that pleasure will make you happy, you will go after pleasure. Because, "as a man thinketh in his heart, so is he," not as he thinketh in his head. There is a vast distance from the head to the heart. In the Greek and Russian Orthodox traditions, they say that whatever spiritual knowledge you have in your head must be brought down into your heart. This takes many, many years.

RELATED PAGES *May 7, August 5*

May 27

Love all that has been created by God, both the whole and every grain of sand. Love every leaf and every ray of light. Love the beasts and the birds, love the plants, love every separate fragment. If you love each separate fragment, you will understand the mystery of the whole resting in God.

FYODOR DOSTOYEVSKY

MOST OF us think of love as a one-to-one relationship, which is the limitation of love on the physical level. But there is no limit to our capacity to love. We can never be satisfied by loving just one person here, another there. Our need is to love completely, universally, without any reservations – in other words, to become love itself.

 RELATED PAGE *December 4*

May 28

Abide in peace, banish cares, take no account of all that happens, and you will serve God according to His good pleasure, and rest in Him.

SAINT JOHN OF THE CROSS

WE HAVE many stories from the Hindu scriptures about gambling, some about kings who lost entire kingdoms gambling at dice. There is the moving story of King Yudhishthira, who lost his kingdom and went into exile, and yet came back, after a terrible battle, to regain everything through the grace of Sri Krishna.

Many people are tempted to gamble, to take risks, when the stakes are high. The mystics would ask us, "Why don't you bet on goodness? Try to be kind to someone who is unkind to you, and look upon it as a gamble."

Of course we are not sure how the other person is going to respond – that is the thrill of it. If they add insult to injury, why not double your bet? Isn't that what people do at roulette? You just keep on doubling your bet until one day you redeem all your losses.

It may not work at the casino, but in life this is the only strategy that pays in the end. After all, what every one of us is trying to do is get our hands on the real treasures of life – rich relationships and resources for contributing to the happiness of all. This is what everybody wants, and to get it we have to gamble on goodness.

RELATED PAGE *August 29*

May 29

Let us not be justices of the peace, but angels of peace.

SAINT THÉRÈSE OF LISIEUX

DEALING WITH acrimonious situations with a calm patience requires toughness as well as love. Sometimes a little creativity helps, too.

A story about one of Saint Francis of Assisi's earliest disciples, Brother Juniper, illustrates this. Once, when a superior had reprimanded him with great severity, Brother Juniper was so disturbed that he could not sleep. He got up in the middle of the night and prepared some porridge with a big lump of butter on top, and took it to his superior's room. "Father, I have prepared this porridge for you and beg you to eat it." The superior told him to go away and let him sleep. "Well," said Brother Juniper simply, "would you be so kind as to hold the light while I eat it?" The superior laughed in spite of himself, and was sporting enough to sit down with Brother Juniper so they could eat the porridge together.

We may not be so ingenuous as Brother Juniper, but we can still learn to head off resentment in every way possible.

RELATED PAGE *June 10*

May 30

Those who eat too much or eat too little, who sleep too much or sleep too little, will not succeed in meditation. But those who are temperate in eating and sleeping, work and recreation, will come to the end of sorrow through meditation.

BHAGAVAD GITA

ONCE, WHEN the Buddha was told that one of his disciples was having trouble, he went to the young man's room to see what the problem was. This young man had been born in a rich family, and he had been trained in music, so he still kept his *vina* – an instrument something like a guitar – in the corner of his room. When the Buddha entered, he saw the vina and said, "Let me see if I can play your vina."

The disciple reluctantly brought it forward. He didn't know that the Buddha had been an expert musician.

The Buddha tightened the strings of the vina until they were about to break. The disciple protested, "You are not supposed to tighten the strings like that, Blessed One; they will break!"

So the Buddha, with tender cunning said, "Oh, yes! Then should I make them loose?" And he loosened all the strings until they couldn't be played at all. "Here, let me do it for you, Blessed One," said the disciple, and he adjusted them. "They are now just right, neither too tight nor too loose."

The Buddha smiled, "Yes, you see, that is what my path is: just right, neither too tight nor too loose. Moderation in everything. Temperance in everything."

 RELATED PAGES *March 2, April 14*

June

What we shall be tomorrow is the result of what we think, say, and do today.

EKNATH EASWARAN

June 1

That one I love who is incapable of ill will, and returns love for hatred. Living beyond the reach of I and mine, and of pain and pleasure, full of mercy, contented, self-controlled, of firm resolve, with all his heart and all his mind given to Me – with such a one I am in love.

BHAGAVAD GITA

IN PERSONAL relationships, we all get troubled when we do our best to be kind to someone and that person treats us with hostility or ill will in return. This is common in life today, and most of us quickly reach the end of our tether. "I don't want to see you again," we say. "I want to get as far away from you as possible!"

All of us have these human impulses. But that is just where the Gita or Jesus or the Buddha would say, "No. That is the way of the timid. That is the way of the weak." Stick it out: not by becoming a doormat, not by blindly obeying whatever command the other person gives you, but by resolutely refusing to hurt anyone no matter how much you have been hurt. It is a great art.

Compassion comes with insight into the heart of life, as we see more clearly the unseen forces that drive a person into action. Ultimately, compassion extends to every creature.

 RELATED PAGE *April 25*

June 2

Dive deep, O mind, dive deep
In the ocean of God's beauty;
If you descend to the uttermost depths,
There you will find the gem of love.

BENGALI HYMN

DON'T THINK the purpose of meditation is to go deep into consciousness, wrap a blanket around yourself, and say, "How cozy! I'm going to curl up in here by myself; let the world burn." Not at all. We go deep into meditation so that we can reach out farther and farther to the world outside.

In meditation we are going deep into ourselves, into the utter solitude that is within. As a counterbalance to this, it is necessary to be with people: to laugh with them, to sing with them, and to enjoy the healthy activities of life.

Meditation and selfless action go hand in hand. When we try to live more for others than for ourselves, this will deepen our meditation. When we deepen our meditation, more and more energy will be released with which we can love and help others.

RELATED PAGE *July 24*

June 3

A desire arises in the mind. It is satisfied; immediately another comes. In the interval which separates two desires a perfect calm reigns in the mind. It is at this moment freed from all thought, love or hate. Complete peace equally reigns between two mental waves.

SWAMI SIVANANDA

THROUGH MEDITATION and the practice of disciplines such as slowing down and keeping the mind one-pointed, we can learn to do something that sounds impossible: when thoughts are tailgating each other, we can slip into the flow of mental traffic, separate thoughts that have locked bumpers, and slowly squeeze ourselves in between.

It sounds terribly daring – the kind of stunt for which professionals in the movies are paid in six figures. Yet we can learn to step right in front of onrushing emotional impulses such as fury and little by little, inch by hard-won inch, start pushing them apart. This takes a lot of solid muscle in the form of willpower; but just as with muscles, we can build up willpower with good, old-fashioned practice.

Once you can do this you will find that there is not the slightest connection between another person's provocation and your response. There seemed to be a connection because your perceptions were crowding together. Now that those thoughts have been separated – even for a hair's breadth – your response has lost its compulsive force.

 RELATED PAGE *February 1*

June 4

As a person abandons worn-out clothes and acquires new ones, so when the body is worn out a new one is acquired by the Self, who lives within.

BHAGAVAD GITA

AS A traditional Hindu, my grandmother believed in reincarnation. For her, death was not a painful topic because she believed so firmly that our real Self cannot die. Even though we cannot but grieve when our dear ones pass away, underneath this grief we should always remember that death is only a change of rooms.

Whether we believe in one life or in a million lives, the basis of meditation remains valid for all of us. Trying to speculate about previous or future lives serves no practical purpose, since this life is headache enough. Let us confine our attention to this life and try as far as our capacity goes to learn to love here and now.

RELATED PAGES *April 20, September 12*

June 5

Speak when you are angry and you will make the best speech you will ever regret.

AMBROSE BIERCE

WHEN WE get tense, it is easiest to vent our frustration by making cracks at our children, our wife, or our husband – it is a simple matter of geographic proximity. When we attack other people, when we become a source of trouble to others, it is not because we want to add to their trouble; we have just become an object of trouble to ourselves. When we are agitated, when we are ready to burst out in anger against others, the immediate solution is to go for a long walk repeating the mantram.

In the ultimate analysis, our resentments and hostilities are not against others. They are against our own alienation from our native state, which is cosmic consciousness, Christ-consciousness, Krishna-consciousness. All the time we are being nudged by some latent force within us, trying to remind us what our native state is.

 RELATED PAGE *April 4*

June 6

They are not following dharma who resort to violence to achieve their purpose. But those who lead others through nonviolent means, knowing right and wrong, may be called guardians of the dharma.

THE BUDDHA

THE HINDU and Buddhist scriptures often use the word *dharma*, which comes from a root meaning "to support." It is a very difficult word to translate into English. In fact, there is really no English equivalent, but dharma is that which supports us, keeps us together. Dharma is the central law of our being, which is to extinguish our separateness and attain Self-realization. This is the universal law inscribed on every cell of our being, and the proof of it is that the more we live for others, the healthier our body becomes, the calmer our mind becomes, the clearer our intellect becomes, the deeper our love and wisdom become.

The Hindu and Buddhist scriptures also speak of a personal dharma. This is our present context, our present assets and liabilities. On the spiritual path, we start from where we stand. Later on, as our capacities grow, our opportunities for service will become greater. What is the right occupation now may not be right later on, but as long as it is not at the expense of others, our job can be made a part of our spiritual journey.

RELATED PAGE *March 19*

June 7

By love may He be gotten and holden, by thought never.

THE CLOUD OF UNKNOWING

THE SUPREME, radiant Being that dwells in our own consciousness cannot be attained by any amount of reasoning, for this Being is one and indivisible, beyond all duality. But by loving Him "with all our heart, and all our soul, and all our strength," we can come to live in Him completely. When we learn to love Her more than we love ourselves, our consciousness is unified.

It is all very well to talk about the Ultimate Reality, the Great Void, but we cannot love a Void. Here it is that we need God in an aspect we can love and understand – the Supreme Poet, the sustainer and protector of all, from whom we came into existence and to whom we shall return. We need a divine ideal like Sri Krishna, Jesus the Christ, the Compassionate Buddha, or the Divine Mother.

Loving the Lord means loving the innermost Self in all those around us. We need only somehow to increase our capacity to love – because we do not live in what we think; we live in what we love.

 RELATED PAGES *January 5, July 25*

June 8

All that is sweet, delightful, and amiable in this world, in the serenity of the air, the fineness of seasons, the joy of light, the melody of sounds, the beauty of colors, the fragrancy of smells, the splendor of precious stones, is nothing else but Heaven breaking through the veil of this world, manifesting itself in such a degree and darting forth in such variety so much of its own nature.

WILLIAM LAW

THE GREAT Hindu scriptures say that God is absolute truth, absolute joy, absolute beauty. Any scientist who is seeking the absolute truth, as Einstein did, is seeking God. Anyone seeking absolute joy, whether in a tavern or in the shopping mall or in Monte Carlo, is seeking God. And anyone who is seeking absolute beauty – on a canvas or a stage or a mountaintop – is seeking God. What lovers of beauty seek in paintings, in sculpture, in dance, in music is just a reflection of the absolute beauty that is God. The real source of all beauty is God, the Beloved.

So, there is nobody who is not seeking God. The scientist in his lab, the gambler at the casino, the artist in her studio: all are seeking God. We are all lovers, restlessly searching for the Beloved, hoping to catch a glimpse of the Face behind the veil.

RELATED PAGE *November 16*

June 9

Being is desirable because it is identical with Beauty, and Beauty is loved because it is Being. . . . We ourselves possess Beauty when we are true to our own being; ugliness is in going over to another order; knowing ourselves, we are beautiful; in self-ignorance, we are ugly.

PLOTINUS

THIS MORNING a friend said to me, "You look good!" I appreciated the compliment, of course, but I also felt a little amused. I almost wanted to reply, "What do you mean? I *am* good." Some people are mostly concerned with looking good. We should not be content with that. If we want a compliment, we should be good; and then others will say, "You are good."

Today, it is said that the image has become the person. If the public relations people can make you look good, you come to believe that you are good.

We should never allow ourselves to emulate or admire images that merely look good. Whether in sports or entertainment or politics, celebrities offer good role models only when they stand for lasting values.

 RELATED PAGE *April 2*

June 10

Lunch kills half of Paris, supper the other half.

MONTESQUIEU

I SUGGEST EATING moderately. Fasting may not be as easy as feasting, but after a while it is not too different. Both are extremes. It is not hard to go the extreme way, but what is really difficult is neither to fast nor to feast, but to be moderate in everything we do. This is what the Buddha called the Middle Path. It requires great artistry and vigilance. Instead of negating the body and senses, we train them to be valuable instruments.

I try to eat good, wholesome food in temperate quantities in order to strengthen the body. If my body is not strong, I cannot contribute to the welfare of society, and I cannot give the best account of myself in life. We harness our physical, mental, and intellectual capacities not to make money or achieve power or fame, but to use these faculties to make our contribution to life.

RELATED PAGES *March 20, May 24*

June 11

Ask, and it shall be given you; seek, and ye shall find; knock, and it shall be opened unto you.

THE GOSPEL ACCORDING TO SAINT MATTHEW

MOST OF us have not tried knocking on the door that Jesus is talking about. We are content to spend all our time exploring the outside of the house. The lawn, the trees, the trellis and the porch swing receive all our attention, so that we never even get inside, never seek out the One who is waiting there. We turn our cottage into House Beautiful, paint it and repaint it, but never so much as knock on the door.

Not only are we not looking for anybody inside, we are convinced that no one is there. If there is a God, we think he is surely outside, as is everything else that catches our attention. Vaguely, fondly even, we may sometimes imagine as we go about our business that Someone is probably keeping an eye on us. But if we will open our ears, we can hear the murmurings from within, the faint stir and rustle of a presence deep inside of us, and a voice hauntingly beautiful. Once we hear that, we will pound on the door with all our might, so that we can enter and meet the One who has been waiting so long.

 RELATED PAGE *May 7*

June 12

I reached in experience the nirvana which is unborn, unrivalled, secure from attachment, undecaying and unstained. This condition is indeed reached by me which is deep, difficult to see, difficult to understand, tranquil, excellent, beyond the reach of mere logic, subtle, and to be realized only by the wise.

THE BUDDHA, ON ATTAINING ENLIGHTENMENT

THE BUDDHA is sometimes quoted as saying that desire is suffering. A more accurate translation is that *selfish* desire is suffering – in fact, the source of all suffering. But desire itself is simply power, neither good nor bad.

Without the tremendous power of desire, there can be no progress on the spiritual path; there can be no progress anywhere. The whole secret of spiritual transformation is turning selfish desire into selfless desire, transforming personal passions into the overwhelming desire to attain life's highest goal. This is not repression; it is transformation.

RELATED PAGES *January 26, April 9*

June 13

When the senses contact sense objects, a person experiences cold or heat or pain. These experiences are fleeting; they come and go. Bear them patiently.

BHAGAVAD GITA

THE GITA does not say that we should not go after pleasure. When I first heard this from my grandmother, I really took to the Gita immediately; but I wasn't expecting what she said next: "The Gita doesn't say not to go after pleasure; it says that when you go after pleasure you are also going after pain."

It is not possible for most of us to accept this. We are always cherishing the distant hope that while no other human being has ever succeeded in isolating pleasure, we are going to perform this miraculous operation and then live in a state of pleasure always. To enter a state of abiding joy we must sometimes say no to pleasure while accepting pain with a smile.

Just as we should not pursue pleasure, we should not pursue pain, either. Pleasure and pain form a single duality of experience. We must learn to remain calm in both, not clinging to either.

 RELATED PAGES *July 12, November 26*

June 14

When the soul is naughted and transformed ... she is so full of peace that though she press her flesh, her nerves, her bones, no other thing comes forth from them than peace.

SAINT CATHERINE OF GENOA

WHEN EVERYTHING you do is to please the Lord, your life is very simple. It is not that you don't face complicated problems; everyday life is likely to bring challenges, but you have learned to face them without inner turmoil. You are no longer interested in pleasing yourself or in pleasing anybody else in particular; you want only to please God.

Putting others first is an area in which the mind can often play tricks on us. Interestingly enough, often when we believe we are thinking of others and putting their needs first, we are really just trying to please – which means we are really thinking about ourselves. When we truly are putting others first, we cannot but feel at peace with ourselves.

RELATED PAGES *January 11, May 12*

June 15

Ahimsa is the attribute of the soul, and therefore, to be practiced by everybody in all affairs of life. If it cannot be practiced in all departments, it has no practical value.

MAHATMA GANDHI

AHIMSA IS usually translated as "nonviolence," but this is misleading and falls far short of the real significance of the word. When all violence has subsided in my heart, my native state is love. I would add that even avoiding a person we dislike can be a subtle form of *himsa* or violence. Therefore, in everyday terms, ahimsa often means bearing with difficult people.

In Kerala we have a giant, fierce-looking plant called elephant nettle. You have only to walk by for it to stretch out and sting you. By the time you get home, you have a blister that won't let you think about anything else. My grandmother used to say, "A self-willed person is like an elephant nettle."

That is why the moment we see somebody who is given to saying unkind things, we make a detour. We pretend we have suddenly remembered something that takes us in another direction, but the fact is that we just don't want to be stung. Whenever I complained of a classmate I did not like, my granny would say, "Here, you have to learn to grow. Go near him. Let yourself slowly get comfortable around him; then give him your sympathy and help take the sting out of his nettleness."

RELATED PAGES *April 11, May 29*

June 16

For now we see through a glass darkly; but then face to face; now I know in part; but then shall I know even as also I am known.

I CORINTHIANS

IN MOMENTS of trouble we are seeing "through a glass darkly," as Paul puts it. At such times we can repeat the mantram to calm our mind and clear our eyes.

In times of distress, when we try to call up the mantram or prayer word, we may have difficulty even locating it. Our attention will be caught in our own turmoil, and every time we try to catch it, it will rebel and slip away again.

Simply bring your attention back to the mantram over and over again until your mind is calm. Repeat *My God and My All*, which is Saint Francis's mantram (or whatever mantram you have chosen). Then, when you go back to the scene that brought you distress, you can stay calm and compassionate. You can speak kindly, even if the response is not kind. You are inwardly secure in your love.

RELATED PAGES *March 2, November 6*

June 17

He who is not tempted, what does he know? And she who is not tried, what are the things she knows?

ECCLESIASTICUS

MISTAKES ARE a natural part of growing up, and there is no need to brood over them. As my grandmother used to tell the young girls in my ancestral home when they began to work in the kitchen, we can all expect to do a little spilling and burning in order to learn to cook.

Even though we have a certain margin for error, the sooner we can learn from our mistakes, the less suffering we will have to undergo in life. The consequences of a mistake may last for many years, and in making a major decision, many of us are prone to overcalculate the satisfaction we are going to get out of it and overlook the suffering involved for ourselves as well as others. We often forget that the action we are contemplating contains the seed of its result.

 RELATED PAGES *February 7, June 30*

June 18

For those who wish to climb the mountain of spiritual awareness, the path is selfless work. For those who have attained the summit of union with the Lord, the path is stillness and peace.

BHAGAVAD GITA

IN ORDER to climb the Himalayas within us, we have to train ourselves, little by little, day by day. Sir Edmund Hillary, who climbed Mount Everest for the first time, did not just stand at the bottom, take one leap, and land on top. He practiced climbing for a long time to learn all the required skills; and for you and me to climb the spiritual mountain, we, too, have to strengthen our muscles over a long period of time.

Most of us get our training in the heart of the family. In mountain climbing, you tie yourself to others with ropes and when somebody slips you haul him up and save him. Similarly, in living with family or friends, if somebody slips you do not say, "Aha! Served him right!" You pull him up. And when you slip, she pulls you up. It is a loving exchange. So there is greater safety when people live together and help one another.

RELATED PAGES *January 31, September 6*

June 19

Do not be dismayed, daughters, at the number of things which you have to consider before setting out on this divine journey, which is the royal road to heaven. By taking this road we gain such precious treasures that it is no wonder if the cost seems to us a high one. The time will come when we shall realize that all we have paid has been nothing at all by comparison with the greatness of our prize.

SAINT TERESA OF AVILA

THOSE WHO offer instant enlightenment mislead us. After all, we have to bring the mind itself under control, and there is no more difficult task in life. We should be prepared for a lifetime of challenge. But then, we need challenges, or we stagnate. If you want to judge your progress, ask yourself these questions: Am I more loving? Is my judgment sounder? Do I have more energy? Can my mind remain calm under provocation? Am I free from the conditioning of anger, fear, and greed? Spiritual awareness reveals itself eloquently in character development and selfless action. Authentic spiritual experience changes the way you see the world and the way you live.

 RELATED PAGE *December 30*

June 20

Heaven lies about us in our infancy.

WILLIAM WORDSWORTH

IN INDIA, stories about Sri Krishna as a little boy remind us of the divinity of children. In one such story, Krishna's mother, Yashoda, was churning curds to make butter in an earthen pot, using a wooden pestle which she moved round and round by means of a rope. Little Krishna was playing nearby but, as usual, he was soon up to mischief.

When his mother tried to get him to obey her, he was defiant. She took the rope she was using and said, "If you don't stop your mischief, I'm going to tie you up." Little Krishna silently put out his arms.

Yashoda tried to tie his hands, but the rope would not reach around his wrists. She got another rope. It, too, was not long enough. Soon everybody on the street had become interested. They all brought ropes and tied them together until the rope was very, very long, yet it would still not reach because of the infinity of the Lord present in baby Krishna. How could anyone tie up those slender hands that held the whole cosmos?

Consciousness of the divinity of children can inspire parents – and all caring adults – to lead more selfless lives.

RELATED PAGE *September 8*

June 21

It is a funny thing about life; if you refuse to accept anything but the best you very often get it.

W. SOMERSET MAUGHAM

WE MUST be careful not to mistake agitation for fulfillment, excitement for joy. When our mind is not turbulent for a little while, we tend to think we're in a slump and start groping about for something that can stir it up again: a thrilling movie, a stiff drink, a spirited quarrel, anything to "get the juices flowing." Taken one by one these may seem like fairly innocuous forms of indulgence, yet in their long-range cumulative impact, they deplete us and deflect us from our real goals.

When we fix our eyes on a higher goal, we begin to see beyond the immediate appeal of short-term satisfactions. Confident that a far greater joy is ours, we can hold out against the voices from all sides that cajole, "Eat this; drink that; watch this; buy that." True joy is found when the mind is still, not when it is excited.

 RELATED PAGES *July 12, August 15*

June 22

There has never been a time when you and I have not existed, nor will there be a time when we will cease to exist. As the same person inhabits the body through childhood, youth, and old age, so too at the time of death he attains another body. The wise are not deluded by these changes.

BHAGAVAD GITA

IN OUR modern civilization we try to cling to time as it rushes past, almost begging time to stop. We want to continue to be what we are now. We don't want to be subjected to the ruthless physical changes that are an inescapable part of life. Yet it is the nature of the body to change, up to the last change we call death. Anybody who tries to cling to what is changing cannot help feeling insecure.

Yet we needn't be helplessly caught in time. There are a number of very simple steps we can take to begin to free ourselves. One of the easiest is to get up early in the morning. This gives us the opportunity to start the day with a leisurely pace – to take a short walk, if we like, and then to have our meditation, without worrying about catching the bus or being on time for school.

RELATED PAGE *February 21*

June 23

As iron put into the fire loseth its rust and becometh clearly red-hot, so one who wholly turneth unto God puts off all slothfulness, and is transformed.

THOMAS A KEMPIS

WE ARE made in the image of God. The image is there, but we need to put in the work to reveal it. Whenever I hear someone say, "This is just the way I am; I've got to learn to live with it," I want to plead, "Don't ever say that!" The miracle of human existence is that we can change. Simply by virtue of being human, we have the capacity to change ourselves completely.

All of us carry a cleansing fire hidden inside. It may be banked with ashes, cold to the touch, but a spark of the divine is there nonetheless, ready to leap into life. It is nothing less than love of God. Latent in every one of us, it wants only encouragement before it flares to vibrant life, burning up everything selfish and impure. Once ignited and coaxed with the fuel of love for others, it sheds light and warmth all around.

 RELATED PAGES *January 1, April 21*

June 24

A soft answer turneth away wrath.

PROVERBS

WHEN YOU feel angry towards someone and want to say something unkind, that is all the more reason to speak kindly. If someone provokes you and you respond with anger, you are reinforcing anger as a part of your personality.

So returning kindness for unkindness is not simply being kind to that particular person. You're being kinder to yourself, because you are undoing a compulsion, taking one more step towards being free. You are turning wrath away from yourself, as well as being kind to the other person.

The deconditioning process is straightforward enough: when anger comes up, don't act on it. When it tries to tell you what to do, say no. Repeat the mantram, go out for a long, brisk walk if possible, and throw yourself into hard, concentrated work, preferably for the benefit of others. When you can shift your attention to your work or to the mantram, you have shifted it away from the anger. Immediately the anger-tendency is weakened a little.

RELATED PAGES *March 2, September 21*

June 25

It is great wisdom to know how to be silent and to look at neither the remarks, nor the deeds, nor the lives of others.

SAINT JOHN OF THE CROSS

MOST OF us cannot help comparing ourselves with others, at least now and then. In fact, this has become so entrenched today that in order to have self-esteem, it seems almost necessary to say, "I am better than he is, so I am good." As long as we compete with each other and compare one with another, a certain amount of envy is inescapable. It is the very rare person who is completely free from jealousy.

But as our spiritual awareness grows, we will know that the Lord is present in everyone and that there is a uniqueness about everyone. The truly spiritual person never tries to compare himself or herself with others, or others among themselves. I have never been able to understand the compelling phrase, "keeping up with the Joneses." It does not matter very much whether I keep up with Tom Jones or anybody else; what is important is to keep up with myself by making my today a little better than my yesterday.

We can keep this ideal before our eyes by not comparing ourselves to others, remembering that all of us have complete worth and value because the Lord is present in us.

 RELATED PAGE *July 19*

June 26

My mind withdrew its thoughts from experience, extracting itself from the contradictory throng of sensuous images, that it might find out what that light was wherein it was bathed. . . . And thus, with the flash of one hurried glance, it attained to the vision of That Which Is.

SAINT AUGUSTINE

EVEN WHEN we are not speaking or acting, most of us find that our mind still goes on working – thinking, day-dreaming, planning, worrying, eating up precious energy that should be going to the body to maintain health. In a sense, our mind is in overdrive all the time. But in meditation we can learn to shift the mind out of overdrive and down into fourth gear, then to third, to second, and eventually to first. We may even learn how to put our mind into neutral and park it for a while by the side of the road.

When we can do that, a much higher faculty – which the Hindus and Buddhists call *prajna*, "wisdom," – comes into play. Then we will find that we see deep into the heart of life, with fathomless patience at our disposal. When we have learned to park the mind even for a short period, so much vitality is conserved that every major system in the body gets a fresh lease on life.

RELATED PAGES *January 30, March 21*

June 27

Hasten slowly and ye shall soon arrive.

MILAREPA

SOME PEOPLE are fortunate enough to have a great wealth of vitality. But when we are feeling especially full of energy, we may be likely to take up too many activities at the same time. We make big plans, but then a great deal of our enthusiasm simply drains away in excitement. When we start to put our plans into action, we find we have run out of steam.

The culprit here is the excitement itself. It is the nature of excitement that it cannot last. It has to die down, and when it does, the same project we began with such enthusiasm looks utterly boring. It is full of dull, drab details that we had not foreseen. And we give up. The project has not changed; our energy that fueled it is depleted. To achieve our highest potential in life, we must cultivate the capacity to carry through. Activity is not achievement. It is not enough to rush about beginning a lot of things and keeping busy. A well-spent life is one that rounds out what it has begun. The life of a great artist or scientist is usually shaped by a single desire, carried through to the very end.

 RELATED PAGES *October 19, November 14*

June 28

He who binds to himself a joy
Doth the winged life destroy.
But he who kisses the joy as it flies
Lives in Eternity's sunrise.

WILLIAM BLAKE

ONE PARTICULARLY painful compulsion in personal relationships is clutching at our partner or friends for security. When we grasp at another person, the real tragedy is that we cease to see that person; in our insecurity, he or she becomes merely an object for propping ourselves up. This is an open invitation to jealousy because we see him or her as a character in *our* drama, not in anyone else's. Finally the relationship may be broken. People may move from one relationship to another, always grasping and always missing what they are looking for.

Real love is the result of a great deal of effort over a long period of time. It is developed through trust and loyalty and patience, learning not to say a harsh word or even show disrespect when we are provoked. Over many years this kind of love can grow to such an extent that those you love will *know* you're incapable of hurting them. Imagine the security this brings, both to you and to them. Your trust and loyalty can be anchored so deep that you never even have a divisive thought.

RELATED PAGES *February 14, November 2*

June 29

It is permissible to take life's blessings with both hands provided thou dost know thyself prepared in the opposite event to take them just as gladly. This applies to food and friends and kindred, to anything God gives and takes away.

MEISTER ECKHART

IN ORDER to live in freedom, we must learn to accept a temporary disappointment, if necessary, when it is for our permanent well-being. Sometimes, when we want to eat something that appeals to us, or when we want to eat a little more than is necessary, we can't help feeling disappointment as we push away from the table. We cannot help thinking that we could as well have stayed on for five more minutes of pleasure, forgetting that it would probably be followed by five hours of stomachache at night. The right time to get up from the meal is when we want just a little more. This is real artistry, real gourmet judgment: when we find that everything is so good that we would like to have one more helping, we get up and walk away.

 RELATED PAGES *April 28, August 15*

June 30

Experience is the name everyone gives to their mistakes.

OSCAR WILDE

OLDER PEOPLE have much to contribute when they are able to draw on the wisdom gained from direct knowledge of life. It takes considerable experience of life to understand the fleeting nature of physical satisfactions and personal profit.

In the first half of life, we all have a wide margin for error, and youth often is a time of experimentation. It is usually in the second half of life that maturity comes – which means we have developed some mastery over personal, self-centered drives. With this spiritual maturity comes an increased capacity to feel for others as much as we feel for ourselves.

This is the great opportunity that we have in the second half of life: our hard-earned wisdom can enable us to bring about a quiet transformation of our society.

RELATED PAGES *June 17, July 29*

July

If you want to live life at its fullest, do everything possible to keep your body in vibrant health in order to give back to life a little of what it has given you.

EKNATH EASWARAN

July 1

To the illumined man or woman, a clod of dirt, a stone, and gold are the same.

BHAGAVAD GITA

GOLD IS not valuable in itself. It is valuable because there is so little of it. If sand were found only in small quantities, people would treasure it in their safe-deposit boxes; they would buy sand certificates, on important occasions they would exchange a little sand, and they would have the expression "as good as sand."

Things cannot give us status. We give status to things. When Tom gets into his BMW, he is giving status to the car. The car is not giving him status. The car says, "I feel good because Tom is at the wheel."

What really gives value to anything is its usefulness in serving others. Our body draws its value from its usefulness in serving others, and our life draws its value, not from the money we make, or the prizes we win, or the power we wield over others, but from the service we give every day to add a little bit more to the happiness of our family and our community.

 RELATED PAGE *February 25*

July 2

Health, a light body, freedom from cravings, a glowing skin, sonorous voice, fragrance of body: these signs indicate progress in the practice of meditation.

SHVETASHVATARA UPANISHAD

IF YOU are practicing meditation regularly, be sure to get adequate physical exercise. This is very important. The deeper your interior life, the greater the need for vigorous physical activity. People sometimes fall into a kind of lethargy in the mistaken belief that this is what it means to work without tension. It is just the opposite. The body is our instrument of physical service, and it thrives on vigorous movement. If you are young or already in good condition, *vigorous* here means vigorous. Swimming, running, and fast-paced sports that require concentration are all excellent exercise. But unless you are in condition, do not jump into such activities immediately. Work up to them gradually. If you are over thirty-five or have any particular physical problems, ask your doctor to start you on an exercise program.

In meditation we gradually reduce our obsessive identification with the body. The body will begin to feel lighter, our step will be more buoyant, and our senses will come more easily under our control. By getting plenty of physical exercise, we help this process along.

RELATED PAGES *February 27, April 6*

July 3

There is nothing so lovely and enduring in the regions which surround us, above and below, as the lasting peace of a mind centered in God.

YOGA VASHISHTHA

STEERING A middle course between being elated and being dejected does not mean resigning ourselves to a flat and monotonous life. Far from it. There is a third state which is neither elation nor depression, and if we can avoid these two extremes, we will find the abiding joy which is our real nature. Most of us have little objection to getting elated, but none of us are very eager to see gloom setting in. We don't mind being told not to get depressed, but "Don't let yourself get elated" sounds puritanical. Yet the time to be cautious is when the mind is starting to get elated. That is not the time to pick up the phone and talk and talk. When you are able to see the specter lurking behind elation and have some personal experience of the joy which transcends both, you will come to look upon excitement with a healthy suspicion.

 RELATED PAGES *April 18, September 24*

July 4

Some people want to see God with their eyes as they see a cow, and to love him as they love their cow – for the milk and cheese and profit it brings them. This is how it is with people who love God for the sake of outward wealth or inward comfort.

MEISTER ECKHART

THE EXTERNAL world, so fascinating, so infinite in its variety, has us firmly in hand and thoroughly mesmerized. Lasting happiness is almost ours – over there, just ahead of us, right around the next corner. When we round that corner and find it has eluded us, something in us says, "Keep running! It's just around the *next* corner." Finally, our life becomes a continual pilgrimage around corners. Such is human credulity that even after rounding a thousand corners, we still say, "The thousand and first, that is *the* corner."

If we believe that happiness arises only when some external condition is fulfilled, we consign ourselves to a perpetual state of discontent. For even when our expectations are fulfilled, sooner or later the little voice inside starts again, "More! More!" It is this habit, this almost mechanical fixation of the mind, that keeps us forever chasing rainbows, until at last we begin to suspect that the kingdom of heaven is within.

RELATED PAGES *April 8, August 8*

July 5

You are quaffing drink from a hundred fountains: whenever any of these hundred yields less, your pleasure is diminished. But when the sublime fountain gushes from within you, no longer need you steal from the other fountains.

JALALUDDIN RUMI

OFTEN WE are most vulnerable during moments of transition. For example, you have wrapped up one assignment and it is time to look over the next. Or you've turned the last page of your novel and it is time to go to bed. Whatever the transition, for a pivotal moment the mind has nothing to hold on to, and in its insecurity it may suggest all kinds of things: a cigarette, an extra piece of pie, a magazine promising the lowdown on your favorite actor's private life. Suddenly any of these can seem fraught with urgency.

Here the mantram can rescue you. If you start repeating it the moment you complete one activity, and do not drop it until the time comes for you to give complete attention to the next job at hand, your will gets a needed boost. A short, fast walk repeating the mantram can be more refreshing than all manner of "treats." Once you are absorbed again, you are home free.

 RELATED PAGES *March 2, August 24*

July 6

Grow old along with me!
The best is yet to be,
The last of life, for which the first was made:
Our times are in His hand
Who saith, "A whole I planned,
Youth shows but half; trust God: see all, nor be afraid!"

ROBERT BROWNING

THE BODY is the temple of the Lord and, if looked after with care, is beautiful even in old age. Childhood has one kind of beauty; youth another; and old age its own special beauty. Even in the evening of her life, my grandmother had a beautiful, healthy body because she was always aware that this temple had to be kept in good order, swept with the mantram broom, and purified through the daily practice of meditation.

We show respect for the Lord, the Self within, by keeping the body healthy and beautiful. Where books, movies, television, and our eating and exercise habits are concerned, we must be vigilant to see we are not indulging the senses at the cost of the health of our body or mind. It is not that we cultivate an ascetic attitude. It is just the opposite. We don't mortify the body, but see that every day it gets what it needs for health, so that it will be a valuable, vital instrument until our last day.

RELATED PAGES *February 27, April 6*

July 7

If thou shouldst say, "It is enough, I have reached perfection," all is lost. For it is the function of perfection to make one know one's imperfection.

SAINT AUGUSTINE

AMONG MY acquaintances on the Blue Mountain in South India was a Britisher who had climbed many of the higher peaks of the Himalayas. One day he confided to me the feeling of exhilaration he felt on reaching the summit of Annapurna, and standing there in awe in the eternal snows. "Then," he added, "you know, old boy, while I gazed out over that magnificent scene, snow-topped mountains as far as the eye could see, the question just popped into my mind: Which peak will be next?" He just couldn't rest on his laurels; he had to keep climbing. That is what gave meaning to his life.

It is the same in meditation. We shouldn't look forward to the day when we plant our flag on the mountain peak and then retire to a life of tedious leisure. Every time we reach a peak, we will feel a legitimate sense of satisfaction; but at the same time a new and more glorious mountain will probably be beckoning us from the far horizon. That is the glory of living. That is the joy of the spiritual ascent.

 RELATED PAGE *December 31*

July 8

The earth is the Lord's, and the fullness thereof; the world, and they that dwell therein.

PSALMS

YOU AND I are trustees. Nothing belongs to us personally. The resources of our planet have been entrusted to every one of us together. Like good bank trustees, we are expected not to squander these resources but to invest them wisely for our beneficiaries: the rest of life, especially the generations to come.

The trust includes not only the lives and natural resources of the planet, but our inner resources as well. This has practical implications. We can lessen our potentially exhausting impact on the earth by simplifying our desires and demands. Simplicity is the key to trusteeship.

RELATED PAGES *September 5, November 12*

July 9

Ahimsa is not a policy for the seizure of power. It is a way of transforming relationships so as to bring about a peaceful transfer of power, effected freely and without compulsion by all concerned, because all have come to recognize it as right.

THOMAS MERTON

BEARING WITH people is the essence of nonviolence. To do this with a feeling of martyrdom, however, is not very helpful; we need to bear with people cheerfully. This does not mean making ourselves into a doormat. Many people suffer from the misguided notion that nonviolence means saying, "Yes, honey, whatever you want is okay with me. You say; I do." Letting people take undue advantage of us is not helpful for them any more than it is for us.

We all know that with a selfish person if we yield an inch he will ask for a yard. With the selfish person, therefore, it is often necessary quietly to say no. Don't accept a situation in which you are exploited, discriminated against, or manipulated. This is the great art of nonviolent resistance, where you love the person, you respect him, but you will not allow him to exploit you, because it is bad for him just as it is bad for you.

 RELATED PAGES *March 19, March 30*

July 10

Know One, know all.

KATHA UPANISHAD

TO KNOW others, you do not have to go and knock on four billion separate doors. Once you have seen your real Self, you have seen the Self in all. It makes it easy to understand and to forgive, and very difficult to quarrel. All of life springs from the same root. The Self in each of us is one and the same.

For this Self, different names are given in different traditions. Christian mystics call it the Christ within. When a person ceases to identify with his perishable self, they say he has become Christ-conscious. The Hindu mystics speak of Krishna-consciousness, or say that such a person has attained complete freedom from the conditioning of time, space, and circumstance. The Buddhists call the same state *nirvana*, from *nir*, "out" and *vana*, "to blow." The ego has been extinguished; there is no more shadow to be mistaken for the real.

RELATED PAGES *February 8, April 9*

July 11

The more we have the less we own.

MEISTER ECKHART

WE HAVE been ruthlessly conditioned to think we can find fulfillment in possessions, to love things rather than people – so much so, that when we feel an emptiness in our hearts, we go to shopping centers to fill it up.

I am all for living in reasonable comfort, but when I go to shopping centers, I cannot help getting alarmed. Not at the money that is being wasted – there is enough money in this country to waste. But there isn't enough *will* to waste. There isn't enough *energy* to waste. When we hear of the energy crisis, this is it. All our vitality, energy, and drive is sapped and undermined by the constant propaganda: go after this, go after that, and you'll be happy. Things are not meant to be loved. They are meant only to be used. People are lovable and loving.

 RELATED PAGES *February 25, July 1*

July 12

Quiet minds cannot be perplexed or frightened, but go on in fortune or misfortune at their own private pace, like a clock during a thunderstorm.

ROBERT LOUIS STEVENSON

WHEN THE mind gets agitated, we do not see life as it truly is, as one. It is the constant agitation going on in our mind that deludes us into believing that you and I are separate.

The question we may well ask is, "If we are to have neither pleasure nor pain in life, are we not likely to become insensitive to the joy of life?" This doubt arises from a wrong assumption, that there is only pleasure and pain and nothing else. Always cutting things up into two classes – everything must be either this or that – is one of the fatal weaknesses of the intellect. Because of this dualistic trap, we find it difficult to understand that the rare person who is able to receive good fortune without getting excited, and bad fortune without getting depressed, lives in abiding joy.

RELATED PAGES *June 13, June 21*

July 13

Love is inseparable from knowledge.

SAINT MACARIUS OF EGYPT

WHEN SELFISH desire is removed from a relationship, there is no hankering to get anything from the other person. We are free to give, which means we are free to love. Then we can give and support and strengthen without reservation.

Interestingly enough, it is only then that we really see each other clearly. The infatuated mind cannot help caricaturing: it sees only what it wants; then, when the desire passes, it sees only what it does not want. Two people who are really in love do not close their eyes to each other's weaknesses. They support each other in overcoming those weaknesses, so that each helps the other to grow.

 RELATED PAGES *June 28, February 14*

July 14

Temperance is love surrendering itself wholly to Him who is its object; courage is love bearing all things gladly for the sake of Him who is its object; justice is love serving only Him who is its object, and therefore rightly ruling; prudence is love making wise distinctions between what hinders and what helps itself.

SAINT AUGUSTINE

LOVE OF God is not something that descends miraculously from the skies. It can be fostered and deepened immensely through our own effort. At present, very little of our love may be flowing to our highest ideals. Most of it is flowing down other channels – towards money, or pleasure, or a new sports car. In some cases, our vital capacity has been flowing down these channels for so long that they are cut very deep. Then, when the time comes to dam these channels up and divert the love in them to flow towards the Lord or the divine Self, we feel we are standing there throwing pebbles into the Grand Canyon. Don't be discouraged by the immensity of the task. Just keep on throwing in the pebbles. They may not seem like much, but after a while they all add up.

RELATED PAGES *July 15, October 2*

July 15

If one wants to abide in the thought-free state, a struggle is inevitable. One must fight one's way through before regaining one's original primal state. If one succeeds in the fight and reaches the goal, the enemy, namely the thoughts, will all subside in the Self and disappear entirely.

RAMANA MAHARSHI

LET ME continue the metaphor of filling in the Grand Canyons of craving. When we learn to toss in our little cravings, every rock we throw in will precipitate an avalanche. Soon, before we even realize it, the Grand Canyon of that particular craving may be completely filled in. But there is another very practical suggestion I can make here.

It is necessary to dam up the old streams down which our love is flowing, but if we do nothing but block the flow, there is always the danger that the dam may break or the water may simply overflow. So instead of giving all of our attention to throwing rocks, we can do our best throughout the day to dig a new channel straight to the Self in those around us – by being patient, by being loyal, by always keeping our eyes on their welfare rather than our own. For a long time this new stream may flow with only a trickle, but if we keep trying, it will begin to drain off a little of the love that is now flowing down other channels. Finally, all our desires will be unified in love.

 RELATED PAGES *July 14, September 2*

July 16

That prayer has great power which a person makes with all his might. It makes a sour heart sweet, a sad heart merry, a poor heart rich, a foolish heart wise, a timid heart brave, a sick heart well, a blind heart full of sight, a cold heart ardent. It draws down the great God into the little heart; it drives the hungry soul up into the fullness of God; it brings together two lovers, God and the soul, in a wondrous place where they speak much of love.

MECHTHILD OF MAGDEBURG

THERE IS nothing on earth like meditation. Each day it is new to me and fresh. I find it difficult to understand why everyone does not take to it. Millions dedicate their lives to art, music, literature, or science, which reveal just one facet of the priceless jewel hidden in the world. A life based on meditation penetrates far beyond the multiplicity of existence into the indivisible realm of reality, where dwell infinite truth, joy, and beauty.

In meditation I see a clear, changeless goal far above the fever and fret of the day. This inner vision fills me with unshakable security, inspires me with wisdom beyond the reach of the intellect, and releases within me the capacity to act calmly and compassionately.

RELATED PAGES *February 1, February 5*

July 17

We have no more right to consume happiness without producing it than to consume wealth without producing it.

GEORGE BERNARD SHAW

SHOPPING FOR things we do not need, even if it is only window-shopping, wastes a lot of vitality; energy flows out with every little desire. It is a surprising connection, but an extravagant shopper will find it difficult to love. He or she scatters love like largesse all over the department store. We can become bankrupt in love this way.

When it comes to our personal vitality, we have no atoms to split, no windmills to set up, no sun to draw on for an alternative source of energy; we have to conserve what we have and make it last. When we find it difficult to love, we can think of it as a personal energy crisis. By not buying things which are neither necessary nor beneficial, we conserve the precious natural resources of the earth, and we save our personal energy, too.

So if you want a good, stiff test of your capacity to love, go into your favorite store some day – preferably when there is a sale – and see if you can walk straight through, looking neither left nor right, and come out unscathed. It may sound unbelievable, but it can be done.

 RELATED PAGES *July 14, July 15*

July 18

I have learned through bitter experience the one supreme lesson to conserve my anger, and as heat conserved is transmuted into energy, even so our anger controlled can be transmuted into a power that can move the world.

MAHATMA GANDHI

MAHATMA GANDHI provides a perfect example of how anger can be harnessed. As a young, unknown, brown-skinned lawyer traveling in South Africa on business, he was roughly thrown from the train because he refused to surrender his first-class ticket and move to the third-class compartment. He spent a cold, sleepless night on the railway platform.

Later, he said this was the turning point of his life: for on that night, full of anger because of this personal injustice, as well as the countless injustices suffered by so many others every day in South Africa, he resolved not to rest until he had set those injustices right. On that night he conquered his anger and vowed to resist injustice, not by violence or retaliation, but through the loving power of nonviolent resistance, which elevates the consciousness of both oppressed and oppressor.

We may never be called on to liberate a people or lead a vast nation, but Gandhi's example can apply in a small way in our own lives, when we decide to return good will for ill will, love for hatred, in the innumerable little acts of daily life.

RELATED PAGES *March 19, September 7*

July 19

I look upon all creatures equally; none are less dear to me and none more dear. But those who worship me with love live in me, and I come to life in them.

BHAGAVAD GITA

THERE IS no need to compare ourselves with others or to feel our contribution is less important than someone else's. Yesterday I read a story that makes this point very well. It was about a Hasidic rabbi named Susya, who said, "When I die, I will not be asked, 'Why weren't you more like Moses?' I will be asked, 'Why weren't you more like Susya?'"

Similarly, the Self is not going to say, "You could have been a doctor! Why were you just a nurse's aide?" He is going to ask, "Were you the best nurse's aide you knew how to be? Did you help your patients not just by your labor, but by your genuine concern for their welfare?" Each of us has a special gift, some special capacity by which we can contribute to the welfare of those around us. What is important is that we use that gift or skill to the very best of our ability.

 RELATED PAGES *April 26, June 25*

July 20

In tribulation, immediately draw near to God with confidence, and you will receive strength, enlightenment, and instruction.

SAINT JOHN OF THE CROSS

I CONFESS THAT I have always been sensitive to pain. When I was a little boy, I hurt my leg playing soccer. It became infected, so my granny took me to our doctor. He washed the wound as gently as he could while I winced. Then he told me apologetically, "I'm going to have to apply tincture of iodine."

Now, I had heard many stories about how much it hurt to have iodine applied to a wound. So I closed my eyes. I felt the doctor's touch on my leg, and then a wave of pain across the wound. I think my yell must have lifted the roof.

Then I noticed the pain had subsided, so I opened my eyes. "Is it over?" I asked. The doctor looked at me with compassion and said, "I haven't even applied the iodine yet."

Often it is fear of pain, and the resistance to pain, that makes pain hard to bear. When fear goes, suffering becomes manageable; and the mantram is the best thing I know for banishing fear. Whether it is a headache, a stomachache, or serious injury, the mantram always helps.

RELATED PAGE *March 2*

July 21

Use the light.
Come home to your true nature.
Don't cause yourself injury:
This is known as seizing the truth.

LAO TZU

AS HUMAN beings, we have been born with the capacity to make choices. No other creature has this capacity, and no human being can avoid this responsibility. Every day, whether we see it or not, we have a choice of two alternatives in what we do, say, and think.

These alternatives are: what is pleasant and what is beneficial. The first pleases us now. The second may be unpleasant at the beginning, as anyone who has begun a physical fitness program knows; but it will improve our health and contribute to our peace of mind.

Both choices promise satisfaction. One we get immediately, but it comes and goes; the other requires effort, but its benefits stay with us and often benefit those around us as well.

 RELATED PAGES *April 27, November 24*

July 22

Old age is the most unexpected of all the things that can happen to us.

LEON TROTSKY

WHEN THE first grey hair appears on our head, it is a critical juncture in life. We go to the mirror with a sinking feeling of dread and try to pluck out the evidence – one here, two there. But the more we pull out, the more seem to come in.

I tease my friends by asking which of them would like to relive their adolescence. It always brings a groan. Youth has a lot to offer, but so does the experience of age. In India we have a joke about a man going to a barber and asking, "Do you have anything for grey hair?" "Yes," the barber says, "respect." Just because we don't have wrinkles or a grey hair, we are not necessarily alive in the fullest sense of the word. Real living comes from making a contribution to life.

This is the paradox of life: when we cling to the body, it loses its beauty. But when we do not cling to the body – and use it as an instrument given us to serve others – it glows with a special beauty, as we can see from the lives of many great saints and mystics. When our consciousness becomes pure, even the body begins to reflect its light.

RELATED PAGES *April 6, July 6*

July 23

Lord, make me an instrument of thy peace.
Where there is hatred, let me sow love.

SAINT FRANCIS OF ASSISI

WHEN WE ask to be made instruments of peace, what we are really asking for is the boundless determination to empty ourselves of every state of mind that disrupts relationships – anger, resentment, jealousy, greed, self-will in any form. Our first priority is to reform ourselves; without that, how can we expect to help other people reform themselves? It is the living example of a man or woman giving all they have to making love a reality that moves our hearts to follow. We do not need a bumper sticker that says, "You are following an instrument of the Lord." Our everyday actions speak for themselves.

 RELATED PAGES *April 21, April 26*

July 24

Still your mind in me, still yourself in me, and without doubt you shall be united with me, Lord of Love dwelling in your heart.

BHAGAVAD GITA

CHILDREN ATTENDING their first swimming lessons have a healthy fear of putting their faces underwater. They are afraid they are going to drown. This is the feeling we can get when we go deeper in meditation and begin to break loose from some of our long-cherished emotional attachments.

When I was first meditating, I had the same fears everyone has. All kinds of struggles were going on inside me, and it took time and effort to overcome them. But once the waters closed over my head and I began to get my bearings in these new realms, I knew this was what I had been looking for and longing for, and all my energy went into diving deeper.

When we put our heads under and dive deep, leaving selfishness on the surface, we find a joy that is a million times what any surface sensation can give, and a love that at its fullest expression embraces all of life. Initially we may fear losing the sensory satisfactions that lie on the surface, but waiting far below are joy, love, life.

RELATED PAGES *June 2, September 13*

July 25

Thou art my glory and the exultation of my heart: thou art my hope and refuge in the day of my trouble.

THOMAS A KEMPIS

SOMETIMES IN our spiritual life, we will find we have come to a point where our progress seems to be stopped cold. Sometimes these dry periods are just that, a boring stretch of ground that we must get over by walking step by step. But sometimes we find before us a chasm, and at that time no amount of plodding at our usual humble pace will get us across.

At those times, devotion to a divine ideal – whether as a personal incarnation of God, or simply complete faith in the Self within us – can enable us to make a leap.

We will close our eyes and say, "I do not have the capacity to go farther without help. Now it is up to You." We'll go forward, secure in the faith that the Self, the Lord within, will never let us fall but will carry us safely to the other side.

 RELATED PAGES *June 7, November 30*

July 26

Like a ball batted back and forth, a human being is batted by two forces within.

YOGABINDU UPANISHAD

AS HUMAN beings we have a divided nature – partly physical, but essentially spiritual. We are constantly batted by two conflicting forces. One force is the fierce downward thrust of our past conditioning as separate, self-oriented, physical creatures. Yet built into our very nature is an inner drive that will not let us be satisfied with a life governed only by biological laws. Some inner evolutionary imperative is constantly exhorting us to grow, to reach for the highest that we can conceive.

RELATED PAGES *July 21, November 8*

July 27

How sweet it is to love, and to be dissolved, and as it were to bathe myself in thy love.

THOMAS A KEMPIS

IN THESE times, a common prescription for a day packed with troubles is to go jump in your hot tub. Relaxation starts immediately; for a time, at least, the body is at peace.

Now imagine a hot tub for the mind. That is what meditation is; it can bathe your mind in peace. This requires a lot of practice, but when you have learned to jump in the hot tub of meditation at the end of a day, instead of rehashing problems with your co-workers or downing a double martini, you can close your eyes, start in with an inspirational passage, and let the accumulated tensions of the day dissolve.

 RELATED PAGES *February 1, July 16*

July 28

Of all things that are, nothing is forbidden and nothing is contrary to God but one thing only: that is, self-will, or to will otherwise than as the Eternal Will would have it.

THEOLOGIA GERMANICA

ALL SPIRITUAL progress requires the sacrifice of self-will. Since most of us have rather large amounts of self-will, we cannot expect to get rid of it overnight. Those who are terribly eager may expect to load all their selfishness in one big truck and in one grand gesture cart it all to the dump. Unfortunately, there is no truck big enough, and even if there were, we would not have the strength to get all our self-will into it.

The safest and simplest method is to cart off a little bit of selfishness every day, day after day, year after year. A thousand and one little acts of thoughtfulness displace a monstrous load. One day we find to our great surprise that all our separateness has vacated the premises. Then we will see that the "sacrifice" was no sacrifice at all. We have lost nothing, but have gained everything.

RELATED PAGES *May 15, September 20*

July 29

Beautiful young people are accidents of nature, but beautiful old people are works of art.

ELEANOR ROOSEVELT

THE MODERN world puts a high premium on youth. By this standard, retirement brings the freedom to take on a second career, or find fulfillment in new hobbies, or to recapture the pleasures of youth. But the last years of life spent in such pursuits are often full of frustrations and regrets.

By contrast, from a spiritual perspective, the second half of life is the natural time to turn from physical satisfactions to inner growth. These are years of opportunity – of continued growth rather than decline. This is the time when we need to concentrate on spiritual development if we are to fulfill our highest potential and realize our immortality. All the world's religions agree that death is not the end of life, only the end of one chapter.

 RELATED PAGES *June 30, October 29*

July 30

But they for whom I am the supreme goal, who do all work renouncing self for me and meditate on me with single-hearted devotion, these I will swiftly rescue from death's vast sea, for their consciousness has entered into me.

BHAGAVAD GITA

WHEN THE lover of God finds somebody in danger, he doesn't turn away; he runs to help. This is one of the unmistakable signs of true love of God.

When someone is in trouble, you don't say, "How did he behave towards me?" You don't ask, "Of what race or color is she?" or "Is this person my countryman? Does she belong to my religion?" None of these questions can be asked by the person who truly loves God. He or she just runs to the rescue of the person in trouble.

When we are trying to help someone, it is *we* who get great joy out of it. If we try to rescue someone who has been unkind, the joy is even greater. This is a secret all but forgotten in our modern world: we find a much more lasting joy in rescuing others than in trying to save ourselves, because in rescuing others we are making sure that we will be saved by the Lord who is within.

RELATED PAGE *June 18*

July 31

Wherever you go, you will always bear yourself about with you, and so you will always find yourself.

THOMAS A KEMPIS

THERE IS only one way to get a real vacation: get as far away from the ego as possible.

Worrying about your problems all the time makes for misery with a capital *M*. For getting away from misery, I recommend this "economy plan": do not feed your ego and your problems with your attention. They will slowly lose weight.

When we feed them, constantly begging them to have one more helping even when they are gorged, we acquire obese problems that hug us tightly and weight us down. So if you really want a vacation, do not brood on your troubles. Do not let yourself get jealous or say uncharitable things about anyone. In other words, do not give the ego breakfast in bed; do not pack it a bag lunch; do not fix its dinner; do not give it pocket money for buying snacks; do not even give it a glass of water. Slowly, surely, the ego will lose weight, until one fine day it will be nothing but a thin ghost of its former self.

You will be able to see right through it, to the divine presence that shines in each of us.

 RELATED PAGES *August 2, September 20*

August

When we go slower, we are more patient – and when we are more patient, we have a choice in how we respond.

EKNATH EASWARAN

August 1

Love seeketh not itself to please,
Nor for itself hath any care,
But for another gives its ease,
And builds a Heaven in Hell's despair.

WILLIAM BLAKE

THOUGH I have lived in this country for many years now, there are still many American expressions that I don't understand. I remember trying to explain meditation to a young fellow who kept shaking his head and saying, "Man, I just don't hear you." In all innocence, I started over again a little louder. Finally it dawned on me what he really meant: "I just don't *want* to hear you. I don't like what you're saying."

This is what most of us do when there is disagreement. We carry around a pair of earplugs, and the minute somebody starts saying something we don't like, we stuff them in our ears until he or she is through. Watch with some detachment the next time you find yourself quarreling with someone you love. It won't look like a melodrama, but like a first-rate comedy – two people trying to reach an understanding by not listening to each other!

An effective way of dealing with a disagreement is simply to listen with complete attention, even if we don't care for what the other person is saying. We are showing how our respect won't waver no matter how vehemently we may disagree.

 RELATED PAGES *January 3, May 20*

August 2

The words of the tongue should have three gatekeepers.

ARAB PROVERB

BEFORE WORDS get past the lips, the first gatekeeper asks, "Is this true?" That stops a lot of traffic immediately. But if the words get past the first gatekeeper, there is a second who asks, "Is it kind?" And for those words that qualify here too, the last gatekeeper asks, "Is it necessary?"

With these three on guard, most of us would find very little to say. Here I think it is necessary to make exceptions in the interests of good company and let the third gatekeeper look the other way now and then. After all, a certain amount of pleasant conversation is part of the artistry of living. But the first two gatekeepers should always be on duty.

It is so easy to say something at the expense of another for the purpose of enhancing our own image. But such remarks – irresistible as they may be – serve only to fatten our egos and agitate others. We should be so fearful of hurting people that even if a clever remark is rushing off our tongue, we can barricade the gate. We should be able to swallow our cleverness rather than hurt someone. Better to say something banal but harmless than to be clever at someone else's expense.

RELATED PAGE *July 31*

August 3

In the first days of my youth I tried to find it in the creatures, as I saw others do; but the more I sought, the less I found it, and the nearer I went to it, the further off it was. For of every image that appeared to me, before I had fully tested it, or abandoned myself to peace in it, an inner voice said to me: "This is not what thou seekest."

HEINRICH SUSO

PHYSICAL ATTRACTION is not a firm foundation on which to build a relationship, for the simple reason that it is never constant. It sets in motion a cycle of expectation and disillusionment that can go on and on. The person who lives in a world of fantasy will often blame the other for letting him down. Perhaps, for example, Juliet expects Romeo to come to her balcony every morning and launch into, "It is the east, and you are the sun . . . ." Three days after the honeymoon, she feels crushed when she is greeted at breakfast with nothing more romantic than, "Where's the toast?" Many relationships sputter because of just such inflated expectations, which demand of life something that it simply cannot give. We should not feel that close relationships are beyond our reach, but they are demanding. Through experience, we come to realize that in love nothing comes as easily as we expected. Everything beautiful has to be worked for.

 RELATED PAGES *May 9, August 20*

August 4

Where there is injury, let me sow pardon.

SAINT FRANCIS OF ASSISI

ONCE, IN wintertime, it is said that Francis and his disciple Brother Leo were making a hard journey on foot through the snowy countryside of Italy. They had been walking along in silence for a long time when Brother Leo turned to Francis and asked him, "How can we find perfect joy?" Francis stopped and replied, "Even if all our friars were perfect in their holiness and could work all kinds of miracles for others, we still would not have perfect joy."

He turned and walked on, and Brother Leo ran after him. "Then what is perfect joy?" Francis stopped again, "Even if we could speak with the birds of the air and the beasts of the field and know all the secrets of nature, we still would not have perfect joy. Even if we could cure all the ills on the face of the earth, we would still not have found perfect joy."

Brother Leo was practically shouting: "Then please, Father Francis, what *is* the secret of perfect joy?"

"Brother, suppose we go to that monastery across the field and tell the gatekeeper how weary and cold we are, and he calls us tramps and beats us and throws us out into the winter night. Then, Brother, if we can say with love in our hearts, 'Bless you in the name of Jesus,' then we shall have found perfect joy."

RELATED PAGES *February 20, August 28*

August 5

People do not know what the Name of God can do. Those who repeat it constantly alone know its power. It can purify our mind completely. . . . The Name can take us to the summit of spiritual experience.

SWAMI RAMDAS

IT'S PROBABLY safe to say that most people do not know how aspirin works. Yet we have faith in aspirin. When you take the bottle off the bathroom shelf and pop a couple of pills into your mouth, you are saying in effect, "I believe. I have faith that this will work." I would say, "Take plenty of mantrams too." It is equally good advice: one relieves fever in the body, the other, the fever of self-will. People sometimes scoff at this and retort, "We don't think it will work." I reply, "Don't you think you can give the Buddha or Jesus as much credence as you give Mr. Bayer?"

Try it. If you feel comforted only by things that come in a bottle, take an empty bottle and write *Rama, Rama* or *Jesus, Jesus* on the label. Then put it on your bathroom shelf. When you have a disquieting afternoon or evening or night, take it down, look at it, and start repeating Rama, Rama or Jesus, Jesus. You have taken the medicine.

 RELATED PAGES *March 1, May 26*

August 6

One who would be serene and pure
needs but one thing, detachment.

MEISTER ECKHART

MOST OF us identify ourselves with our pet opinions. Then, when we are contradicted, we take it personally and get upset. If we could look at ourselves with some detachment, we would see how absurd this is. There is scarcely any more connection between me and my opinions than there is between me and my car. I have a close friend who is devoted to her Volkswagen Bug. If I compliment her on it, she is pleased; if I tell her what her neighbor says about Volkswagens, she feels insulted. But why? Where is the connection? *She* is not a VW Bug.

Once we realize at a deeper level of consciousness that we are not our opinions, most of the resentment in differences of opinion disappears. There is nothing wrong with disagreement; in fact, sometimes it is necessary to disagree. But we should do so with complete respect for the other person.

RELATED PAGES *March 18, May 20*

August 7

Where are you searching for me, friend?
Look! Here am I right within you.
Not in temple, nor in mosque,
Not in Kaaba, nor Kailas,
But here right within you am I.

KABIR

MANY HAVE begun the spiritual search while still suffering from severe personal problems. Saint Augustine was deeply enmeshed in the life of the world, and pulled himself free only after great anguish of mind. Others suffered physically. Saint Thérèse of Lisieux endured the constant pain of tuberculosis. So there is no need for any of us to feel downcast about our situation or the particular difficulties we face, provided we do everything we can to purify our mind.

Meditation is essentially a discipline for slowing down the furious pace of thinking; if you can gradually bring your mind to a state so still that no movement, no thought, can arise except those you yourself approve, your mind will have become pure. We have no need to teach pure motives to the mind. All that is necessary to make the mind pure is to undo the negative conditioning to which it has been subjected; then we will be left with pure, unconditioned awareness.

 RELATED PAGES *February 1, December 20*

August 8

A sheltered life can be a daring life as well. For all serious daring starts from within.

EUDORA WELTY

I AM SITTING in my chair at home in the country, looking out on the green hills. There is everything right here to satisfy me: birds, flowers, trees, reasonable comfort, loyal companions, and the precious opportunity of selfless service. Right here is everything I need for complete happiness always.

But as I look out of my cottage window I see a camper in the distance traveling along the road. Somewhere in my mind is the uneasy stirring of a desire to jump into that camper and go out chasing rainbows to find the pot of gold at the end. This belief that somewhere out there is the land of joy dogs our footsteps wherever we go. As long as we look upon happiness as something outside us, we shall never be able to find it. Wherever we go it will still be beyond our reach, because "out there" can never be "in here."

As Jesus says, "The kingdom of heaven is within."

RELATED PAGES *April 8, July 4*

August 9

As oil is in the oil seed,
So is the Lord within thee, unrevealed.

KABIR

IF WE could interview a negative tendency, say, Resentment, it might say, "I don't worry! I've been living safely in this fellow's mind for years. He takes good care of me – feeds me, dwells on me, brings me out and parades me around! All I have to do is roar and stir things up from time to time. Yes, I'm getting fat and feeling grand. And I'm proud to tell you there are even a few little rancors and vituperations running around now, spawned by yours truly!"

So he may think. But when you repeat the mantram, you are prying him loose. You are saying, in a way that goes beyond vows and good intentions, that resentment is not part of the real you. You no longer acknowledge its right to exist.

We use something genuine to drive out impostors that have roamed about largely through our neglect and helplessness. We move closer and closer to our divine Self, because these impostors, resentment and ill will, are no longer coming between us.

RELATED PAGES *March 1, April 22*

August 10

I went to the root of things, and found nothing but Him alone.

MIRA BAI

THE LORD is not someone outside us who lived in a given place at a given time. He is right within.

Throughout creation, God is the principle of creativity itself. Even some of the greatest scientists and philosophers have yet to grasp this simple truth. One well-respected astronomer calls it cowardly to conclude that God created the universe just because we cannot comprehend the conditions of its creation. This great scientist is still thinking of God as someone outside, holding court beyond the Andromeda galaxy; he hasn't glimpsed that all this is God, and wherever there is light, or beauty, or excellence in anything, we are seeing a little more of His glory.

But, as Mira says, to see this vision we cannot just stay on the surface of life picking up a few baubles of pleasure and prestige. We have to get deep, deep below, and go to the root of all things.

RELATED PAGE *September 28*

August 11

Acquire a firm will and the utmost patience.

ANANDAMAYI MA

WE BEGIN our journey towards the supreme goal of life from where we stand. Just as it is good to be patient with others, it is equally necessary to be patient with ourselves. After all, when the desire to live for others comes to us, we can be haunted by our past mistakes, by the amount of time we have wasted in selfish pursuits. But we must accept ourselves with all our strengths and weaknesses.

There are many obstacles on the spiritual path which can strengthen us, and these cannot be overcome unless we have infinite patience with ourselves. If we are patient with others, shouldn't we be patient with ourselves as well? Each of us is individual, with our own special qualities. We start now, where we are, with our partial love for money, partial love for pleasure, partial love for prestige, and a little love for God. We will progress at our own pace. It is not good to compare one person's progress with another's.

 RELATED PAGES *August 28, October 1*

August 12

We ought to fly away from earth to heaven as quickly as we can; and to fly away is to become like God, as far as this is possible; and to become like him is to become holy, just, and wise.

PLATO

WE ARE all capable of flying like eagles high in the sky of love, but often we prefer running on the ground instead.

Have you seen that curious bird, the quail? We have many of them where we live. When we are driving down the lane, they won't get out of the way. They won't fly. They try to outrun the car. It is only when they conclude their number is up that they start flying. They know how to fly, but they would rather stay on the ground.

Most of us are like that. But our wings are there; we have only to spread them to experience the exhilaration of soaring into the sky and looking down to see all life as one.

RELATED PAGES *March 8, December 3*

August 13

The Perfect Way is only difficult for those
who pick and choose;
Do not like, do not dislike;
all will then be clear.
Make a hairbreadth difference,
and Heaven and Earth are set apart.

SENG-TS'AN

HAPPINESS AND sorrow, good and bad, pleasure and pain – these are the very texture of life on the superficial level. The less you are bound by these dualities, the more clearly you will be able to see the core of purity and selflessness that is the real Self in everyone, even in people who cause trouble.

My grandmother had a pungent phrase for difficult people: "a lash in the eye." We all know from experience how an eyelash in the eye can be so irritating that we just cannot think about anything else. That is exactly how difficult people affect those around them, so naturally most of us try to avoid such people.

But this lash in the eye is an opportunity for learning the skills that matter most in life: patience, forgiveness, and freedom from likes and dislikes. It is only the spiritually mature person who can go and put his arm around someone who has given him a really difficult time, and say sincerely, "Without you, how could I ever have learned to be patient? How could I have learned to forgive?"

 RELATED PAGES *June 15, July 9*

August 14

Endurance is one of the most difficult disciplines, but it is to the one who endures that the final victory comes.

THE BUDDHA

PEOPLE OFTEN find that meditation is easy for the first few months; but then, just when they think things are going well, it becomes difficult. It is like digging in your garden. The surface level of consciousness is soft loam, easy digging for the first twelve inches or so. The blade of the shovel is turning over the soil so easily that you say, "This is great! Isn't meditation wonderful?" Then you strike something hard and impenetrable. Your hands sting from the shock, and your arms ache. That is the first stratum of bedrock – a dense, rock-hard layer of sheer resistance. Congratulations! You are getting somewhere at last!

How do you know you have hit something? The most common sign is a wave of sleep during meditation. Your mind is saying, in effect, "My shovel is getting blunted, and my arms are tired. Why not stop digging and have a snooze?" It is extremely important not to yield to this inclination. Sit up straighter and draw away from your back support until the wave of sleep has passed. This problem of sleep may be with you for a long time. You have a lot of strata to dig through, and there is great joy in this digging.

RELATED PAGE *September 11*

August 15

The joy of the spirit ever abides, but not what seems pleasant to the senses. Both these, differing in their purpose, prompt us to action.

KATHA UPANISHAD

WHEN WE let the senses follow their own lead, they cannot help going after pleasure; that is their nature. As a result, it should come as no surprise to see that most of the world today is on the road to sensory satisfaction.

It takes real toughness, and a lot of practice, to wait out all of the blandishments of passing pleasure when they lead us away from our real goal. When we lack this toughness, despite better goals we may cherish in our hearts, we will not be able to take the road that leads where we want to go. It is a poignant paradox: wanting only happiness, yet going systematically in the other direction. But if we keep choosing the joy of the spirit, I can assure you, we will reach our goal.

RELATED PAGES *June 21, June 29*

August 16

If someone takes your coat, give him your cloak as well; if he makes you go a mile with him, go with him two.

THE GOSPEL ACCORDING TO SAINT MATTHEW

IF YOU really want to land a blow at a compulsion, defy it. Do just the opposite of what it says. It is a daring approach which appeals to everyone with a sense of adventure. If somebody has been unkind to you, go out of your way to be kind to him. It can require a lot of endurance simply to be patient with such a person, but we're talking about more than endurance now; we're talking about daring.

Try it: there is an exhilaration in it, and a special delight in seeing the other person rub his eyes in disbelief, "I was just rude to him, and now he's being thoughtful. What's wrong with him?"

RELATED PAGE *October 23*

August 17

Those who are selfless rejoice here and rejoice there; they rejoice wherever they go. They rejoice and delight in the good they have done.

THE BUDDHA

WHEN WE live for others, we'll find we are less oppressed by the natural changeability of life. Instead of wanting, even demanding, that everything go our way, we'll feel at peace when everything is going everybody else's way. In other words, we will be less likely to get discouraged or depressed by the normal ups and downs of life.

And when we are able to function freely in all the varied relationships and vicissitudes of life, we will gradually find an inner certitude that we are equal to every challenge. Then, just because somebody is agitated, we won't be afraid. Just because someone is unfavorably disposed towards us, we will not get diffident or annoyed. The Buddha says these outward changes of fortune can never affect our joy, which is permanent.

 RELATED PAGE *September 24*

August 18

The soul that is attached to anything, however much good there may be in it, will not arrive at the liberty of divine union. For whether it be a strong wire rope or a slender and delicate thread that holds the bird, it matters not, if it really holds it fast; for, until the cord be broken, the bird cannot fly.

SAINT JOHN OF THE CROSS

REMEMBER JONATHAN Swift's description of Gulliver tied with thousands of little strings anchored to the ground with thousands of little pegs? Similarly, we are tied down by numerous selfish attachments, large and small.

We can get attached to anything, from our heirloom china to our comic books. Things are not meant to be loved but to be used wisely. People are to be loved, but there, too, we must be careful not to come to see people as possessions – which is quite different from loving them. Through the practice of meditation, we can learn to recall all our selfish desires and slip free of the fetters that bind us to a limited way of life. For it is then, when we are not selfishly attached to anything, when we are living for the welfare of everybody around us, that we are likely to be given a long life, health, and plenty of energy to go on contributing to the peace of the world in whatever way we can.

RELATED PAGES *October 25, November 25*

August 19

The wine of life is oozing drop by drop,
The leaves of life are falling one by one.

OMAR KHAYYAM

LIKE LEAVES, we come into this life, are here for a few days, and then are gone. Nobody remembers us, and nobody misses us.

As long as we believe that we are separate, we inevitably have to die. Our immortality is in the whole, which never dies. In living just for personal profit and pleasure, no matter under what philosophical name we may call it, our real personality withers away. It cannot be otherwise.

When you become aware that you are not a leaf but the tree, something amazing happens in your life: you are able to act spontaneously, almost effortlessly, for the good of all.

This is the proof of your awareness that you are the tree: everywhere it will motivate you, everywhere you will see what contribution you can make. You won't have to deliberate the pros and cons. You won't need a computer to provide you with a plan of action. You will know instinctively, intuitively, the needs of those around you. What's more, it will seem natural to change even long-established habits, to drop something that before would have given you pleasure, if it means the tree may flourish.

 RELATED PAGES *February 9, April 26*

August 20

Beauty is all very well at first sight; but who ever looks at it when it has been in the house three days?

GEORGE BERNARD SHAW

OFTEN WE try to build relationships on what is pleasing to us, particularly on physical attraction. But if there is anything sure about physical attraction, it is that it has to change. We cannot build on it; its very nature is to come and go.

Physical attraction is a sensation – here one minute and gone the next. Love is a relationship. It is pleasant to be with someone who is physically attractive, but how long can you enjoy an aquiline nose? How long can you thrill to the timbre of a voice when it doesn't say what you like? It's very much like eating: no matter how much you are attracted to chocolate pie, there is a limit to how much of it you can enjoy. Beyond that limit, if somebody merely mentions chocolate, your stomach stages a revolt.

If you want to build a relationship, build it on what endures. To build on a firm foundation, we have to stop asking, "What do I like?" and ask only, "What can I give?" Then there is joy in everything, because there is joy in the relationship itself – in ups *and* downs, through the pleasant and the unpleasant, in sickness and in health.

RELATED PAGES *January 11, August 3*

August 21

Late have I loved thee, O Beauty so ancient and so new; late have I loved thee! For behold, thou wert within me and I outside; and I sought thee outside and in my unloveliness fell upon these lovely things that thou hast made. Thou wert with me and I was not with thee. I was kept from thee by those things, yet had they not been in thee, they would not have been at all. Thou didst call and cry to me and break open my deafness. . . . I tasted thee, and now hunger and thirst for thee; thou didst touch me, and now I burn for thy peace.

SAINT AUGUSTINE

WHEN WE use the word *love*, let us use it very carefully, in the deeply spiritual sense, where to love is to know; to love is to act.

If you really love, from the depths of your consciousness, that love gives you a native wisdom. You perceive the needs of others intuitively and clearly, with detachment from any personal desires; and you know how to act creatively to meet those needs, dexterously surmounting any obstacle that comes in the way. Such is the immense, driving power of love.

 RELATED PAGE *September 30*

August 22

Place your mind before the mirror of eternity; place your soul in the brightness of His glory.

SAINT CLARE OF ASSISI

WE ARE shaped by what gains our attention and occupies our thoughts. Today, amidst all of the conditioning to the contrary, we need constant reminders of our higher nature, and that is why spiritual reading can be very helpful. The media drown us in such a low image of the human being that it is essential to remind ourselves constantly of something higher.

All of the world's religions provide nourishment for the spirit distilled from centuries of spiritual exploration. It is a wise investment of time to take half an hour or so each day for reading from the scriptures and the writings of the great mystics of all religions. Just before bedtime is a particularly good time, because the thoughts you fall asleep in will be with you throughout the night.

Our consciousness takes on the color of what we think about. By reading the words of a favorite saint or mystic, we imbue our mind with thoughts that are beautiful, true, and full of light.

RELATED PAGE *February 12*

August 23

The test of a man or woman's breeding
is how they behave in a quarrel.

GEORGE BERNARD SHAW

WHEN TEMPERS are frayed, and an argument is in progress, it is very difficult for anyone to listen with courtesy to an opposing point of view. If we could ask the mind on such occasions why it doesn't listen, it would answer candidly, "Why should I? I already know I'm right." We may not put it into words, but the other person gets the message: "You're not worth listening to." It is this lack of respect that offends people in an argument, much more than any difference of opinion.

But respect can be learned – in part by acting as if we had respect. We show respect by simply listening with complete attention. Try it and see: the action is very much like that of a classical drama. For a while there is "rising action." The other person's temper keeps going up; language becomes more and more vivid; everything is heading for a climax. But then comes the denouement. The other person begins to quiet down: his voice becomes gentler, his language kinder, all because you have not retaliated or lost your respect for him.

 RELATED PAGES *April 25, May 20*

August 24

O good Jesus, thou has bound my heart in the thought of thy name, and now I can not but sing it; therefore have mercy upon me, making perfect that thou hast ordained.

RICHARD ROLLE

WHEN YOU are walking is one of the best times to repeat the mantram, especially if you walk briskly. The rhythm of your footsteps, the rhythm of the mantram, and the rhythm of your breathing all harmonize to soothe and invigorate the body and mind. Breathing is closely connected with your state of mind. People who are tense or angry breathe rapidly and irregularly; those who are calm, loving, and secure breathe smoothly, slowly, and deeply. A brisk walk helps to make your breathing rhythm deep and even, and the mantram will help to calm your mind.

RELATED PAGES *March 1, March 2*

August 25

By two wings we are lifted up from things earthly: by simplicity and purity.

THOMAS A KEMPIS

TO SOAR to the heights, the soul needs two wings. One is purity, which enables us to keep our eyes on the one thing in life that matters: awareness of the divinity within every human being. The other is simplicity: of lifestyle, but also simplicity in our desires.

This raises a worry that many serious-minded people have today. Living in the workaday world, surrounded by all manner of influences we cannot control, can purity and simplicity ever be anything for us but beautiful abstractions? It is one thing to grasp intellectually how we want to live; it is quite another to put our ideals into practice.

Yet, it is possible to learn to tug our attention away from lesser things, and focus on what really matters. And, to our great surprise, we will actually hit on some remedies. One person may start with his teenaged son, discovering a way to give him support that hadn't occurred to him before. Another may mobilize help for children dying of hunger in Ethiopia or help the homeless in the inner city.

 RELATED PAGES *January 14, November 14*

August 26

If you let your mind dwell on ghosts, you'll become a ghost yourself. If you fix your mind on God, your life will be filled with God. Now – which are you going to choose?

SRI RAMAKRISHNA

IN MEDITATION, we learn the skill of bringing our attention back to the words of the inspirational passage whenever it strays away. Attention is like a restless puppy, fond of running after anything new that comes along. When it sees an intensely charged memory, it cannot let it roll by; it has to chase the memory and keep yapping, yapping, yapping.

Just as with a dog, we have to call the mind back over and over again, whenever we sit down for meditation. This may go on for years. But if we keep practicing diligently and systematically, the day will come when we can put our attention where we want it with little effort, and it will stay without movement or protest. Then, however unkind somebody may have been, we will not be mastered by resentment; our attention will not turn to the past at all.

RELATED PAGES *October 9, October 27*

August 27

There are many going afar to marvel at the heights of mountains, the mighty waves of the sea, the long courses of great rivers, the vastness of the ocean, the movements of the stars, yet they leave themselves unnoticed!

SAINT AUGUSTINE

TODAY MANY people who enjoy traveling are not content with visiting London or Paris; they want to travel by camel in the Sahara, or kayak in the Antarctic. But no matter how exotic, this is horizontal travel, where we stay on the surface of life. Much more fascinating is vertical travel – that is, meditation, which takes us to the Land of Love in the utmost depths of consciousness.

For a long time we may not get very far, but if we insist on traveling deep, meditation will become a daring adventure. We will pass through level after level of consciousness, just the way one travels from one country to another. There is this difference: when we pass from the United States into Mexico, we know when we have crossed the border. We must stop and speak to the guard. Then the language changes. We know we are in a new land. In meditation, it is rather different. The changes are likely to take place so gradually that we may not even be aware of it immediately. But slowly and surely we will begin to have a strong feeling of coming home to our native land.

 RELATED PAGE *July 24*

August 28

It is in pardoning that we are pardoned.

SAINT FRANCIS OF ASSISI

THERE ARE times when past mistakes swim into our vision and do their best to consume us in guilt or regret. At such times it is essential to turn all our attention outwards, away from ourselves.

Analyzing our mistakes and developing a guilt complex benefits no one. If, when you were in Milwaukee, you happened to say something insulting about your girlfriend's dog, it is not necessary to go to Milwaukee and find your old girlfriend or her dog and make amends. Every dog you treat with kindness will be a proxy for that dog. In this way, if you have treated a particular person badly, even if you can no longer win that person's forgiveness, you can still win the forgiveness of yourself, of the Lord of Love within, by bearing with people who treat you badly and doing your best not to treat anyone badly again. Whatever we have done, we can make amends for it without looking back in guilt or sorrow.

RELATED PAGES *August 4, August 11*

August 29

And what rule do you think I walked by? Truly a strange one, but the best in the whole world. I was guided by an implicit faith in God's goodness; and therefore led to the study of the most obvious and common things. For thus I thought within myself: God being, as generally believed, infinite in goodness, it is most consonant and agreeable with His nature that the best things should be most common.

THOMAS TRAHERNE

A STATE OF permanent joy, hidden at the very center of consciousness, is the Eden to which the long journey of spiritual seeking leads. There, the mystics of all religions agree, we uncover our original goodness. We don't have to buy it; we don't have to create it; we don't have to pour it in; we don't even have to be worthy of it. This native goodness is the essential core of human nature.

We are made, the scriptures of all religions assure us, in the image of God. Nothing can change our original goodness. Whatever mistakes we have made in the past, whatever problems we may have in the present, in every one of us the uncreated spark in the soul remains untouched, ever pure, ever perfect. Even if we try with all our might to douse or hide it, it is always ready to set our personality ablaze with light.

 RELATED PAGES *February 8, December 20*

August 30

When the heart grieves over what it has lost, the spirit rejoices over what it has found.

SUFI PROVERB

DURING THE early stages of the spiritual journey, we can feel a certain deprivation when we have to keep saying no to the senses as they clamor for things that will only add to the burden of the journey later on. "Don't eat this. Don't drink that. Don't smoke this. Don't watch that." This is what you hear from your spiritual teacher. There is no rapture; there is no ecstasy; only "keep plugging along."

This discriminating restraint of the senses is not asceticism. Its purpose is not to subjugate the body. We need to train the senses to be faithful allies on our journey for two compelling reasons: first, the body is our vehicle, and we need to keep it healthy, strong, and resilient so that it can carry us steadily and safely to the summit of consciousness; second, training the senses strengthens the will day by day, enabling us gradually to gain control over the fierce passions that rage beneath the surface of consciousness. Without a trained will it is not possible to move up out of the Valley of the Shadow of Death which is our physical world. Untrained, the will becomes self-will, our worst enemy; but trained, the will can become our most powerful ally.

RELATED PAGES *January 24, March 22*

August 31

When on the bridge, the pilgrim says Rama, Rama, but afterwards, it's Kama, Kama.

HINDU PROVERB

PILGRIMS TRAVELING in the Himalayas sometimes must cross deep ravines on rope bridges. While on the bridge, which is swinging like a pendulum, everyone says *Rama, Rama, Rama,* "Lord, Lord, Lord," with as much devotion as he or she can muster. But as soon as the first step is taken on terra firma, it is likely to be *kama, kama, kama,* "Pleasure, Pleasure, Pleasure." When we are in the middle of turmoil we are very responsive to the mantram; but as soon as our health is good, our income is steady, and pleasures are flowing smoothly, we forget.

The Lord is a good psychologist: he knows the way our minds run. Turmoil can be his way of tapping us on the shoulder and saying, "Don't forget me."

 RELATED PAGES *March 2, November 23*

September

When the mind is completely still, unstirred even in its depths, we see straight through to the ground of our being.

EKNATH EASWARAN

September 1

Love your enemies, bless them that curse you, do good to them that hate you.

THE GOSPEL ACCORDING TO SAINT MATTHEW

THIS IS love at its most magnificent. In order to love like this, we cannot be attached to ourselves. It is because we think so much about ourselves that we strike back, show resentment, speak harshly, move away.

Jesus' words do not mean agreeing with everything people say or supporting whatever they do. We sometimes have to oppose people we love. Yet, if we do it tenderly, it is not likely that it will cost us a single friend. In fact, that person might say, "I've found a friend who will support me and stand beside me always."

 RELATED PAGES *April 25, August 23*

September 2

The affairs of the world will go on forever. Do not delay the practice of meditation.

MILAREPA

THE HUMAN being simply does not have enough fuel in one lifetime to explore every byway that presents itself. If we had a thousand years to live, we could explore every roadside attraction, doing all the little things that appeal to us, and still have time left for realizing the goal of life. But even the most long-lived of us will be given a hundred years at most – and but a fraction of that time before vitality and resolution begin to wane.

People approach spiritual growth in one of two ways: there are the "locals" and the "express" trains. The "locals" stop at every little station along the way to sample the food and enjoy the local color. But the "express" goes straight through to the destination. Fortunately, there seems to be an inner law: we start as "locals" but become "expresses" as we make progress on our journey.

When we take to meditation and put all our heart into practicing spiritual disciplines, we find ourselves speeding towards the goal.

RELATED PAGES *February 13, October 19*

September 3

Grant what thou commandest and then command what thou wilt.

SAINT AUGUSTINE

ASSESSING HIS own inner resources and finding them meager, Augustine strikes a humble bargain with the Lord that has endeared him to spiritual aspirants down the ages. He says, "I'll do whatever you like, Lord. I'll overcome the most towering passion. But only if you make it possible."

It would be poor sportsmanship indeed if the Lord were to throw us into the arena of life, loose the lions upon us, and then leave us to our own devices. But this is not his way. When he sends us a temptation, he also grants the weapons with which to resist it. By moving closer to the Lord in meditation, by calling on him with the mantram, by striving to carry out all the disciplines that wise spiritual counselors have recommended through their own lives, we can gradually ally ourselves with the Lord so completely that we have access to everything that is his. We learn love without limit, courage without fail, wisdom that can penetrate the toughest problems life offers.

 RELATED PAGE *March 1*

September 4

Unto those that hath shall be given, and they shall have abundance: but from those that hath not shall be taken away even that which they have.

THE GOSPEL ACCORDING TO SAINT MATTHEW

THIS IS a strange paradox, a little-known secret. Jesus isn't speaking of worldly goods. He is speaking of a very rare kind of treasure: the more you draw on it, the more you will have. The more patient you are with people, for instance, the more patience you will have. The more generous you are today, the more generosity you will have tomorrow. The more love you give, the more loving you become.

The principle can be stated in the plainest of terms: if you are selfish with your love, the scant security you cling to will be battered by life. But if you give of yourself freely, your security will be unshakable. Your joy will be limitless. You will always have more to give.

RELATED PAGES *January 26, March 5*

September 5

An attitude to life which seeks fulfillment in the single-minded pursuit of wealth – in short, materialism – does not fit into this world, because it contains within itself no limiting principle, while the environment in which it is placed is strictly limited.

E.F. SCHUMACHER

THE VERY air we breathe is not inexhaustible. If we love our children as we profess to, we should remember that the air is limited, exhaustible, a perishable member of the family of life. Treat it gently. Treat it with care. Don't blow fumes into the air or dump poisons into the rivers and oceans just because it increases profits. Don't fan overconsumption by buying things you do not need. It is not only corporations who carry the responsibility for pollution. Insofar as we tell them, "Produce all you want! We'll buy whatever you make," the rest of us are responsible too.

It is a wise commentator on today's world who points out that we do not inherit from our parents: we borrow from our children. Let us do all we can from today onwards to ensure that our children's children will live in a world unthreatened by radioactive waste and chemical pollution.

RELATED PAGES *July 8, November 12*

September 6

The heart benevolent and kind
The most resembles God.

ROBERT BURNS

IT IS through personal relationships that we learn to function beautifully in life throughout its ups and downs. We all need the little human contacts of life, and we all need intimate personal relationships with family or friends. Many people today do not live with a family, but that is not really the issue. Whether we live alone, with family, or with friends, we can cultivate personal relationships that are kind and genuine.

We can cultivate personal relationships everywhere, in everything, every day, with each person in our life – even the bank teller and the mail carrier.

Most of us, in moments of candor, will probably admit that we want to be liked by those around us. We like to please and be loved by those we love. And nothing makes us feel so secure as knowing that we have brought a little joy into the life of someone we care about. That is why putting others first can be such a natural, beautiful part of life.

RELATED PAGES *January 10, March 16*

September 7

Man must evolve for all human conflict a method which rejects revenge, aggression, and retaliation. The foundation of such a method is love.

MARTIN LUTHER KING

ALL OF us can play an important part in the conquest of violence. We can do this by throwing our full weight behind peaceful, effective programs for eliminating the situations from which violence arises. But just as importantly, we need to do everything we can to remove every trace of hostility in ourselves.

The violence that is flaring up on our streets and in many corners of the world is the inevitable expression of the hostility in our hearts. Hostility is like an infectious disease. Whenever we indulge in a violent act or even in hostile words, we are passing this disease on to those around us. When we quarrel at home, it is not just a domestic problem; we are contributing to turmoil everywhere.

A teacher of meditation in ancient India, Patanjali, wrote that in the presence of a man or woman in whom all hostility has died, others cannot be hostile. In the presence of a man or woman in whom all fear has died, no one can be afraid. This is the power released in true nonviolence, as we can see in the life of Mahatma Gandhi. Because all hostility had died in his heart, he was a profound force for peace.

RELATED PAGES *March 19, July 18*

September 8

Give a little love to a child, and you get a great deal back.

JOHN RUSKIN

THOSE WHO have children can become masters of patience, endurance, and steadfastness, because children will test you at every turn. Little ones are ruthless observers. When I see a five-year-old watching me, I feel as though Sherlock Holmes is on my track. I can almost hear him saying, "Elementary, my dear Watson. I can see the inconsistency between his word and deed quite clearly." The way to make our children patient and loving is to be that way ourselves. When we are upset or agitated, the mantram can come to our rescue. By continually calling on the source of strength within us, we can make our lives an inspiring example to our children.

RELATED PAGES *March 29, June 20*

September 9

Even as a tortoise draws in its limbs, the wise can draw in their senses at will.

BHAGAVAD GITA

WHAT A marvelous simile! Just imagine a tortoise being approached by a group of school children with sticks in their hands. He sees the children coming, and the command is given to the limbs, "Retire!" Immediately, the head, the tail, and the four legs withdraw into the shell. The children come; they tap on the shell with their sticks, trying to get the tortoise to come out. He is safe inside.

After the children leave and all is quiet, the tortoise ventures to stick his neck out, then his tail and legs. He continues his journey, unconcerned. He goes where he likes.

If we want to live in freedom, we must train our senses. We learn when to welcome an experience, and when to withdraw for our own safety. We become masters of our lives. Then we will be like the giant tortoise I saw at the zoo – wandering freely while all the other animals were in cages. A notice on his back read: "I am free. Don't report me to the management."

RELATED PAGES *May 3, October 2*

September 10

As you repeat the Holy Name, gather quietly, little by little, your thoughts and feelings and will around it; gather around it your whole being.

ON THE INVOCATION OF THE NAME OF JESUS

THE LITTLE waits and delays that life is so full of are all opportunities to repeat the mantram. In the morning, when you're waiting for the coffee to perk, you can repeat the mantram instead of staring blankly at the wall. When you are standing in line at the bank or the supermarket, the mantram will make the wait seem shorter, and your patience will help those around you too. When you are waiting for an interview, or for the doctor to come in, the mantram can save you a good deal of anxiety.

In all these cases, you are putting your time to better use than if you were letting your mind run on about what might be troubling it. You are saving yourself from unnecessary tension and anxiety. You are sending the mantram deeper into your consciousness.

It is many of these little moments that finally add up to impressive spiritual growth. Patience and concentration blossom in the space that you have cleared for them.

RELATED PAGES *March 1, March 2*

September 11

As butter lies hidden within milk,
The Self is hidden in the hearts of all.
Churn the mind through meditation on it;
Light your fire through meditation on it:
The Self, all whole, all peace, all certitude.

AMRITABINDU UPANISHAD

MEDITATION ENABLES us to understand the teachings of the scriptures and apply them in our daily life. It is meditation that reveals the inner Self dwelling in all things.

But the practice of meditation is like a long journey: some days we make wonderful progress, and others we seem barely able to go one step. Like a veteran traveler who knows the road, when we gain a little experience of the benefits, we'll look forward to our meditation period. We'll sit down for meditation with eagerness and enthusiasm each day.

 RELATED PAGES *May 5, August 14*

September 12

Each day is a little life; every waking and rising a little birth; every fresh morning a little youth; every going to rest and sleep a little death.

ARTHUR SCHOPENHAUER

MY GRANDMOTHER, my spiritual teacher, used to tell me that the pain we associate with the great change called death arises from our innumerable selfish attachments. One day she illustrated this in a simple way by asking me to sit in a chair and hold tight to the arms. Then she tried to pull me out of the chair. She tugged and pulled at me, and I held on tight. It was painful. She was a strong person, and even though I held on with all my strength, she pulled me out.

Then she told me to sit down again, but this time not to hold on anywhere, just to get up and come to her when she called. With ease I got out of the chair and went to her. This, she told me, is how to overcome the fear and pain of death. When we hold onto things – houses, cars, books, guitars, our antique silver teapot – we get attached and tied down.

RELATED PAGE *June 4*

September 13

Do not you believe that there is in us a depth so profound as to be hidden even to the one in whom it is?

SAINT AUGUSTINE

IN TALKING about deeper levels of consciousness, metaphors can be helpful. So let's talk about the "lake of the mind." It is a deep lake, but we are familiar only with the surface. We know how to swim effortlessly on the surface; modern life is quite good at teaching us all kinds of ingenious strokes for this. It even supplies us with flotation devices that keep us bouncing pleasurably on the surface of life forever.

Yet over time we become aware of how much distress is involved in the struggle merely to stay afloat. For some reason, peace of mind simply doesn't seem attainable; the mind keeps stirring up a never-ending succession of waves.

Life on the shimmering surface of consciousness, we may someday be forced to admit, isn't everything it's supposed to be. We come to the uncomfortable realization that there is simply no guarantee of security anywhere as long as we're living on the surface of life. At some point, every sensitive person is ready to dive – deep into consciousness in meditation. He or she wants to find out whether something more reliable lies below. Often it is the spiritual teacher who gives us the courage to dive. We ask ourselves, "If he has done it, why can't I?"

 RELATED PAGES *June 2, July 24*

September 14

Whoever approaches Me walking, I will come to him running; and he who meets Me with sins equivalent to the whole world, I will greet him with forgiveness equal to it.

MISHKAT AL-MASABIH

THE LORD, the Self, wants nothing more than that we should all be united with him. He is very eager to see us take the first step, but he knows us very well by now: he watches carefully to see that we take that step and do not wobble back and forth. It is not enough just to put your foot forward and touch it lightly to the ground; you must put your weight on it completely. When we do take that step – by bearing patiently with those around us, or by changing some unhealthy habit – we can be sure that he will run toward us. But we must take the first step.

RELATED PAGE *February 24*

September 15

We are not holier or higher for the outward works that we do. Truly God that is the beholder of the heart rewards the will more than the deed. The deeds truly hang on the will, not the will on the deeds.

RICHARD ROLLE

IT IS because we don't have any real challenge in life that we do not grow to our real height. We need a challenge that is worthy of our capacities, and making money, if I may say so, is not much of a challenge. Neither is becoming famous or achieving power; and as for pleasure, challenge is conspicuous by its absence.

But becoming rich in personal relationships, learning to return love for hatred, being always aware of the unity of life, these things are the most difficult achievements on the face of the earth. Only when we see a person who has accomplished such feats do we begin to glimpse the heights a human being can attain. This is our real stature, and no matter what our problems or liabilities, every one of us can attain these heights through regular, enthusiastic spiritual practice.

 RELATED PAGES *March 13*

September 16

The best, like water,
Benefit all and do not compete.
They dwell in lowly spots that everyone else scorns.
Putting others before themselves,
They find themselves in the foremost place
And come very near to the Tao.

LAO TZU

IN TODAY'S competitive climate, often those who are aggressive about imposing their will on others are labeled "successful." But the accomplishments of such people are often sadly short-lived, while the damage they do themselves and others can be far-reaching. When competitiveness is excessive, we end up offending others, feeling offended, and lashing back, and that undoes everything worthwhile we might achieve.

People who do not compete, on the other hand, seldom get upset when life goes against them. They do not try to impose their way on others, or get agitated or depressed or defensive when people hold different views.

Gandhi was an excellent example of this. It is said that he was at his best when he was criticized; it made him even more respectful and compassionate, and made him reach deeper into himself to find new ways of explaining his stand.

RELATED PAGES *February 18, March 17*

September 17

In vain our labours are, whatsoe'er they be,
Unless God gives the Benedicite.

ROBERT HERRICK

THERE ARE some people who are action-oriented. If they finish all of their work during the day and have a few free hours at night, they say, "I can't get to sleep, so I'll just stay up and do some work on the computer."

It is wonderful to have abundant energy, for then no obstacle is too big to overcome. But there can be danger when we have more energy than we know what to do with. We feel we have to act. We just cannot be idle. We get involved in activities and relationships out of restlessness.

It is not enough if we just keep busy. The question is, what are we busy about? This is a very useful question. To know when to plunge into an activity and when to refrain from it requires judgment – detachment and discrimination.

 RELATED PAGE *January 7*

September 18

Suffering is the ancient law of love; there is no quest without pain; there is no lover who is not also a martyr.

HEINRICH SUSO

PRACTICALLY SPEAKING, in order to learn to love, we need a tool for transforming anger into compassion, resentment into sympathy. We need some kind of brake to apply when the mind shifts into high gear under the influence of anger and other negative emotions. The mind is so used to having its own way in almost everything that all it knows is how to race out of control.

How many of you would ever step into your Pontiac or Toyota if you knew the brakes could suddenly fail. I could say, "You have plenty of gas, a big engine, gorgeous upholstery, and radial tires. Why don't you go ahead?" You would reply, "But I can't stop the thing!" Amazingly enough, most of us manage to travel through life without knowing how to brake the engine of the mind.

We can all install a simple but effective brake – the mantram. Whenever you feel agitated, annoyed, impolite, or downright angry, keep repeating the mantram. Gradually the mind will race less and less. When the brake is thoroughly road-tested, you will have the equipment to be patient and kind in every situation. You will be ready to face the tests that real love demands.

RELATED PAGES *March 1, April 22*

September 19

He that is slow to anger is better than the mighty; and he that ruleth his spirit than he that taketh a city.

PROVERBS

IN THE interest of good health, in the interest of a long life, in the interest of loving relationships, it is essential to learn how to deal with our anger creatively and constructively. If we do not, in time it will no longer be isolated outbursts of anger; we will become the victims of an unending stream of rage, seething just below the surface of life, with which no human being can cope.

Through meditation and the mantram every one of us can learn to reduce the speed of our thinking, and install a reliable speedometer in our mind. Then, whenever the speed of thinking goes over, say, fifty-five, one of those recorded voices will automatically whisper, "Be careful. You may not be able to keep your car on the road."

Positive thoughts travel slowly, leisurely. The slow mind is clear, kind, and efficient; in the beautiful phrase of the Bible, it is "slow to wrath." Patience means thoughts puttering along like Sunday drivers, taking the trouble to notice the needs of people around.

 RELATED PAGES *February 16, September 25*

September 20

What does God ask of thee, except thyself? Since in the whole earthly creation He made nothing better than thee.

SAINT AUGUSTINE

THE SCRIPTURES of all religions have a great deal to say about renunciation. They are not asking us to renounce our stamp collection or our tickets to the World Series; they are asking us to sacrifice our self-will. This is a painful renunciation to make, because the ego will try every trick in the book to undermine our efforts.

Just as the mountain climber does not begin with Mount Everest, you cannot get rid of all your self-will immediately. Practically speaking, it is best to start on a very small scale. When you go out to dinner with a friend, instead of painstakingly choosing just what you like, have what the other person is having. More likely than not it will be something you would just as soon pass over. That is the time to smile and enjoy it. If two people who care deeply about one another can do this, can learn to like what the person they love likes, they cannot help moving closer to each other.

RELATED PAGES *July 28, July 31*

September 21

A tree is known by its fruit; we by our deeds. A good deed is never lost; one who sows courtesy reaps friendship, and one who plants kindness gathers love.

SAINT BASIL

I AM THE first to admit that it takes a lot of endurance to mend a relationship, especially when your efforts seem to be met with indifference. When you start giving another person your best, especially in an emotionally entangled relationship, he may not notice it for weeks. This kind of indifference can really sting. You want to go up to him, tap him on the shoulder, and say, "Hello, Thomas, I've just been kind to you." Thomas would say, "Oh, thank you, I didn't even know it" – not because he was trying to be rude, but because he was preoccupied with himself.

To be patient and go on giving your best, you can't have expectations about how other people are going to respond. You can't afford to ask, "Does he *like* me? Does he even care?" What does it matter? You're growing. You're learning how to rub off the edges and corners that make human relationships difficult. You are becoming the kind of person that everyone wants to be with, that everyone admires and feels comfortable with.

RELATED PAGES *January 10, April 10*

September 22

God has created the world in play.

SRI RAMAKRISHNA

A SIMPLE, CHILDLIKE story in India's ancient scriptures tells how multiplicity emerged from unity. The Lord, the One without a second, felt very lonesome one morning. After all, he was the only thing that existed in the entire universe, so when he looked around him, he could see no one but himself. This did not satisfy him at all. He wanted to play.

So he made playmates. Out of himself he created the myriads of creatures, the two-footed and the four-footed. He started playing with them, playing hide-and-seek, which is what life is all about. We are all playing this game with the Lord. We are all seeking him, and he is hiding playfully from us.

It is easy to talk about this, sing about this, paint this, but it is an entirely different matter to experience it. Yet in deepest meditation, the veil separating you and me can drop. Then, beneath the varied costumes, we will be able to perceive the same supreme Reality whom we call God, who is playing his game in the world.

RELATED PAGE *January 8*

September 23

To me every hour of the light and dark is a miracle,
Every cubic inch of space is a miracle.
Every square yard of the surface of the earth
Is spread with the same. . . .
What strange miracles are these!
Everywhere . . .

WALT WHITMAN

ONCE WHEN I was giving a talk I used the word "miracles," and someone in the audience asked skeptically, "Tell us about one."

Every moment you remain alive is a miracle. Talk to medical people; they will tell you there are a million and one things that can go wrong with this body of ours at any given instant. It is only because we haven't developed the capacity for appreciating miracles that we don't see them all around us. Life is a continuous miracle: not only joy but sorrow too; not only birth but death too.

But the most precious miracle of all is to see the divinity in every creature – when we see that the divinity in our hearts is our real Self, and that it is the same Self shining in all.

 RELATED PAGE *December 2*

September 24

We must not wish anything other than what happens from moment to moment, all the while, however, exercising ourselves in goodness.

SAINT CATHERINE OF GENOA

A TREMENDOUS AMOUNT of our vital energy is squandered in the vacillations of the mind. If things go our way, we get elated; if things do not go our way, we get depressed. Yet elation and depression are made from the same cloth.

It is when the mind is getting elated that we need to be very vigilant, because what goes up will inevitably come down. If, through the practice of meditation and repetition of the mantram, we can keep the mind calm when good things are coming our way, then when bad things come, we won't be dejected. Our mind will stay calm.

Only then will we be free to be truly spontaneous in our responses to life.

RELATED PAGES *April 18, July 3*

September 25

Know well what leads you forward and what holds you back, and choose the path that leads to wisdom.

THE BUDDHA

BLAMING OURSELVES when we get angry is not going to be of much help in the long run. What is helpful is to gain a clearer understanding of how anger comes about. Getting angry is like having a malfunctioning engine. The mind is like the engine of the body, which can be compared to the chassis of the car we drive. But the sad fact is that most of us know a lot more about our car engine than we do about our own minds.

We don't even have the slightest idea of where the ignition switch of the mind is located. As a result, the engine goes on cranking out thoughts of every description throughout the day and throughout the long night in dreams. Worry and resentment and anger use up enormous quantities of vitality. It's like leaving our car idling in the garage all night long; in the morning when we need to get to work, we have to push it down the road.

What we need to do is learn how to slow down the mind, and eventually to park it at the side of the road when travel isn't necessary. Then we will have all the vitality, all the fuel, we need when we want to reach a worthwhile destination.

 RELATED PAGE *September 19*

September 26

A human being fashions his consequences as surely as he fashions his goods or his dwelling. Nothing that he says, thinks, or does is without consequences.

NORMAN COUSINS

THE HINDU and Buddhist scriptures give us the same truth in what is called the law of karma, which is the psychological equivalent to the physical law that every action has a reaction equal and opposite to it. The Buddha says we can fly higher than the heavens or hide in the depths of the earth, but we will not be able to escape the consequences of our actions. Though we drive to another city or fly to another country, though we change our job or our name, our mistakes will pursue us wherever we go.

Paradoxically, the only way we can begin to escape from the consequences of our actions is to stop running from them and to face them with fortitude. In this sense, every difficult situation is a precious opportunity. When we find ourselves in some situation where we always make the same mistake, if we can manage *not* to make that mistake, the chain can be broken. Often, if we face it squarely, that situation will not come up again.

RELATED PAGES *June 17, August 28*

September 27

Know the Self within and go beyond all sorrow.

BRIHADARANYAKA UPANISHAD

WHEN ALL hostility, fear, and insecurity are erased from your mind, the state that remains is pure joy.

That state, hidden at the very center of consciousness, is the Eden to which the long journey of spiritual seeking leads. It is "the peace that passeth all understanding," that resolves all conflicts, fulfills all desires, and banishes all fear.

The purpose of all valid spiritual disciplines, whatever the religion from which they spring, is to enable us to return to this native state of being – not after death but here and now, in unbroken awareness of the divinity within us and throughout creation. Theologians may quarrel, but the mystics of the world speak the same language, and the practices they follow lead to the same goal.

 RELATED PAGES *January 23, December 31*

September 28

God is not external to anyone, but is present with all things, though they are ignorant that he is so.

PLOTINUS

I HAVE HEARD people claim that mysticism denies the physical world. A good mystic would answer, "We are not belittling Sir Isaac Newton. We don't deny the Pythagorean theorem. All we are saying is that we have discovered another dimension to life, another realm – changeless, eternal, beyond cause and effect – on which the entire physical universe rests."

Because our lives are oriented outward, we may doubt the existence of the Self within. I have been telling people about this Self almost daily for more than thirty years, but occasionally I still am asked, "Are you talking about something outside us?" Compared with this Self – whom we call Krishna or Christ, Allah or Adonai or the Divine Mother – my own body is "outside." Compared with the Self, my own life is not more dear.

RELATED PAGES *August 10, October 10*

September 29

By faithfulness we are collected and bound up into unity within ourselves, whereas we had been scattered abroad in multiplicity.

SAINT AUGUSTINE

SENSORY PLEASURES are only nickel-and-dime satisfactions. It is only when we don't have a wider frame of reference that we believe they hold out the promise of great pleasure. When we widen our horizons to encompass a greater breadth of life, we can evaluate these pleasures more shrewdly.

Some of the greatest saints and mystics experimented with their senses rather freely in their earlier days. Augustine himself admits to having painted ancient Carthage red. But when they reach a state of unlimited compassion and concern for others, they say, "Those were mere pennies. Now I am in possession of limitless wealth."

 RELATED PAGES *May 3, October 11*

September 30

Love makes everything that is heavy light.

THOMAS A KEMPIS

IT IS love that teaches us our real stature and reveals the heroism we never thought we possessed. The renunciation that might be well-nigh impossible in a vacuum can be blessedly simple when someone we love stands to gain. Turning down a second glass of wine might take some doing in ordinary circumstances, for example; but when you're in the company of an impressionable teenager, you'll gladly set it aside.

Suppose you're tempted to add to your collection of antique fire screens: hard to resist, maybe, if your aim is *solely* to reduce your own acquisitiveness. But if the money you save can be spent on a tent for family camping trips, it can be a breeze. You feel so good inside! A knack for quiet self-sacrifice is the very life and soul of friendship. Reducing self-will needn't be a joyless deprivation – it can be so many little acts of love, performed over and over throughout the day.

RELATED PAGES *August 21, September 20*

October

We all need tasks that draw out our deeper resources – the talents and capacities we did not know we had.

EKNATH EASWARAN

October 1

Adopt the pace of nature, her secret is patience.

RALPH WALDO EMERSON

POETS LIKE to write about love, popular singers like to glorify love, but nobody bothers to sing the praises of patience. I once heard of a man who prayed to God, "Give me patience, O Lord, and give it to me now!" That man was not born with a patient nature. Most of us aren't – but we can develop it through practice.

You will find opportunities every day if you look for them. In a situation where there is a lot of friction, where people differ from you and aren't shy about letting you know it, don't run away. Move closer to them. You may have to grit your teeth; you may have to bite your lip to keep from giving vent to a harsh retort. And then, of course, you need to smile too, which doesn't come easily with your lip between your teeth. It is a demanding art to do this gracefully. But it is an art that can be learned.

 RELATED PAGES *January 22, August 11*

October 2

The senses have been conditioned by attraction to the pleasant and aversion to the unpleasant: we should not be ruled by them; they are obstacles on our path.

BHAGAVAD GITA

WE ARE conditioned to like some things and to dislike others. There is not necessarily any logic to it – it is often just a matter of habit.

Take food, for example. We like what we learn to like. In Kerala we have a particular kind of mango that is eaten green, when it is acutely sour. There is nothing inherently pleasant about this sensation; in fact, a detached observer would call it painful. But everybody likes it; everybody eats it; so you learn to like it too. And in the end, you cannot do without it.

Beneath all likes and dislikes is a basic compulsion of the mind to pass judgment on everything: "I like this, I don't like that." When this compulsion is rigid, it is rigid everywhere – with food, with philosophies, and especially with other people.

So, when we free ourselves from a compulsive liking for sour green mangos – or chocolate cake or red chilis – the whole likes-and-dislikes compulsion is weakened. As a result, all our other likes and dislikes will have a looser hold on us, giving us greater freedom, which will affect even our personal relationships for the better.

RELATED PAGES *January 18, March 20*

October 3

Lord, how can I ever find rest anywhere else when I am made to find rest in thee?

SAINT AUGUSTINE

THE VAST majority of human beings spend their lives in the pursuit of cherished goals which, when they are achieved, often leave them even more restless and unfulfilled. There is nothing wrong with desire. Like electricity, which can light a home or electrocute the tenant, desire is neither good nor bad. It is the most powerful force we have to drive us to action. Tragedy comes when desire is not subject either to the intellect or to the conscious will. Then we have a powerful vehicle speeding without anybody in the driver's seat.

Imagine all the cars in your hometown coming out of their garages and going about anywhere they like without drivers. How many accidents there would be, how much damage to life and property! When I go after what I desire, and you do the same, sometimes we collide.

We need to learn to distinguish between purely personal goals and those that include the happiness of other people. These latter desires provide a more lasting fuel for our actions, and lead to the kind of fulfillment that doesn't fade.

 RELATED PAGES *January 14, May 2*

October 4

Love does not insist on its own way; it is not irritable or resentful; it does not rejoice at wrong, but rejoices in the right.

I CORINTHIANS

IN *MY FAIR LADY*, Rex Harrison sings in exasperation: "Why can't a woman be more like a man? . . . Why can't a woman be like *me*?"

It did not surprise me to learn that this was a very popular song. In every emotional relationship, even if we don't put it into words, each of us has a rigid set of expectations which requires the other person to act and think in a particular way. Interestingly enough, it is not *that* person's way; it is our own.

When he or she acts differently, we get surprised and feel irritated or disappointed. If we could see behind the scenes, in the mind, this sort of encounter would make a good comedy. Here I am, relating not to you but to my idea of you, and I get irritated because you insist on acting your own way instead!

It is really no more than stimulus and response. If you behave the way I expect, I'll be kind. If you behave otherwise, I'll act otherwise too: rude, or irritated, or disappointed, or depressed, depending on my personality, but always something in reaction to you. It means, simply, that none of us has much freedom; our behavior is dependent on what other people say and do. To live without self-centered expectations is the secret of freedom in personal relationships.

RELATED PAGE *April 4*

October 5

Trifles make perfection, and perfection is no trifle.

MICHELANGELO

MOGUL ART, one of the great periods of artistic achievement in India, often is in miniature. The artist concentrated on very small areas, on little things, and worked with tenderness and precision. Only somebody who understands art will be able to see all the love and labor that has gone into it. Family living is like Mogul art, worked in miniature. The canvas is so small, and the skill required is so great, that most of us really do not appreciate the vast potentialities of family life.

Today we hear a great deal about the family becoming obsolete. Let us hope this is just the fantasy of those who do not understand the value of the family. To me, the family is like a free university, where we can get our finest education in living for others. Family does not just mean Papa, Mama, Junior, and Janie, but all the members, including grandparents, uncles and aunts and country cousins. The family can include dear friends and those who participate closely in all our endeavors.

We begin by being tender and unselfish and putting up with innumerable discomforts for the sake of adding to the joy of our family. Then, gradually, we extend our love to include our friends, our community, our country, and our world.

 RELATED PAGES *January 10, September 6*

October 6

As an archer aims the arrow, the wise aim their restless thoughts, hard to aim, hard to restrain.

THE BUDDHA

THOUGHTS ARE things, even though we cannot hold them in our hands or see them with our eyes. This is very different from our usual view. Usually we consider thoughts as immaterial, so we are not aware of how a fleeting thought can affect us. If I throw a beach ball at you, it won't hurt much; in five minutes you will have forgotten about it. But if I say something harsh to you, you will not be able to forget that thought; you will take it home in your mind, have nightmares about it, and wake up oppressed the next morning. We all know from personal experience how a harsh comment from a parent or a friend can rankle in our consciousness for years. This is the immense power of thoughts.

October 7

No one hath so cordial a feeling of the Passion of Christ, as one who hath suffered the like himself.

THOMAS A KEMPIS

THE PRINCIPLE underlying the Passion of Christ is that out of his infinite mercy, the Lord has taken our suffering upon himself. As long as any living creature is in pain, so is Jesus, for he lives at the heart of all. Wherever violence breaks out, no matter how cleverly we try to justify it, we are crucifying the spirit of Christ.

Patience and *passion* both come from a Latin word meaning to suffer or endure. When we speak of the Passion of Christ, we are recalling the suffering he endured on the cross. Whenever we practice patience – cheerfully bearing with somebody who is irascible, or enduring discomfort rather than imposing it on others – in a small way we are embracing the principle of the Passion.

This does not mean becoming blind to what others are doing. I know when somebody is being rude or unkind, but it does not impair my faith in that person. I keep my eyes on the core of goodness in him; and I act towards her as I would have her act towards me. There is only one way to make others more loving, and that is by loving more ourselves.

RELATED PAGES *March 30, May 4*

October 8

Just as a flower gives out its fragrance to whomsoever approaches or uses it, so love from within us radiates towards everybody and manifests as spontaneous service.

SWAMI RAMDAS

MANY OF us find it difficult to be compassionate towards other people for the simple reason that most of our sensitivity is directed towards ourselves. The less we dwell on ourselves, the more our sensitivity will open out to the needs and feelings of others.

Every time you hurt someone and then grieve inside because of it, you are attending a valuable seminar on sensitivity. It is a seminar at the deepest and most personal level, the experiential, and it is infinitely more effective than anything we can attend for college credit. The credit comes to us directly, when we change our behavior and don't hurt people again. "Everybody's feelings can be hurt," we realize, "just like my own. I have to take others' feelings into consideration in what I do."

RELATED PAGES *January 26, August 28*

October 9

The spirit of man is the candle of the Lord.

PROVERBS

CLAY LAMPS are still used today in India, where they are lit and placed in an alcove of the shrine. Since there is no wind in the protected niche, the tongue of the flame burns without a flicker.

In the depths of your meditation, when you are concentrating on an inspirational passage such as the Prayer of Saint Francis, your mind will be like the tongue of flame in a windless place – motionless and steady. At that time you will be concentrating completely on the words of the prayer, which means that you are slowly becoming like Saint Francis in your daily conduct and consciousness. It requires enormous endeavor to do this, but through ceaseless effort every one of us can reach the state in which the mind, like the flame of the clay lamp, does not flicker or waver at all.

 RELATED PAGES *January 30, August 26*

October 10

The knower and the known are one. Simple people imagine that they should see God, as if he stood there and they here. This is not so. God and I, we are one in knowledge.

MEISTER ECKHART

IN ORDER to say that there is no one in our deeper consciousness, we have to go there, knock on the door, and find that no one is at home. Until he has made that journey, knocked on the door, and heard a voice saying "There is no one here," no one should call himself an atheist. "Agnostic" is more correct.

Of those who tell me they are atheists, I ask, "Don't you believe in yourself?"

Their answer is, "Of course."

"Then," I say, "you believe in God."

When we use terms like "God" or "Lord" it is not referring to someone "out there." We are invoking someone who is inside us all the time, who is nearer to us than our body, dearer to us than our life.

RELATED PAGES *June 11, September 28*

October 11

When I was a child, I spake as a child, I understood as a child, I thought as a child: but when I became an adult I put away childish things.

I CORINTHIANS

I HAVE SOMETIMES heard adults, who should show more wisdom, complaining, "I want all the pleasures of the senses I enjoyed in my teens." I would like to put before them the example of my young friend Jessica. It wasn't very long ago that I saw her playing with dolls. I understand there are dolls now which, if you press a button, actually get a fever. Perfect for playing hospital! But Jess has graduated from dolls to people. She has worked hard to become an accomplished nurse, and now she is helping and comforting real patients. She also has two beautiful children of her own. Of course, she no longer has any need for dolls.

In the same way, now that we are grown up, our joy should consist in helping others. Once we so much as taste this joy, we will feel no need to play at being children again.

RELATED PAGES *June 30, September 29*

October 12

You are not the same, nor are you another.

THE BUDDHA

THE BUDDHA is saying that we change from moment to moment. Personality is not cast in a rigid mold; the whole secret of personality is that it is a process. The nature of a process is that it can be changed. For a time, it is true, the changes you are trying to make will not seem natural. When someone is rude to you, you will still feel a wave of resentment inside. It does not matter; at the outset, it is enough to *act* kind, to pretend to be kind, to stage a sort of kindness performance.

Gradually, if you put your whole effort behind this transformation, using the tool of meditation, the seething will subside. Then it will not just be a flawless performance, you will actually transform anger into compassion. You will feel sorry for the person who has offended you. You will not be the same angry person you used to be; and yet you will not be someone else, either. To be patient, kind, and secure is our real nature; anything else is being false to ourselves.

RELATED PAGE *January 1*

October 13

Be ye kind one to another, tenderhearted, forgiving one another, even as God for Christ's sake hath forgiven you.

EPHESIANS

OFTEN IT is nothing more than our likes and dislikes that keep us from seeing the core of purity and selflessness that is in everyone. We don't like the way he cuts his hair, we don't like the way she drops her *r*'s, and we can't get beyond these surface obstacles. Yet if we free ourselves from the rigid dictates of our own likes and dislikes, we will see people more clearly – even those whom we find difficult to love.

Some people *are* a little more irritating and self-willed than others. But instead of criticizing such people, which only makes their alienation worse, we can focus all our attention on what is best in them. This most practical skill can help those around us tremendously – while it helps us get over our likes and dislikes as well. It is like turning a flashlight onto one particular spot, concentrating on what is kind, generous, and selfless in the other person. We'll find that this kind of support draws out and strengthens these very qualities in him or her.

 RELATED PAGES *February 20, August 13*

October 14

All, everything that I understand, I understand only because I love.

LEO TOLSTOY

THERE IS nothing easy about learning to love. The real romantic must be very practical: it takes a lot of hard, unromantic work to sustain any human relationship. Naturally there are going to be differences between you and your partner. Identical twins have differences of opinion, so why should two people from, say, New York City and Paris, Texas, expect life together to be smooth sailing?

Even on the honeymoon there may be difficulties. You open Pandora's box expecting a lot of doves and out come a couple of bats instead. You have to be ready to say, "The doves are there; they're simply lying low. Why don't we get to work and shoo away these bats?" Rather than dwelling on the negative, try to respect the potential in the other person and help him or her to realize that potential through your support. If you want a relationship to get deeper and deeper with the passage of time, you will go on strengthening it all your life.

RELATED PAGES *January 20, March 7*

October 15

In order to overcome our desires and to renounce all those things, our love and inclination for which are wont so to inflame the will that it delights therein, we require a more ardent fire and a nobler love.

SAINT JOHN OF THE CROSS

MOST OF us are not aware to what extent our desires are compulsive. We do not realize how often they push and shove us about without any say on our part. But when we think "*I* would like a hot fudge sundae," it would be more accurate to say that the desire is thinking *us*. Intellectually we may know that a hot fudge sundae means more calories than we need; but the desire has a hold on us, and we believe, temporarily, this is what will satisfy us. Not until we have eaten the sundae do we reflect, "That's not what I *really* wanted. Why did I go and eat it?"

Not that there is anything wrong in eating sundaes. The important point is that we do not have the capacity to *choose*. For "hot fudge sundae" we can substitute our own favorite pleasures. Some may not be harmful in themselves, but when the inability to choose extends to destructive habits such as smoking, drinking, or taking drugs, we begin to cause suffering to ourselves and to those around us.

 RELATED PAGES *January 24, March 20*

October 16

Manifest plainness,
Embrace simplicity,
Reduce selfishness,
Have few desires.

LAO TZU

DETACHMENT FROM likes and dislikes, habits and opinions, is not a sign of weakness. It is an enormously strong and positive quality. Nor does freedom from likes and dislikes mean that life is insipid for us, but rather that we are not driven compulsively by rigid ways of thinking. Even if we don't get what we want – or if we do get what we don't want – we can still function cheerfully and efficiently.

Detachment from habits does not mean that we have no habits. Good habits can be very useful to cultivate in life. But we should be able to change our habits gracefully, or drop them altogether when necessary, especially if we learn that they are harmful to us or are not exactly endearing us to those around us. If we are used to a cup of coffee every morning with our breakfast and one morning we discover that we are out of coffee, we don't say, "I can't function without my coffee," and go back to bed. We should be able to say cheerfully, "I'll have tea instead – or soy milk."

RELATED PAGES *January 18, March 18*

October 17

We should take care not to make the intellect our god; it has, of course, powerful muscles, but no personality.

ALBERT EINSTEIN

THE TEACHINGS of great spiritual figures such as the Buddha are practical, not theoretical. The Buddha will say beautifully, "I have no theories." It's one of his most disarming statements. He did not engage in intellectual discussion, and often he would meet questions with a noble silence.

The scriptures are meant for translation into our daily lives over a long period of years. And in order to practice the teachings of the Compassionate Buddha, or any other teacher, we need an immense tool like meditation by which we can work on our consciousness. In this, it is not of much help to have only an intellectual understanding.

The Buddha doesn't talk about theory. Like all great teachers, he says, "These are things that you can verify for yourself." He is a supreme scientist who will say, "Undertake this experiment and discover the results for yourself."

 RELATED PAGES *April 9, December 28*

October 18

He that loveth, flieth, runneth, and rejoiceth. He is free, and cannot be held in. He giveth all for all, and hath all in all, because he resteth in one highest above all things, from whom all that is good flows and proceeds.

THOMAS A KEMPIS

THIS SPRING I watched six baby swallows learn how to fly. They were huddled on the telephone wires observing their mother, who came flying slowly by in front of them, doing the easier turns and showing them the basics of flying. There was no need for these baby swallows to read books or attend lectures on how to fly. They have an inborn instinct for it. Learning to fly may not be easy, but this is what birds are born to do.

The Lord sees us sitting on a perch made of pleasure, profit, power, or prestige, quaking with every variation in our bank account and every critical comment that comes our way; and he asks us if we would not rather forget our failings and learn to fly.

This is what we are born to do: to leave our perch of selfish interests and soar aloft. To soar to union with God means that all the faculties and resources which have been hidden in us can come into our lives, to the great benefit of those around us.

RELATED PAGE *August 12*

October 19

One cannot collect all the beautiful shells on the beach. One can collect only a few, and they are more beautiful if they are few.

ANNE MORROW LINDBERGH

IF YOU are determined to stick to what is really important in life, then from day to day you will see that the unimportant pastimes, the distractions that lead you away from your purpose, will gradually weaken their hold.

On the list of priorities, first and foremost is meditation. It will clear your eyes and bring the detachment and discrimination we all need to make wise choices. So right at the top of your list should be the resolution to practice meditation, and not to let anything come in the way.

Not even the greatest of worldly achievements will satisfy us completely. Nothing finite can ever satisfy us. Sooner or later, all the vitality that has gone into pursuing countless goals in the outer world must flow into one huge desire to discover the divine presence within. This supreme discovery is what matters most in life. We are all born to seek the supreme truth.

 RELATED PAGES *January 14, May 13*

October 20

"This is myself and this is another." Be free of this bond which encompasses you about, and your own self is thereby released.

SARAHA

TO LOVE completely, it is not enough if I care deeply; I must also be detached from myself. To know what is best for someone, I have to be able to step aside from my own prejudices and preconceptions, slip into that person's shoes and become one with him temporarily, looking at life through his eyes rather than my own. When I step back again, I will have seen his needs from the inside; only then can I see clearly how to serve those needs with detachment and compassion.

Why, then, do we find it so difficult to get ourselves out of the way? The reason, quite simply, is that we live rather superficially, on the surface of life. On the surface, we feel that it is natural for people to quarrel, for nations to go to war. "It's only human," we say. Only in the depths of the soul can we realize that quarreling and fighting are not natural at all. What is natural is loving everybody, seeing everybody as one.

RELATED PAGES *January 17, February 4*

October 21

Why are we not happy? Because we are much more concerned over things which are more powerful to make us unhappy than truth is to make us happy, in that we remember truth so slightly.

SAINT AUGUSTINE

IF SOMEONE were to pull over to the side of the road in San Francisco and ask me how to get to Los Angeles, I wouldn't say, "Go north." Everyone knows you have to go in the other direction. Similarly, spiritual figures like Saint Augustine tell us, "Don't follow your selfish desires and angry impulses; that is the way to emotional bankruptcy." But we reply, "Oh, no! I know what I'm doing."

Saint Augustine would insist, "Please believe me. If you go that way, you will become more insecure. Instead, let me show you a secret trail that will take you slowly round to security."

The route is always there and it is always open. We must be prepared for arduous hiking over rough terrain. Very likely we are going to have lapses; some attractive detours may distract us temporarily. All that we should ask for is the determination to do our best to stay on the right trail and go forward.

 RELATED PAGES *January 26, September 4*

October 22

Mind is consciousness which has put on limitations. You are originally unlimited and perfect. Later you take on limitations and become the mind.

RAMANA MAHARSHI

MUCH OF our daily behavior is conditioned by forces deep below the conscious level of our minds. This means we are limited to a conditioned, automatic way of thinking and responding to the events of life around us. When such a conditioned behavior is strong, we think of it as a fixed part of the personality. Othello *is* jealous, Hamlet indecisive, Macbeth ambitious; that, we say, is their nature. To many biologists, this is something that is built into our very genes.

I do not agree. Jealousy, vacillation, competition, and the rest are not permanent mental furniture; they are a process. A mental trait is a thought repeated over and over a thousand times, leading to words repeated a thousand times, resulting in action repeated a thousand times. At the beginning it is only a burgeoning habit of thought; you do not necessarily act on it. But once it becomes rigid, it dictates behavior. It is possible, through the practice of meditation and the other disciplines, to go against these conditioned ways of thinking and actually change ourselves from the inside out.

RELATED PAGES *January 2, December 20*

October 23

It is the mind that makes one wise or ignorant, bound or emancipated.

SRI RAMAKRISHNA

MENTAL HABITS are like ditches in the mind. They have to be dug laboriously. But they can also be filled in and new channels can be dug. Take resentment for example. It does not burst full-blown into the mind; it grows. At first you simply expect people to behave towards you in a particular way. If they behave in their own way instead, you get surprised, then irritated. You are digging a little channel in consciousness.

In the early stages, this channel may be only an inch or so deep. Thought may flow down it, but it may also flow somewhere else. Also, the walls are still soft and crumbly; they may cave in and fill the channel a little – for example, when someone you dislike says something kind. There is an element of choice. But every time we respond to a situation with resentment, the channel gets a little deeper. Finally there is a huge Grand Canal in the mind. Then anything at all is enough to provoke a conditioned resentful response. Consciousness pours down the sluice of least resistance. We can dig new mental channels – kind ways of thinking instead of resentful ones, patience instead of anger. Every time you try to return good will for ill will, love for hatred, you have dug your new, beneficial channel a little deeper. Transforming character, conduct, and consciousness is not a moral problem. It's an engineering problem.

 RELATED PAGES *July 14, August 16*

October 24

In every veil you see, the Divine Beauty is concealed, making every heart a slave to him. In love to him the heart finds its life; in desire for him, the soul finds its happiness. The heart which loves a fair one here, though it knows it not, is really his lover.

JAMI

IT IS very difficult for most of us to understand to what extent our love can be expanded. Everybody has a few people with whom he can be friendly, with whom she can be tender, but the Lord tells us, "That's not enough. If you want to become whole and never be separate again, you should have love and respect for everyone."

Jesus said, "What is the special achievement in loving those who love you? Even selfish people are prepared to do that. Bless those that curse you." I can see the twinkle in his eye as the gathering gasps. This is the daring of Jesus. Today we talk about revolution, but I think there has never been a greater revolutionary than Jesus the Christ. He tells us that by loving those who hate us, we can win our freedom, because we will no longer be dependent on how others act towards us. The person who practices this can reach the summit of human consciousness, for it is only by loving people who oppose us and learning to bear with them that we can heal ourselves and heal them too.

RELATED PAGE *January 4*

October 25

There is no greater glory than love, nor any greater punishment than jealousy.

LOPE DE VEGA

IT IS good to admire beauty, but it is neither good nor practical to want to take beauty home, put it on a shelf, and say, "You stay right there." When we see something beautiful, we may begin to want it for ourselves. It may be a dramatic house, it may be a lovely flower, it may be a graceful dancer – we just want it. If this wanting becomes a compulsion, it is likely we will lose what we want so much.

Jealousy comes into a relationship when we try to possess someone for ourselves. It is a very difficult secret to discover: that when we do not want to possess another person selfishly, when we do not make demand after demand, the relationship will grow and last. And it is something we have to learn the hard, hard way. This is the secret of all relationships, not only between husband and wife, boyfriend and girlfriend, but between friend and friend, parents and children. Instead of trying to exact and demand, just give, and give more, and give still more. This is the way to earn love and respect.

 RELATED PAGES *August 18, December 19*

October 26

Love feels no burden, thinks nothing of trouble, attempts what is above its strength. . . . It is therefore able to undertake all things, and it completes many things, and warrants them to take effect, where one who does not love would faint and lie down.

THOMAS A KEMPIS

WITHOUT A tank full of gas, no car can drive very far. The mind, too, needs a full tank of vitality to draw on for patience, resilience, and creativity. Filling that tank every morning is one of the most practical purposes of meditation. The test of your meditation is: How long can you be patient with those around you? In the beginning, you should aim to make it at least to noon acting like the proverbial angel.

Most of us, however, even if we start with a full tank, have little control over the thousand and one little pinpricks that drain vitality as we go along: worry, vacillation, irritation, daydreaming. By lunchtime the indicator may be hovering around empty.

Then it is that you have to be acutely vigilant. The tank is nearly empty, but by sheer effort and deft defensive driving, and using the mantram, you manage to coast through to the end of the day without any serious accidents.

The more effort you make, the more endurance you gain. The next day you may find the tank itself a little larger; you start the next day with a greater capacity for love and patience than before.

RELATED PAGES *February 13, April 1*

October 27

We must do our business faithfully, without trouble or disquiet, recalling our mind to God mildly, and with tranquility, as often as we find it wandering from him.

BROTHER LAWRENCE

A FAST MIND is like a race car in the hands of a dubious driver. Fear, resentment, greed, anger, self-will, and jealousy rush through the mind at a hundred miles an hour. At such speeds we cannot turn, stop, or keep from crashing into people. At speeds like this we are not really driving at all. We are hostages, trussed up in the trunk. And who knows who is at the wheel?

The function of passage meditation is twofold: it slows the mind, and by absorbing the words of an inspirational passage deep into consciousness, it gradually transforms negative emotions into positive states of mind. The slower the thoughts go, the greater the control you have over them, and the more positive they become.

 RELATED PAGES *February 1, August 26*

October 28

As pure water poured into pure water becomes the very same, so does the Self of the illumined man or woman verily become one with the Godhead.

KATHA UPANISHAD

FOR SOME reason, it is very difficult for us to accept our divine nature. This has always puzzled me. We pay money for books about how destructive we are. We stand in line to see movies that emphasize our capacity for making trouble. Then, when Jesus comes to tell us that the kingdom of heaven is within us, we say, "There must be some mistake."

It is to convince us that our real Self is always pure and eternal that men and women of God keep arising among us. More than anything, we need to hear their good news that the source of all joy and security is right within. In the Hindu scriptures there is a precise term for our real nature: the Atman. All it means is "the Self" – not the little self, the changing personality with which most of us identify, but the higher Self, our real, changeless personality.

RELATED PAGES *January 21, August 22*

October 29

Nothing is more beautiful than the love that has weathered the storms of life. . . . The love of the young for the young, that is the beginning of life. But the love of the old for the old, that is the beginning of – of things longer.

JEROME K. JEROME

EVERY MORNING, just after you step on the bathroom scale to make sure you haven't put on an extra ounce when you weren't looking, you can step on the scale of love and make sure your ego hasn't put on any weight. The critical measure is your capacity to be equable and kind in everyday relationships.

We all tend to feel impatient when something we want is waiting round the corner; and we all occasionally get angry when that something slips away. The positive approach is to be aware enough of this cycle to say sincerely, "Tomorrow I am going to be a little more patient than I was today. The day after, I am going to be a little more self-controlled." Working on equability every day yields results.

Where intimate relationships are concerned, your love should grow. Don't ever be satisfied with telling your partner, "I love you every bit as much as that first time I saw you at the supermarket!" Love should never be static; it must never become stagnant. Fifty years later you should be able to say, "I love you fifty times more than I did that first day." That is true love speaking.

 RELATED PAGES *July 6, July 29*

October 30

Thoughts of themselves have no substance; let them arise and pass away unheeded. Thoughts will not take form of themselves, unless they are grasped by the attention; if they are ignored, there will be no appearing and no disappearing.

ASHVAGHOSHA

LIFE IS a kind of play in which we are called upon to play our part with skill. But in meditation we are sometimes more like the audience, while our thoughts are the actors. If we could go backstage, we could see all the actor-thoughts getting made up. Anger is there putting on his long fangs. Fear is rattling his chains. Jealousy is admiring herself in the mirror and smearing on green mascara.

Now, these thought-actors are like actors and actresses everywhere: they thrive on a responsive audience. When Jealousy comes out on stage and we sit forward on our seats, she really puts on a show. But on the other hand, what happens if nobody comes to see the performance?

No actor likes to play to an empty house. If they're real professionals, they might give their best for a couple of nights, but after that they're bound to get a little slack. Jealousy doesn't bother with her makeup any more; who's going to admire it? Anger throws away his fangs. Fear puts away his chains. Whom can they impress? Finally, the whole cast gives it up as a bad job and goes home.

In other words, when you can direct attention, your thinking will never be compulsive again.

RELATED PAGES *May 23, December 11*

October 31

Existence is a strange bargain. Life owes us little; we owe it everything. The only true happiness comes from squandering ourselves for a purpose.

WILLIAM COWPER

WE OFTEN think that if we go after what we want, we will probably get it; then we will be happy and secure. The mass media have latched onto this line of thinking and intone it like a litany: grab, grab, grab! Yet sooner or later the whole smorgasbord of things begins to lose its luster. Then the sensitive person asks, "If I go on grabbing and grabbing, at what point do I become secure and feel no more need to grab?" This question can lead to some far-reaching changes in our lives.

Our needs are much too big to be satisfied with things, no matter how many we can manage to acquire. The more we try to get, the more acutely we feel those bigger, undeniable needs. Our deepest need is for the joy that comes with loving and being loved, with knowing we are of genuine use to others. The more we give of ourselves to others, the more the Lord within wants to give us. Every day we empty ourselves by giving all we can in the way of kindness and loving help. Then every morning we will find ourselves full again – of love, of understanding, of forgiveness, of energy.

 RELATED PAGES *March 29, September 4*

November

When we simplify our lives, we can give our time and attention to what matters most.

EKNATH EASWARAN

November 1

The loathsome mask has fallen, the man remains
Sceptreless, free, uncircumscribed, but man
Equal, unclassed, tribeless, and nationless,
Exempt from awe, worship, degree, the king
Over himself.

PERCY BYSSHE SHELLEY

NONE OF us wants to be artificial. We all want to be natural and spontaneous. But true spontaneity is not simply doing what we feel like doing and not doing what we don't feel like doing. That is simply reacting as we have been conditioned to react. It is really no more spontaneous than a rubber ball which bounces when we drop it on the sidewalk.

We are being truly spontaneous when we can change the habits of a lifetime. We are being truly spontaneous when we are able to drop our pet project and work for the welfare of those around us without a ripple of protest in the mind. We are being truly spontaneous when we can respond calmly, constructively, and compassionately to a difficult situation. The secret of spontaneity is training. We cannot just decide to be spontaneous overnight; but we can all make these marvelous transformations in our lives if we are prepared to put in the sustained effort they require.

RELATED PAGE *October 4*

November 2

Love and pity and wish well to every soul in the world; dwell in love, and then you dwell in God.

WILLIAM LAW

LOYALTY IS the quintessence of love. When two people tell each other, "As long as you do what I like, I'll stay with you, but as soon as you start doing things I don't like, I'm packing my bags" – that is not love; that's convenience. Loving somebody means that even when they trouble you, you don't let yourself be shaken. Even when they are harsh to you, you don't move away. Even when they make a mistake that hurts you, you don't go off and make the same kind of mistake to hurt them.

All of us are so liable to human error that unless we have some capacity to bear with the errors of others, we will not be able to maintain a lasting relationship, which is the tragic situation that many people find themselves in today. We should never settle for this unhappy state of affairs.

RELATED PAGES *February 14, June 28*

November 3

The earth which sustains humanity must not be injured; it must not be destroyed.

HILDEGARD OF BINGEN

IN THE ancient Indian tradition, many timeless truths underlying life – on which the health of the world depends, and our life too – are conveyed in simple, beautiful allegories. The earth is Goddess Earth. She is a person. She is a living personality. Today we have forgotten that the earth is our mother, and that unless she is healthy, that with which she nourishes us will not make us healthy.

Air is also considered to be a great god, whom we are expected to worship by keeping it pure, because our very life depends upon it. It is incomprehensible to me how this vital necessity of ours has been ignored in our modern civilization in the frantic pursuit for material possessions, many of which are not necessary. We needn't embrace poverty, but a beautiful life can be a simple life. Isn't pure air more precious than anything else?

This is not a pessimistic outlook; it is a very optimistic one, because environmental problems can be solved by little people like us, working together.

 RELATED PAGES *July 8, November 12*

November 4

God doth not need
Either man's work or his own gifts. Who best
Bear his mild yoke, they serve him best. His state
Is kingly: thousands at his bidding speed
And post o'er land and ocean without rest.
They also serve who only stand and wait.

JOHN MILTON

I INTERPRET THIS "standing and waiting" as inexhaustible patience, as bearing with people, particularly in close personal relationships. When everything around us is swirling, when we feel our feet are slipping, we get terrified. We fear that we are going to be swept away, and even with our very good intentions, we are not sure whether unkind words may not come out of our mouth, whether unkind actions may not come from our body.

It is when everything is uncertain like this, when the whirlpool is going round and round, that we must be able to draw upon enormous patience to stay firm and steadfast. Calling on the Self, the Lord in our heart, by repeating the mantram, we find access to our deeper reserves of devotion, firmness, and love.

RELATED PAGES *January 22, September 19*

November 5

One that is not prepared to suffer all things, and to stand to the will of the Beloved, is not worthy to be called a lover of God. A lover ought to embrace willingly all that is hard and distasteful, for the sake of the Beloved; and not to turn away for any contrary accidents.

THOMAS A KEMPIS

LOVE IS a sacred skill that we must work to maintain. And learning to bear up under changes in attitude and circumstance with an inner toughness is the best practice for loving. If we do not develop this kind of toughness, our love will not be strong enough to support the weight of close relationships.

One of my quarrels with contemporary civilization is the way it trivializes life. We have very little left that is sacred. In a scientifically advanced era, with the benefit of culture and education, we should grieve to discover that our love barely scratches the surface of life – no wonder, then, that it fails to nourish us. Loving is already something of a lost art.

When we finally realize we are missing out on something sacred, we may no longer know where to turn. Love is so exquisitely elusive. It cannot be bought, cannot be badgered, cannot be hijacked. It is available only in one rare form: as the natural response of a healthy mind and healthy heart.

 RELATED PAGES *January 4, March 9*

November 6

Be patient. The path of self-discipline that leads to God-realization is not an easy path: obstacles and sufferings are on the path; the latter you must bear, and the former overcome – all by His help. His help comes only through concentration. Repetition of God's name helps concentration.

SWAMI RAMDAS

IN DIFFICULT situations the mantram offers immediate, effective first aid. When you are getting angry or afraid, or when you feel you have to get your way or you will explode, start repeating the mantram and head for the door. Go for a good, fast walk around the block. Repeat your mantram as if your life depended on it – in some respects it really might.

Walk briskly. There is a close connection between the rhythm of the mantram, the rhythm of your footsteps, the rhythm of your breathing, and the rhythm of your mind. You will find that the furious pace of your thoughts begins to slow down, that your breathing becomes deeper and steadier. By the time you get back, your mind will be clearer. A good deal of your agitation will be gone. That is the power of the mantram. The effect on yourself and on other people has to be seen to be believed.

RELATED PAGES *March 2, June 16*

November 7

Wandering with thee, even hell itself would be to me a heaven of bliss.

RAMAYANA

FOR THE long spiritual journey, ongoing support, guidance, and inspiration are necessary for everyone. We all need the support of people who share our aspirations, and to whom we can turn in difficult times. So we should not overlook the importance of spiritual companionship.

Meditating with two or three friends gives tremendous support. When husband and wife practice meditation together, they strengthen one another immeasurably. The challenges of self-transformation become so much easier to bear when we can face them with the support of those we love.

But if we find that there seems to be no one to share our interest in meditation, the important thing is to be patient – to have faith that we will eventually find the spiritual companions that we need. Until then, we can turn to a few invaluable books in which spiritual aspirants share their experiences. These books can become old friends: the writings of Swami Ramdas, the *Gospel of Sri Ramakrishna*, the works of Saint Teresa of Avila, *Of the Imitation of Christ*, the teachings of the Buddha, to give a few examples out of a vast storehouse of spiritual wisdom.

 RELATED PAGE *February 11*

November 8

When you move amidst the world of sense, free from attachment and aversion alike, there comes the peace in which all sorrows end, and you live in the wisdom of the Self.

BHAGAVAD GITA

THE GRACE of God sometimes comes in the form of sorrow. If we are not prepared to realize the unity of life, the Lord in his infinite love will let us suffer until we are forced to change our ways.

Of course, it isn't at all easy to change: often it is quite painful. It's very much like learning to use a stiff arm again. If your arm has been injured, and twisted into a rigid position, even the slightest movement becomes painful. Yet you have to learn to move it in order to regain the use of your arm. There is suffering in this, as there often is in any kind of growth.

We should never conclude that our lives are hopeless, that we can never improve, that we are condemned by God or fate or chemistry or conditioning to repeat the same mistakes. We always have a choice. That is the glory of our human nature: not only that we can always choose a better path, but that someday we will. We can never alienate ourselves from our divine Self, and the whole force of evolution is pushing us towards the divine vision, in which we see ourselves as we really are.

RELATED PAGES *January 2, February 7*

November 9

A human being is part of the whole, called by us "universe," a part limited in time and space. He experiences himself, his thoughts and feelings, as something separate from the rest – a kind of optical delusion of consciousness. This delusion is a kind of prison for us, restricting us to our personal desires and to affection for a few persons nearest to us. Our task must be to free ourselves from this prison by widening our circle of compassion to embrace all living creatures and the whole of nature in its beauty.

ALBERT EINSTEIN

NONE OF us see life as it is, the world as it is. We all see life as *we* are. We look at others through our own likes and dislikes, desires and interests. It is this separatist outlook that fragments life for us – man against woman, community against community, country against country. Yet the mystics of all religions assure us on the strength of their own experience, if only we throw away this fragmenting instrument of observation, we shall see all life as an indivisible whole.

 RELATED PAGES *January 28, March 8*

November 10

Before us are life and death, good and evil. That which we shall choose shall be given us.

ECCLESIASTICUS

THE CAPACITY to discriminate between right desires and wrong desires is very precious. Right desires benefit everyone – including ourselves. Wrong desires may be pleasing, but they benefit no one – again, not even ourselves. The criteria are simple to state, but not so simple to apply in everyday life.

The problem that arises is that wrong desires can be very skillful impersonators. They put on a three-piece suit and a false mustache and present themselves suavely as Mr. Right, the benefactor of all; if they happen to be just what we like, that is only happy coincidence. To live wisely, we need to be able to recognize right desires and yield to them, which is a pleasant but rare state of affairs. But much more important, we need to be able to recognize wrong desires and resist them.

This can be very difficult. There are times when we have to take on the desire face to face, like a boxer in the ring. The very attitude of resisting in the face of a wrong desire is the beginning of good health, vitality, and love.

RELATED PAGES *January 14, November 24*

November 11

We can only learn to know ourselves and do what we can – namely, surrender our will and fulfill God's will in us.

SAINT TERESA OF AVILA

FROM WHAT I have seen of life, problems are a repertory theater. We may see all sorts of characters, but only a very few problems are playing all the roles. Self-will, of course, is the most versatile of actors. In fact, in a sense, he is the *only* actor. He can play any part, anytime. He throws us off guard by continually changing his costume, so that we think we are dealing with a brand-new problem, instead of the famous ham, Mr. Ego. Today he may star as Alf, The Amazing Palate Craving, tomorrow as Why-don't-you-love-me Winifred.

Give us a problem that we recognize – dressed in a particular costume, cast in a particular role, appearing at a particular place and time – and we know how to deal with it. But the moment the same problem appears in a way we do not expect – say, wearing a false mustache and a fez – we go to pieces. The mind looks through its catalog and throws up its hands: "Boss, this isn't supposed to happen! I don't know what to do."

We can learn to see the underlying problem, self-will, and deal with it, instead of trying to deal with each individual disguise.

 RELATED PAGE *May 15*

November 12

You never enjoy the world aright, till the Sea itself floweth in your veins, till you are clothed with the heavens, and crowned with the stars; and perceive yourself to be the sole heir of the whole world, and more than so, because men are in it who are every one sole heirs as well as you.

THOMAS TRAHERNE

IN OUR relationship with the environment, the real power does not lie in the hands of technologists or politicians or directors of multinational corporations. It is individuals like you and me who make the final decisions about what is bought and sold in the stores, how much carbon dioxide is pumped into the atmosphere, and what is dumped into the sea. Each of us can begin to heal the environment right away by changing our daily habits.

And beyond that, there is another area which deserves our immediate attention: the world within. For each of us has an entire world within, an internal environment as real as the one we see around us. This internal environment has a powerful effect on the external environment: the way we think affects the way we treat the earth. When we purify this inner environment, we are not only making ourselves more secure and fulfilled, but we are also making an important contribution to the health of Mother Earth.

RELATED PAGES *July 8, September 5*

November 13

Love, all alike, no season knows, nor clime,
Nor hours, days, months, which are the rags of time.

JOHN DONNE

LOYALTY IS a precious quality that we have almost lost sight of today. Instead of loyalty, almost everyone talks about freedom, especially in relationships. The idea is that if two people come together in freedom, each can walk out of the arrangement. This is supposed to be a complete safeguard against unhappiness. But even where both are free to walk out – where there are no obligations, no bonds, not even any ties – they go on doing this over and over and do not acquire the capacity to love. Without loyalty, it simply is not possible to love deeply.

 RELATED PAGES *February 14, October 29*

November 14

I think the world today is upside-down and is suffering so much because there is so very little love in the homes and in family life. We have no time for our children, we have no time for each other; there is no time to enjoy each other.

MOTHER TERESA OF CALCUTTA

AN OBSESSION with hurry has been so worked into our social system that we scarcely notice we do not have time to love. Everywhere the slogan is "Hurry, hurry, hurry." Yet to be aware of the needs of others, to spend time with others, to speak and act with thoughtfulness, patience, and consideration, we must give time – a lot more time than most of us are willing to give at present.

We all need warm, deep, personal relationships to thrive, but modern life seems to place such a small value on them – compared with the high value placed on money and prestige and pleasure. It is so easy to be distracted and to fritter our attention away in countless ways, until we find we have little left for family and friends. By simplifying our lives, dropping less important activities, we allow more time for what matters most. But it is also essential to slow down our pace of living, so that we can free ourselves from the grip of time-driven thinking and behavior.

RELATED PAGES *March 15, June 27*

November 15

If there is righteousness in the heart, there will be beauty in the character. If there is beauty in the character, there will be harmony in the home. If there is harmony in the home, there will be order in the nation. If there is order in the nation, there will be peace in the world.

CONFUCIAN TRADITION

IN A home where one person can be patient and forgiving, even if the rest of the family does not see eye to eye with him or her, they will share in a spiritual bonus. All of us benefit by living with someone who does not live for himself or herself.

It is misleading to think that people who meditate are seeking only their own illumination. They are contributing to the removal of selfishness and separateness in the world.

By some unwritten law our hearts and respect gradually go out to such people.

 RELATED PAGE *January 27*

November 16

People see his pleasure-ground; him no one sees at all.

BRIHADARANYAKA UPANISHAD

WHEN I was a boy in my ancestral home in South India, the children used to play a game called *kooee.* One little boy or girl would run and hide in a room of the labyrinthine building. Then he would call out "kooee," and we would hear "kooee" echoing from all corners. "Kooee" would be coming from upstairs and downstairs; from the ceiling "kooee" would reverberate. We would race through the halls, tear through each room in search of the one who was crying "kooee." Then at last we would catch her, and the game would be over.

This is the game we are all playing. Some people hear the call coming from the bank. Others hear the call from the haunts of pleasure. Many hear it coming loud and clear from status and prestige. Still others, tragically, seek power that calls to them with a loud voice.

We need to open our ears, so that when we hear the elusive call we will say, "Oh, that is Krishna playing on his flute. That is Jesus beckoning to us to follow him. That is the Divine Mother calling us home. That is the Buddha trying to wake us up." Finally, we learn how to trace the sound to its source and say, "Caught you at last!"

RELATED PAGES *June 8, July 4*

November 17

But charity means pardoning what is unpardonable, or it is no virtue at all. Hope means hoping when things are hopeless, or it is no virtue at all. And faith means believing the incredible, or it is no virtue at all.

G. K. CHESTERTON

EVERY ONE of us can learn to love without qualifications or reservations. Naturally, we start with imperfections. But there is no need to throw up our hands as so many are doing today and say, "Let us be separate *and* have a relationship. Here are my duties, here are yours. This is the boundary line. If you stay on your side, I'll respect you; but if you cross over, you're an invader." Wherever people go their separate ways like this, love cannot grow. It is not possible to have both separateness and intimacy.

RELATED PAGES *January 4, March 9*

November 18

Attachment is the great fabricator of illusions; reality can be attained only by someone who is detached.

SIMONE WEIL

ONE OF the profoundest laws of spiritual psychology is: you see what you are, and you are what you see. The observer cannot help conditioning what he or she observes.

Those who cannot love see a world where love has little place. Those who live to enlarge their love, by contrast, see a world of hope: a world of men and women who, despite their failings, are capable of love in the core of goodness in their hearts.

To see life from this lofty vantage, we need detachment, not from others but from ourselves.

RELATED PAGES *May 1, December 11*

November 19

We know only that we are living in these bodies and have a vague idea, because we have heard it, and because our faith tells us so, that we possess souls.

SAINT TERESA OF AVILA

I AM NOT my body. This body is like a jacket that I wear. I have a brown jacket with a Nehru collar, made in India, which has served me very well. I take good care of it, and I expect it to last me at least another five years. This body of mine is another brown jacket, made in South India and impeccably tailored to my requirements by a master tailor, whose label is right inside. This jacket has to last me much longer than the other, so I am very careful with it. I give it the right amounts of nutritious food and exercise. Just like my Nehru jacket, this body-jacket will someday become too worn to serve me well. When death comes I will be able to set it aside, with no more tears than I would shed when I give my old Nehru jacket away.

 RELATED PAGES *February 27, May 9*

November 20

Roll on, thou deep and dark blue ocean, roll!
Ten thousand fleets sweep over thee in vain;
Man marks the earth with ruin, – his control
Stops with the shore.

LORD BYRON

ALAS, LORD Byron, no more! Industrial society's reach has extended deep into the sea. Pollution, depletion of the ozone layer, global warming – threats like these are changing the ocean.

In the Bhagavad Gita, the Lord says, "Among bodies of water, I am the ocean." He does not say merely, "I made the ocean"; he says, "I am the ocean." To me, this is the basis of all our environmental efforts, and it accords with what ecologists tell us about the importance of the sea. The sea supports us, balances our climate, provides a home for whales and seals and dolphins. When we look at the sea, we should remember the infinite tenderness and compassion of God. When we pollute the ocean we are ignoring and abusing that compassion in a manner unworthy of us.

RELATED PAGES *July 8, November 12*

November 21

Beloved, let us love one another: for love is of God.

I JOHN

THE IDEA of romance held by the modern world seems to be taken from the world of business. We are told that love should not be freely given, but that it is a commodity that must be bargained over. Some wary couples are even drawing up "contracts" to specify who will do the dishes and who will wash the car. As long as the contract is observed to the letter, peace reigns, but any breach brings serious consequences. We model our personal lives after our business lives. If it works when negotiating a contract with your supplier, why shouldn't it work when negotiating with your domestic partner?

Yet no one is content with this state of affairs. None of us really wants to strike back at those we love. We do not get satisfaction out of hurting people who have let us down. We have simply fallen into the habit of brooding on wrongs done to us, until we finally explode.

Love means that regardless of what someone does to us, we will not strike back in anger.

 RELATED PAGES *February 14, November 2*

November 22

Death be not proud, though some have called thee
Mighty and dreadful, for thou art not so,
For, those, whom thou think'st thou dost overthrow,
Die not, poor death, nor yet can'st thou kill me.

JOHN DONNE

"AND TIME passes so quickly," Death whispers in our ear. Only a while ago we were toddlers, as sweet and angelic as any baby we see today. Just look at your old baby pictures and you cannot help wondering what happened to that wide-eyed child of not too many years ago.

With the passage of time the body inevitably undergoes certain natural changes, the last of which is death. This is something every creature has to undergo. The immortal dweller within the body, however – our real Self – is unaffected by these changes. It was never born; it can never die.

RELATED PAGES *February 22, May 19*

November 23

Undisciplined love dwells in the senses, for it is still entangled with earthly things. . . . Disciplined love lives in the soul and rises above the human senses and forbids the body its own will.

MECHTHILD OF MAGDEBURG

IN THE Hindu scriptures, the Sanskrit word *kama* means selfish desire, or any kind of private gratification. The opposite of kama is *prema*: love pure and perfected, a selfless love that does not ask what it can get but what it can give. The first leads only to spiritual starvation; the latter nourishes and heals.

In Hindu mythology kama is sometimes personified as the god Kama, who is a little like the Greek Cupid. Like Cupid, Kama is armed with a bow, and he has five arrows tipped with flowers, one for each of the five senses. Prema might also be said to have five arrows: five things we need to acquire in order to love. The first is time. Second is a one-pointed mind, which is the capacity to direct attention as we choose. Third comes energy, vitality. Fourth, we need discrimination. And fifth, we must have awareness of the unity of life.

 RELATED PAGE *August 31*

November 24

Goodness is the only investment which never fails.

HENRY DAVID THOREAU

DISCRIMINATION IS the precious capacity to see the difference between what is pleasant for the moment and what is fulfilling always. Today we are surrounded by a bewildering array of glittering lifestyles and models of behavior, most of which deliver just the opposite of what they promise. We need to make wise choices every moment just to keep from being swept away. For a long time, these choices are not easy. Often they go against the grain of our conditioning. It takes real courage and endurance to go on making such choices day in and day out. But once you begin to taste the freedom it brings, you will find a fierce joy in choosing something of lasting benefit.

RELATED PAGES *July 21, November 10*

November 25

I was held back by mere trifles, the most paltry inanities, all my old attachments.

SAINT AUGUSTINE

SOONER OR later, most of us encounter the haunting fear that if we turn our senses inwards, which is what diving into the murky water of consciousness means, we may lose everything enjoyable in life. This fear is one of the most formidable obstacles between us and deepening meditation. But if we persevere, we will see the day when these old attachments will fall away, almost of themselves, and no one will be as surprised as we are.

Gradually, with experience, our faith grows that deep within us the Self is willing and able to take responsibility for our ultimate welfare. Slowly we can surrender our personal will to an immeasurably more profound purpose. Bit by bit, we can work ourselves loose from the grip of compulsive entanglements in the faith that our capacity to love and be loved will thereby be magnified a millionfold.

 RELATED PAGE *August 18*

November 26

In truth, to attain to interior peace, one must be willing to pass through the contrary to peace. Such is the teaching of the sages.

SWAMI BRAHMANANDA

I ONCE ASKED my grandmother, "Why shouldn't we go after pleasant things, Granny? It's only human. And what's wrong with wanting to stay away from unpleasant things?" She didn't argue with me. She just told me to eat an amla fruit.

It was easier said than done. The fruit was so sour that I wanted to spit it out, but she stopped me. "Don't give up. Keep chewing." Out of love for her, I did, and the sourness left. The fruit began to taste sweeter and sweeter. "Granny, this is delicious," I said.

"But you didn't like it at the outset. You wanted to spit it out." That is how it is with spiritual disciplines.

RELATED PAGE *June 13*

November 27

And ye shall seek me, and find me, when ye shall search for me with all your heart.

JEREMIAH

THE MANTRAM is most effective when we say it silently, in the mind, with as much concentration as possible. Saying the mantram aloud a few times can help you get started, and it is so rhythmical that it can be sung aloud. But we need not dwell on the tune and rhythm. Anything which takes attention away from the mantram itself, such as counting, or worrying about intonation, or connecting the mantram with physiological processes, only weakens the mantram's effect.

The mantram is a force, and in order for this force to work, it must be working from deep inside. At first, we will be repeating the mantram only at the surface level of the mind. But if we repeat it with regularity and sustained enthusiasm, it will take root deep in our consciousness.

 RELATED PAGES *March 1, March 2*

November 28

Whatever I am offered in devotion with a pure heart – a leaf, a flower, fruit, or water – I accept with joy.

BHAGAVAD GITA

WE CAN look upon everything we do as a gift to the Lord. If we hoe the garden carefully so that our family – or a neighbor's family, or someone in need – can have fresh vegetables for dinner, that is an offering to the Lord. If we work a little more than is expected of us at something that benefits others, that too is an offering to the Lord. Everywhere, in every detail of daily living, it is not a question of quantity or expense that makes our offering acceptable; it is cheerfulness, enthusiasm, and the capacity to forget ourselves in helping others.

RELATED PAGES *March 29, April 26*

November 29

When thoughts arise, then do all things arise. When thoughts vanish, then do all things vanish.

HUANG PO

WHEN MEDITATION deepens, and the thinking process slows down, we will find that we don't have to think all the time. It sounds simple, even scary, but it is a mighty achievement that yields unimaginable peace. Thoughts are no longer compulsive.

Just as we turn the key in the ignition of our car when we want to go somewhere, we should be able to find the ignition switch in our own mind. When we want to think constructively we switch the mind on and drive all the way to Los Angeles without any detours or breakdowns. Anger is a breakdown. Resentment is a protracted detour that often makes us forget our original travel plan entirely and then leaves us out of gas in the middle of nowhere. But when we know where to find the ignition switch, we can start the mind out in Seattle on Interstate 5 and drive straight through to Los Angeles. We have a wonderful trip, and when we arrive and our project is completed, we switch the mind off and let it rest.

There may be a certain pleasure in letting the mind wander, but for how long? What the spiritual teacher asks us is simple: Don't you want to decide your destination? And don't you want to get there with your body still healthy and your mind at peace?

 RELATED PAGES *April 1, May 18*

November 30

O Lord, how entirely needful is thy grace for me, to begin any good work, to go on with it, and to accomplish it. For without that grace I can do nothing; but in thee I can do all things when thy grace doth strengthen me.

THOMAS A KEMPIS

ONE WAY of representing God is with a holy hammer in his pocket. When he finds we are being irresponsible, when he sees us going in the wrong direction, he takes out this little hammer and gives us a gentle rap on the knuckles. If we are really good students we shall be able to learn with just this one small rap.

There *are* a few rare creatures who have this capacity to learn. Most of us, however, would not be able to change our ways if the only guidance the Lord gave us was, "Won't you please consider this very carefully and act upon it if you approve?" The vast majority of us go on making the same mistake over and over again. It is only when the raps become painful that we bother to ask where they come from and how we can put an end to them. We have to be shocked into awareness that we are injuring ourselves and others. Then, through all the little decisions we make day in and day out, we have to work to transform our sorrow-producing habits into acts that lead to increasing joy.

RELATED PAGES *February 7, July 25*

December

When you live for give to life, beneficial forces will support you and give you greater health, longer life, and deeper creativity.

EKNATH EASWARAN

December 1

At the center of our being is a point of nothingness which is untouched by sin and by illusion, a point of pure truth, a point or spark which belongs entirely to God, which is never at our disposal, from which God disposes of our lives, which is inaccessible to the fantasies of our own mind or the brutalities of our own will.

THOMAS MERTON

THE IMPETUS to gain mastery over one's mind and senses does not come from a distant deity. It doesn't come from any monastic rule, or even from one's spiritual teacher. It comes from deep within yourself. You have had a fleeting glimpse of the shining presence within, and in its bright remembered light, all your flaws and blemishes are thrown into sharp relief. You can't wait to start removing them.

To have the desire to travel deep into consciousness is a sure mark of divine grace. To be no longer content to pick up what is floating on the surface of life, and to want only the pearls at the bottom of the sea, this is grace, welling up from deep inside.

RELATED PAGE *May 2*

December 2

If your heart were sincere and upright, every creature would be unto you a looking-glass of life and a book of holy doctrine.

THOMAS A KEMPIS

THE PURE in spirit, who see God, see him here and now: in his handiwork, his hidden purpose, the wry humor of his creation. The Lord has left us love notes scattered extravagantly across creation. Hidden in the eye of the tiger, the wet muzzle of a calf, the delicacy of the violet, and the perfect curve of the elephant's tusk is a very personal, priceless message.

Watch the lamb in awkward play, butting against its mother's side. See the spider putting the final shimmering touches on an architectural wonder. And absorb a truth that is wordless. The grace of a deer, the soaring freedom of a sparrow hawk in flight, the utter self-possession of an elephant crashing through the woods – in every one of these there is something of ourselves. From the great whales in the blue Pacific to the tiniest of tree frogs in the Amazon basin, unity embraces us all.

RELATED PAGES *January 8, February 28*

December 3

Most people live, whether physically, intellectually or morally, in a very restricted circle of their potential being. They make use of a very small portion of their possible consciousness, and of their soul's resources in general, much like a man who, out of his whole bodily organism, should get into a habit of using and moving only his little finger.

WILLIAM JAMES

WE THINK we are very limited creatures, very small, good for maybe only fifteen minutes of love or patience before we have to crack. Instead of identifying with our deepest Self, we are identifying with some biochemical-mental organism.

But when you calm the mind in meditation every morning, you will see how far you can stretch your patience and your love during the day. You will see for yourself how comfortable you feel with everybody, how secure you feel wherever you go. You will find that you have a quiet sense of being equal to difficult situations.

These discoveries give a hint of the heights to which a human being can rise. Once we see this for ourselves, we will catch the exhilaration of the mystics when they say that because the Lord is our real Self, there is no limit to our capacities.

 RELATED PAGES *March 8, August 12*

December 4

I believe in person to person. Every person is Christ for me, and since there is only one Jesus, that person is the one person in the world at that moment.

MOTHER TERESA OF CALCUTTA

VIRTUALLY EVERYONE today believes that it is possible to love only two or three people. When Jesus talks about loving our neighbor as ourselves, or the Compassionate Buddha tells us to love the whole world as a mother loves her only child, we believe it is all metaphorical. Mother Teresa says no, it is literal. Two or three people are not enough for our capacity to love. We should be able to love everyone – not feel a vague sentiment for a faceless mass, but actually be in love with every individual.

RELATED PAGES *January 26, May 27*

December 5

Precious gems are profoundly buried in the earth and can only be extracted at the expense of great labor.

ANANDAMAYI MA

A FEW DAYS ago I was watching a woodpecker, a creature I hadn't seen since I left India. This one had a red turban. While I watched, he came and alighted on a huge tree. He was quite a small creature, and the trunk of the tree was enormous. I wanted to go up to him and say, "What, make a hole in that huge trunk with your tiny beak? Impossible. Preposterous!"

But this little woodpecker was not intimidated by size. He did not throw up his legs in despair; he just alighted and went about looking for the right place to begin operations.

It is the same with transforming consciousness; you have to look for the right spot. In some people it is a particular compulsive craving; in some it is jealousy; in some, blind fury. Some may be fortunate enough to have all three. Each person has to look for that spot where urgent work is most needed.

 RELATED PAGES *January 2, December 6*

December 6

O God! make me busy with Thee, that they may not make me busy with them.

RABIA

LET ME continue with the story of the woodpecker. Once our red-turbaned chap had checked out possible areas for working, he settled down at what looked like a solid, unyielding spot and started pecking away rhythmically. He didn't just give a peck or two and then fly off in search of a worm, not to return for half an hour. He went on pecking systematically, with sustained enthusiasm, until he was done. I was amazed at his dexterity. When he had finished, he left such a large hole that if he had gone on, I have no doubt the entire tree would have fallen.

That is the kind of work required to transform personality. For a long time, all we are doing in meditation is pecking away at what we want to change in ourselves. At best it is tedious; often it is downright painful. The problem is that we identify ourselves with the accumulation of habits and opinions, likes and dislikes, which we have developed over the years. We think this is who we are, and are not prepared to let it die.

RELATED PAGES *January 2, December 5*

December 7

And I marveled to find that at last I loved you and not some phantom instead of you; and I did not hesitate to enjoy my God, but was ravished to you by your beauty.

SAINT AUGUSTINE

TO DEEPEN our love, to unify our desires, the Lord – the Self within – on occasion gives us a fleeting taste of the joy of union. Once we taste this joy, all we want is to be permanently aware of him in everyone, everywhere, every minute. This intense longing is the mark of genuine spiritual experience.

At the same time we experience the joy of union, we see clearly the great mass of self-will that weighs us down and keeps us from our most cherished goal.

Yet none of us need feel disheartened. Remember how even great figures like Saint Augustine almost despaired when they saw how powerful was the pull of selfish satisfaction. That is our human conditioning, and it is no reason to give up. All of us can learn to reduce our excess baggage.

 RELATED PAGES *June 12, July 25*

December 8

As clouds are blown away by the wind, the thirst for material pleasures will be driven away by the utterance of the Lord's name.

SRI SARADA DEVI

WHEN WE are getting angry, or are driven by some craving, the mind is taking off like a sports car that can accelerate from zero to sixty in a matter of seconds. It's gone before we even know what has happened. What the mantram can do, when we use it regularly and become established in it, is exactly what a power brake does: stop the car quickly. In all loving relationships, one of the most vital faculties to cultivate is a power brake.

When the mind is getting agitated, when angry words are rushing to our lips and our blood pressure is going up, that is the time to step on the power brake; you just touch it lightly and the car stops. Try it. You'll be amazed at the mantram's power in such situations.

RELATED PAGES *March 1, March 31*

December 9

Love is swift, sincere, pious, joyful, generous, strong, patient, faithful, prudent, long-suffering, courageous, and never seeking her own; for wheresoever we seek our own, there we fall from love.

THOMAS A KEMPIS

OUR ENGLISH word *love* has become almost impossible to use. We say he's "falling in love" as if it were something that could happen every day, like falling into a manhole. Is it so easy to fall in love?

Listen to our popular songs; look at our magazines and newspapers. When they say, "I love you," that's not what I hear; I hear "I love me." If we could listen in on a marriage proposal with the ears of Thomas a Kempis, this is what we would hear. The man gets down on bended knee and says, "Sibyl, dear, I love me; will you marry me?"

There is a little undertone of this in almost all relationships. This is how we have all been conditioned, to put ourselves first at least part of the time. Most relationships begin with some passionate "I love you's" and some undertones of "I love me." But if we want our relationship to blossom, we'll gradually change the focus from *me, me, me* to *you, you, you.* Then our selfish passion is transformed into pure love.

 RELATED PAGES *February 14, August 3*

December 10

The only thing necessary for the triumph of evil is for good men to do nothing.

ATTRIBUTED TO EDMUND BURKE

SOME OF our most trying difficulties are caused by plain old inertia. Inertia shows itself in not wanting to move, not wanting to act – in other words, in wanting to be a stone just lying on the road. It is all right for a stone to be inert; that is its role in life. But it is not all right for you and me to just lie down and try to avoid problems, saying, "What does it matter?"

When I hear the phrase "well adjusted," I do not always take it as a favorable comment. Mahatma Gandhi has said that to be well adjusted in a wrong situation is very bad; in a wrong situation we should keep on acting to set it right. When Gandhi, at the peak of his political activity, was asked in a British court what his profession was, he said, "Resister." If he was put in a wrong situation, he just could not keep quiet; he had to resist, nonviolently but very effectively, until the situation was set right.

RELATED PAGES *March 3, May 16*

December 11

Each of us sees the Unseen in proportion to the clarity of our heart, and that depends upon how much we have polished it. Whoever has polished it more sees more – more Unseen forms become manifest.

JALALUDDIN RUMI

AS YOUR meditation deepens, there will still be occasions when you get upset, but you will be able to watch what goes on in the lab of your mind. It's like getting into a glass-bottomed boat, where you venture out onto the ocean and watch all the deep-sea creatures lurking beneath the surface: resentment sharks, stingrays of greed, scurrying schools of fear. You slowly gain a certain amount of detachment from your mind, so you can observe what is going on, collect data, and then set things right.

Some of the chronic problems that millions of people suffer from today might be solved by gaining a little detachment from their minds and emotions, so they can stand back a little when the mind is agitated and see the ways in which it makes mountains out of molehills. Many problems simply are not real; they start to seem real only when we dwell on them. The thorniest problems to solve are those that are not real; yet most of us go on giving them our best efforts.

 RELATED PAGES *October 30, November 18*

December 12

A good action is never lost; it is a treasure laid up and guarded for the doer's need.

CALDERON DE LA BARCA

IN HINDUISM and Buddhism this principle is called the law of karma. The word *karma* has been much misunderstood, but its literal meaning is simply action, something done. So instead of using exotic language, we might as well refer to the "law of action," which states that everything we do – even everything we think, since our thoughts condition our behavior – has consequences: not "equal and opposite" as in physics, but equal and alike.

The comparison with physics is deliberate, for this is not a doctrine of any particular religion. It is a law of life, which no one has stated more clearly than Saint Paul: "Whatsoever we sow, that shall we also reap." The working of this law, we should bear in mind, is not necessarily negative. If we sow mercy, we shall receive mercy in ample harvest. If we give love, we shall receive love; if we are kind and patient to others, others will be kind and patient to us.

RELATED PAGES *June 17, December 14*

December 13

Envy and wrath shorten the life.

ECCLESIASTICUS

ALL OF us have a need to forgive, whether in large or small matters. All of us suffer little irritating pinpricks every day. It is not very effective to analyze these small wrongs and then forgive them one by one. Much more effective is not to dwell on them at all. Whenever a stray bit of wrath arises and wants to talk over some incident from the past, don't invite that thought in.

When we can withdraw our attention completely from the past, it is not possible to get resentful; it is not possible to be oppressed by mistakes in our past, no matter who made them. All our attention is in the present, which makes every moment fresh, every relationship fresh. Staleness and boredom vanish from our life.

 RELATED PAGES *January 25, February 3*

December 14

All things by immortal power
Near or far,
Hiddenly
To each other linked are,
That thou canst not stir a flower
Without troubling of a star.

FRANCIS THOMPSON

THE SCIENCE of ecology teaches us that everything in the universe is connected. We cannot separate ourselves from the consequences of even the least of our actions: whatever we do *here* comes back *there*. This is the law of the unity of life. Like gravity or any other law of nature, you cannot break it; you can only break yourself against it.

If you throw a bottle into the air, it will return to earth and shatter. Similarly, if you act in a way that violates the unity of life – polluting the atmosphere, wasting precious resources, ignoring the needs of others – you will find your health, your peace of mind, and your happiness destroyed. We are not separate fragments. Like all the animals and plants, we depend on each other and on the environment.

RELATED PAGES *February 4, February 9*

December 15

They do much who love God much, and they do much who do their deed well, and they do their deed well who do it rather for the common good than for their own will.

THOMAS A KEMPIS

WE NEEDN'T rule out the exchange of useful, thoughtful gifts at Christmas, but when we expect something in return, it is not a gift but a contract. Using this strict definition, we might wonder if all of those packages under the Christmas tree are really gifts.

Rather than giving expensive, perhaps not really useful gifts, there are so many more meaningful things that all of us can give. If you have been a smoker, you can give it up – not as an act of self-denial, but as a loving gift to your family. It will be a most precious, most treasured gift. If you have been drinking heavily, you can give up alcohol as an act of love. It is a gift that will keep on giving. If you have been overeating, you can start eating nutritious food in temperate quantities, and exercising regularly. It's a beautiful gift for everybody in the family. These are real gifts.

 RELATED PAGES *September 20, September 30*

December 16

Know that when thou learnest to lose thy self
Thou wilt reach the Beloved.
There is no other secret to be revealed,
And more than this is not known to me.

ANSARI

TO KNOW completely, the knower has actually to become one with the known. To know you as you really are, I must somehow get out of my own shoes and step into yours. I must get myself out of the way in order to know you as you really are. This is what we catch some glimpse of in totally faithful love, where we forget ourselves completely in the happiness of another. The mystics of all faiths and all ages testify that then we know directly, intuitively, what the needs of the other are, and we do our utmost to make sure those needs are fulfilled. It is this direct awareness that we can develop through the sustained and enthusiastic practice of meditation.

RELATED PAGE *July 10*

December 17

Amor saca amor.

SAINT TERESA OF AVILA

THE SAINTS and mystics are the world's greatest authorities on love. When Saint Teresa says, "Love begets love," she is giving us the precious secret. One of the most beautiful things about love is that even today it cannot be purchased. It cannot be stolen; it cannot be ransomed; it cannot be cajoled; it cannot be seduced. *Amor saca amor:* only genuine love begets love.

All of us have been conditioned, even though we may not put it in such crass terms, to believe that if you love me six units, I should love you at most six units in return. I can feel secure in loving you six units because you have already committed yourself that far. But if you get annoyed with me and stomp out, slamming the door, I should pull back, at least temporarily, my six units of love.

Everyone can learn to love and urgently needs to learn to love. After all, even if you don't learn Esperanto, your life is not necessarily going to be dull and drab. But if you do not learn how to love, everywhere you go you are going to suffer.

 RELATED PAGES *April 23, November 21*

December 18

Give all thou canst; high Heaven rejects the lore
Of nicely-calculated less or more.

WILLIAM WORDSWORTH

THIS MORNING, when I was reading an important New York paper, I noticed an article on the dynamics of gift-giving. This article quoted a distinguished professor of sociology as saying that in every gift there is a reciprocal relationship, even if it is not conscious. In other words, when you are making a gift, you are expecting a gift in return.

Not only that, there are very subtle social gradations: gifts to longtime friends, to recent friends, to acquaintances, to possible benefactors. All these factors come into play when choosing the gift. No wonder shopping for gifts is so terribly time-consuming. No wonder people feel confused and inadequate about what to give.

But the spiritual approach is very simple. Whatever you give – it may be a check to a worthy cause, it may be clothes to a person who is cold, it may be food to the hungry, it may be medical help to the sick – do it without thinking of getting anything in return. Do it as a service to God, not reluctantly, but with joy.

RELATED PAGES *March 5, September 4*

December 19

What I needed most was to love and to be loved. I rushed headlong into love, eager to be caught. Happily I wrapped those painful bonds around me; and sure enough, I would be lashed with the red-hot pokers of jealousy, by suspicions and fear, by bursts of anger and quarrels.

SAINT AUGUSTINE

EVEN IN the most intimate of personal relationships, most of us still live inside our own private mental worlds. Our attention is often preoccupied – sometimes more in the past and future than in the present – so that we have very little attention to give to those we want to love. Despite our best intentions to draw closer, all kinds of distracting thoughts – likes and dislikes, attachments and aversions, private moods, dreams and desires – come in any time they like, keeping other people at a distance. We yearn for closeness and find, more often, disappointment.

Here Augustine echoes the experiences that almost all of us go through, starting often in our adolescence. The journey into deeper consciousness is one we must take up if ever we are to find the love, the closeness, and the fulfillment we all so earnestly desire.

 RELATED PAGE *May 1*

December 20

If we had to seek for virtue outside of ourselves, that would assuredly be difficult; but as it is within us, it suffices to avoid bad thoughts and to keep our souls turned towards the Lord.

PHILOKALIA

TO REMAKE ourselves, we don't have to bring goodness, love, fearlessness, and the like from without and force them into our hearts somehow. They are already present in us, deep in our consciousness. If we work to remove the impediments that have built up over many years of conditioning, to dislodge the old resentments and fears and selfish desires, our life will become like a fountain of living waters, as it was meant to be.

An old fountain may be clogged so that not much water can get through. But with a lot of cleaning, you can get the water to start playing again. Then grass and flowers will grow around it, and birds will come there to have their bath. Just so, love can flow from us as from a living fountain, and those we live and work with will come to us to be refreshed.

RELATED PAGES *August 7, August 29*

December 21

If Winter comes, can Spring be far behind?

PERCY BYSSHE SHELLEY

I AM AN incorrigible optimist. I'm aware of the threats that surround us, but I haven't lost my faith, I haven't lost my hope. And I haven't lost my confidence that people working together harmoniously can bring about a change for the better in the world that our children will grow up in.

It's not for governments to improve our lives. It is for each individual to ask himself or herself, "Should I continue to make things which destroy life, or can I lend my expertise and my experience to benefit life, to help life?"

We get discouraged because we don't see life as it is. We feel we can't make a difference because we don't see things as they really are. When we see life as it is, when we see people as they are, all sorrow will fall away, all suffering will come to an end. This is the great message of all religions. When we see life as it is, all sorrow falls away.

 RELATED PAGE *November 8*

December 22

Knowledge of ourselves teaches us whence we come, where we are and whither we are going. We come from God and we are in exile; and it is because our potency of affection tends towards God that we are aware of this state of exile.

JAN VAN RUYSBROECK

LIKE THE story of the prodigal son in the Bible, in India we tell a simple story of a prince who is kidnapped by robbers when he is very young. He forgets all about the palace, even about his father and mother. He just grows up as a bandit, learning to master the bow and arrow, ambush passersby, and disappear without getting caught.

Then one day the king's spiritual teacher happens by. Many years have passed; the little child is a grown man, rough and cocksure. But the teacher recognizes him, and with great love embraces him, and calls him "your royal highness." The young man, outraged, pushes him away.

But the teacher's faith is unshaken. He begins to tell the young man stories about his childhood, how life used to be in the palace. Gradually the prince begins to remember. Finally, memory clears. He draws himself up: "Now I recall," he says slowly, as if awakening from a dream. "I'm not a bandit. I simply forgot who I was." Truly a prince, he goes home to his father and mother. We are all children of God, but we've forgotten who we are.

RELATED PAGE *January 28*

December 23

Let the wise guard their thoughts, which are difficult to perceive, which are extremely subtle, which wander at will. Thought which is well guarded is the bearer of happiness.

THE BUDDHA

WHEN THE mind has become completely still, when there is no movement at all – neither on the conscious level nor in the unconscious depths – then there is no anger, fear, or greed.

When in deep meditation the turbulent factory of the mind closes down for just a few minutes, we find a soothing stillness which heals the body, mind, intellect, and spirit. In this stillness we feel the enormous draw of the ocean of pure love deep within, pulling us into a union that is complete peace, complete joy, and complete fulfillment. Then it is we realize that boundless joy has been right there within us all the time, joy that cannot be limited by separateness and does not depend on any circumstances outside, but is an abiding legacy that never leaves us. This is what is meant by everlasting life, which we can find here and now.

The stilled mind is spirit – eternal, infinite, immutable, and indivisible. When the mind has been completely stilled from top to bottom there can be no separateness.

 RELATED PAGES *January 30, June 26*

December 24

Ah! would the heart but be a manger for the birth,
God would become once more a little child of earth.
Immeasurable is the Highest! Who but knows it?
And yet a human heart can perfectly enclose it.

ANGELUS SILESIUS

IN ONE of his inimitable images, Sri Ramakrishna says that a great incarnation is like a mighty ship that takes people across the sea. Jesus the Christ, the Buddha, and Sri Krishna can be compared to the *Queen Elizabeth,* able to cross the sea of life to what the Buddha calls the "other shore," beyond change and death. But little people like you or me can at least serve as humble rafts.

We don't have the spiritual capital to build a big boat, but we can improvise by picking up a few planks, maybe a piece of driftwood or two, and tying it all together well enough to float on the sea. That way we may at least be able to carry across our families and friends. Nobody has an excuse to say he or she lacks the wherewithal to cross the sea of life; we can always go on a raft.

December 25

We are celebrating the feast of the Eternal Birth which God the Father has borne and never ceases to bear in all Eternity. . . . But if it takes not place in me, what avails it? Everything lies in this, that it should take place in me.

MEISTER ECKHART

THE LORD of Love, immortal and infinite, comes as a divine incarnation in times of great crisis to rescue mankind from disaster. In age after age, whenever violence and hatred threaten the world, the Lord comes down to inspire and protect those who turn to him, who live in harmony with the law of unity. He comes to protect such people from the heavy odds ranged against them, and to reestablish peace on earth and good will among all.

Yet there is another level on which this divine birth can take place. Every one of us has this choice: shall I prepare for the divine birth to take place in my consciousness by abolishing my own selfishness? It is up to you and me to keep our doors open, to put up a little sign, "Ready for receiving an incarnation." But our house must not be cluttered up. It must be empty of selfishness and self-will. Only then can the blessed child be born in our humble hearts.

 RELATED PAGE *June 7*

December 26

Those who are good and pure in conduct are honored wherever they go. The good shine like the Himalayas, whose peaks glisten above the rest of the world even when seen from a distance.

THE BUDDHA

PEOPLE WHO are good, kind, selfless, and hardworking for the welfare of others will be very deeply loved, very deeply respected wherever they go. It is a simple law of human nature that we love the highest. We want to be like such people, and we want to lead the kind of life they lead. This is the saving grace of human nature: when we see someone who is patient, kind, forgiving, and forbearing, we begin to trust him, to love her.

Such people have such a deep, loving concern for us that they will block our way when we are going astray. They will point out, very sweetly, very tenderly, when we are on the wrong path, and then they will support us and help us to change our direction. This is the role of the spiritual teacher, the person we can trust to stand in our way when we aren't strong enough, wise enough to make the right choice.

RELATED PAGE *May 21*

December 27

The last enemy that shall be destroyed is death.

I CORINTHIANS

MOST OF us find the death of another person or creature deeply unsettling, yet after a time we manage to submerge our feelings and carry on. For someone deeply sensitive to the transitory nature of life, however, an encounter with death can leave scars that last a lifetime. As a teenager Saint Augustine witnessed the untimely death of a bosom friend, and suddenly a trapdoor opened into deeper awareness. He was devastated. "I thought death suddenly capable of devouring all men, because he had taken this loved one."

The word *anxiety* is a weak term for expressing this continuing uneasiness, this unsettled sense of being out of place and running out of time. Generally we can only ascribe it to external events, if we succeed in linking it to anything at all. But what is actually happening is that a wisp of memory is rising, whispering to us from deep within that nothing external in life is secure, nothing physical ever lasts.

No matter how hard we may try, in the long run none of us can escape the devastating fact of death. Yet an encounter with death, as in the case of Augustine, can leave us changed decidedly for the better. It can prompt us forward on the long search for something secure in life, something death cannot reach.

 RELATED PAGES *February 22, November 22*

December 28

Reason is like an officer when the King appears.
The officer then loses his power and hides himself.
Reason is the shadow cast by God; God is the sun.

JALALUDDIN RUMI

THINKING, HOWEVER useful it may be at times, is not the highest human faculty; it is only a stage in development. If, for example, in the throes of evolution we had stopped with instinct, saying, "This is the highest possible mode of knowing," our human future would have been stunted: I would not be seated here writing these words, nor would you be reading them.

Like instinct, reason is only a way station. When friends and I go to San Francisco to see a play, we sometimes stop halfway along to stretch our legs. But we don't get so involved in stretching legs that we forget to go on to the theater. Thought is a useful but temporary stopping station; it should not be considered a permanent solution to the problems of living. Just as we were able to rise above instinct and to develop reason, we must one day pass beyond discursive thinking and enter into a higher mode of knowing.

We cannot solve the problems of the mind with the mind. We cannot solve our problems by thinking about them, analyzing them, talking about them. In meditation, we often simply leave personal problems behind – we move out of the neighborhood where they live.

RELATED PAGE *October 17*

December 29

Out of compassion I destroy the darkness of their ignorance. From within them I light the lamp of wisdom and dispel all darkness from their lives.

BHAGAVAD GITA

WITH INFINITE tenderness, the Lord lets it dawn on us only gradually that we are not separate, that we belong entirely to him. If this realization were to come overnight, ordinary people like you and me would not be able to withstand it; it would be more than our nervous systems could bear. That is why the Lord is so gentle with us; he spreads the transformation from separateness to unity out over many years so that all these changes in the mind and body can take place gradually. Often we are not even aware they are taking place until we look back and remember how we were some years before.

We should not ask when illumination will come. We should have a patient impatience to reach the goal. Finally, after many years, no matter what our past has been, we will begin to live in the light that knows no night. The temple may have been dark for a thousand years, but once the lamp is lit, every corner will be ablaze with light.

 RELATED PAGES *April 9, December 22*

December 30

On the one hand I felt the call of God; on the other, I continued to follow the world. All the things of God gave me great pleasure, but I was held captive by those of the world. I might have been said to be trying to reconcile these two extremes, to bring contraries together: the spiritual life on the one hand and worldly satisfactions, pleasures, and pastimes on the other.

SAINT TERESA OF AVILA

SAINT TERESA of Avila was a remarkably spiritual woman. Even as a girl she could say passionately, "I want something that will last forever!" Yet this woman who was to become one of the world's greatest mystics went through twenty years of doubt and struggle before becoming established in God. If Teresa took twenty years, can people like you and me think of doing it in less? Her words can inspire all of us, for everyone begins with doubts and conflicts. Little people like us are likely to be haunted by them – and to feel frequently disheartened for a long, long time.

When you have doubts about your capacity for spiritual progress, don't be defeatist. Remember these words of Saint Teresa and keep striving, keep on trying. This is all we are expected to do.

RELATED PAGES *June 19, December 7*

December 31

Imagine if all the tumult of the body were to quiet down, along with our busy thoughts. Imagine if all things that are perishable grew still. And imagine if that moment were to go on and on, leaving behind all other sights and sounds but this one vision which ravishes and absorbs and fixes the beholder in joy, so that the rest of eternal life were like that moment of illumination which leaves us breathless.

SAINT AUGUSTINE

As I reach the spiritual summit, I hardly feel my body. My mind is still; my ego has been set at rest. The peace in my heart matches the peace at the heart of nature. This is my native state, the state to which I have been striving through the long travail of evolution to return. No longer am I a feverish fragment of life; I am indivisible from the whole.

I live completely in the present, released from the prison of the past with its haunting memories and vain regrets, released from the prison of the future with its tantalizing hopes and tormenting fears. All the enormous capacities formerly trapped in past and future flow to me here and now, concentrated in the hollow of my palm. No longer driven by desire for personal pleasure or profit, I am free to use all these capacities to alleviate the suffering of those around me. In living for others, I come to life.

 RELATED PAGES *July 7, September 27*

Passage Meditation
An Eight-Point Program

by Eknath Easwaran

On the next page are listed the eight points of the program for a fuller, healthier, more spiritual life that I have used myself. The heart of this program is meditation. The principle of meditation is simple: we are what we think. When we meditate on inspired words with profound concentration, they have the capacity to sink into our consciousness, alive with a charge of spiritual awareness. Eventually these ideals become an integral part of our personality, which means they will find constant expression in what we do, what we say, and what we think.

These eight points are explained and illustrated in my book *Passage Meditation,* which has a chapter on each one. (The full text of *Passage Meditation* is also available online at www.easwaran.org/meditation.)

PASSAGE MEDITATION

AN EIGHT-POINT PROGRAM

1. Meditation on a Passage Slow, sustained concentration on the words of inspirational passages. Practiced for one-half hour each morning.

2. Repetition of a Mantram Silent repetition of a sacred name or phrase with the power to transform consciousness. Practiced whenever possible, day or night.

3. Slowing Down Setting priorities and reducing the tension caused by hurry.

4. One-Pointed Attention Giving full concentration to the matter at hand.

5. Training the Senses Overcoming conditioned habits and learning to enjoy what is beneficial.

6. Putting Others First Gaining freedom from selfishness and separateness; finding joy in helping others.

7. Spiritual Fellowship Spending time regularly with other passage meditators for inspiration and support.

8. Spiritual Reading Drawing inspiration from writings by and about spiritual figures and the scriptures of all religions.

Index

D

E

F

T

U

W

Y